Grey & McLaughlin plc

The NINTH DEVICE

KLAUS SCHIRMER

Published by Klaus Schirmer,
Durban, South Africa
klausauthor@gmail.com

Edited by Cathy Eberle
Cover design and typesetting by Wendy Bow, Apple Pie Graphics
Printed and bound by Pinetown Printers (Pty) Ltd

AUTHOR'S FOREWORD

At the end of this story I have included a brief chapter on some of the technical issues surrounding nuclear devices and the construction of these weapons. Initially I was going to open the novel with this chapter, but (and rightly so) was advised by my wife and most avid critic, that it would detract from the actual story and the plot. Good advice indeed, yet it still makes for interesting reading. Not that it is so technical of nature as to become mind-numbingly boring, but for the layman with a bent towards the technical, I recommend reading those last pages. Otherwise, and as with the first book in the Grey & McLaughlin plc series, Cold Factor, I dedicate this work to my wife Liesel - for her support, understanding and belief in what I do.

Last but not least, special thanks to Ginger Weirich, a lady I have not met in person, who has helped me tremendously with initial editing and critique. Having someone who tells you how it is - "warts and all" – is invaluable! We will meet one day!

Enjoy "The Ninth Device"

PROLOGUE

November 1994 – Farm Vredendal – North West of Pretoria, South Africa

The five elderly men ascended the stairs from the basement room buried deep below the sand-covered concrete floor of the large farm shed. They made their way slowly up the stairs, the last of them pausing for a brief moment to turn and look back into the depths of the cavernous crypt. Illuminated by a multitude of ceiling-mounted fluorescent lights, the underground structure resembled a military bunker, the grey concrete walls, roof and ceiling, coupled with the harsh light, creating an environment even the most ardent of minimalists would have found depressing.

Stacked neatly against the walls on either side of the 20-metre-long room stood a series of crates, each stencilled with a series of black numbers. The last man in the silent procession, his silhouette a dark shape against the glare of the fluorescent tubes, paused for a brief moment, his mind wandering. Had they been right? Was this what they had dedicated their lives to? They had failed, hadn't they? But now was not time to procrastinate. They had to go, time was running out. He sighed deeply and switched off the lights. It was done. He joined his four colleagues at the top of the stairs, and they proceeded to lower a heavy concrete trap-door over the opening in the centre of the floor leading to the tomb-like basement. Once closed, they filled the space between the trap-door edges and the recess it had been lowered into, with dirt, then covered the floor with a layer of straw. Satisfied with their work, they left the farm shed, closed the large roller-door and locked it with an industrial padlock.

"Johannes!" Pieter van Zyl called across to the farm house, some 50 metres away. Soon after a middle-aged African man opened the front door and made his way across to the group of men.

"Meneer?"

"Here, take these." He handed him two keys for the padlock. "Hide these where I have told you to."

"I will." The African man was nervous, frightened.

"Good, Johannes, very good. Now repeat what I told you this morning."

"If anyone comes here looking for the owner, you are away and I do not know when you will be back. I have been told to look after the buildings and the cattle while you are gone. Your name is Hein Grobbelaar and you only come here three or four times a year. I do not know where you stay when you are not here. I only work here. That is what you told me."

"Yes Johannes, it is. Excellent!" He glanced across at the farmhouse, noting Johannes's wife and two young children watching from the doorway. "Remember this well, Johannes. You will be paid every month. You will keep this farm tidy and clean. You may go everywhere and do whatever you want to, but you may never go into the shed. You will look after the cattle, and, as of now, they are your own." Johannes's face lit up like a Christmas tree. "But remember this, too, I have paid a *sangoma* 20 head of cattle to put a mighty curse on you and your whole family if you fail to obey the simple instructions I have given you. If you do obey, you will be a wealthy man and nothing will happen. But, Johannes," the man's voice became quiet, threatening, "if you do not, first your children will die, one by one, then your wife, then the rest of your family, and then finally you. It will be of a disease for which there is no cure, and death will be slow, terrible and painful. This, the *sangoma* has assured me of. Do you understand?"

Johannes trembled, cold sweat beads of abhorrent fear forming on his forehead. He knew the man facing him had been to see a *sangoma* and not just any *sangoma*. No, it had been the most powerful *sangoma* in the area, an old, wild, strange and evil woman who resided in a cave in the mountains not far from the farm. It was said that she had eaten the hearts of two infants, whose parents had been forced to witness the sacrifice. Johannes shuddered. This *sangoma* surely spoke directly to the spirits of darkness. Yet he knew too that, if he obeyed the instructions, no harm would come to him or his family and he would be richer than he had ever dared to dream of.

"Yes, baas," he replied, reverting back to the humiliating form of address of the apartheid years. "You have my word. May the ancestors bear witness!"

Half an hour later the five men left the farm, leaving Johannes and his family behind them. The same evening, the daily gaggle of scheduled international flights to Europe commenced, leaving what was, at the time, the Jan Smuts International Airport in Johannesburg. Five of those flights each carried one of the five men, bound for different destinations across continental Europe and the United Kingdom. Francois Labuschagne, Pieter van Zyl, and the three other men had left South Africa.

For the next 19 years the concrete vault would remain sealed, the contents of the chamber all but forgotten. Until the latter half of 2013.

CHAPTER 1
CREDIBLE THREAT

London, United Kingdom

Not uncommon for London, it was raining; a steady, persistent drizzle lasting for days on end. The temperature had not moved much beyond 11 degrees Celsius either. It was utterly miserable, perhaps typical of the south-east of England in late autumn. Shortly after 17:00 Michael Grey parked his car in an available space just opposite the Red Lion, pulled up the collar of his coat and crossed the slick road. Standing outside the entrance to the pub, as always, was Darryl, the large, immaculately dressed African doorman, whose salary was paid by Grey & McLaughlin plc. It was Grey's personal contribution to the establishment and it ensured that there were never any problems. On the rare occasion that a patron had gotten out of line, it had ended very quickly - messing with gentle giant Darryl was simply not something anyone did voluntarily, no matter how inebriated. Grey stopped for a minute to chat to Darryl about his young family – Darryl's wife had just given birth to a third baby girl who Darryl was over the moon about – asked him to keep an eye on his car and entered the pub. Gary Logan, manager of the Red Lion and a personal friend, saw him come in and came across to greet him.

"Hey Mike! How's things going? Tough week?"

"Hi Gary." Grey unbuttoned his coat and took it off. "Nah, nothing out of the ordinary. Usual day-to-day grind. All good here?"

"No problems." He pointed at a corner table. "Billy's here already. The usual for you?" Grey typically stuck to the house bitter, London Pride, as he had ever since he and his business partner, Billy McLaughlin, had started frequenting the pub. Over the years it had become the norm, that, every Friday afternoon, the two would meet up at the Red Lion to go through the developments of the week.

"Yeah, thanks." Grey, Chief Operating Officer of Grey & McLaughlin plc, took the offered pint glass from Logan and walked towards the corner table where Billy McLaughlin, his partner, was sitting going through a couple of notes lying on the table in front of him. McLaughlin was not only the Chief Financial Officer, he was also an IT genius of considerable proportions - so good at his chosen specialty that he was viewed by an elite handful of "in the know" individuals as being right up there at the top of the pile. Jointly, the two men ran Grey & McLaughlin plc. Ostensibly a company dealing in corporate security matters, there was a more clandestine side to the business most people had no idea about, the provision of solutions to the somewhat delicate problems experienced from time to time, not only by major global corporations, but also by governments. As long as a brief was in line with the overall principles of democracy, freedom and free economic activity, Grey & McLaughlin plc would consider accepting an assignment. Not all were accepted; some were simply far too risky. But the accepted assignments, and of those there were not many, were - without exception – executed to the fullest satisfaction of the respective client or government. It had made Michael Grey and Billy McLaughlin very wealthy indeed.

There was one other oddity, something known to only a handful of people. Michael Grey, 49 years of age, with the looks and physique of a 36-year-old, had not always been known by that name. In his early 20s, he had been Kobus Botha, a special forces operator in the South African Defence Force. Colloquially known as a *Recce* in South Africa, he had survived a botched operation in Angola and ended up becoming a reluctant hero in the Republic of South Africa. The government of the day, intelligent enough to realise that Botha would forever be under the spotlight in South Africa for his exploits, gave him a new identity. He became Michael Grey, born in South Africa, the son of British immigrants. The rest is history. Kobus Botha, aka Michael Grey, left South Africa and moved to London where he met Billy McLaughlin and Grey & McLaughlin plc had been born.

As Grey approached the table McLaughlin looked up, skipping the usual greeting. *Uh oh,* thought Grey, *something's brewing...*

"Hi Billy. What's up?"

McLaughlin frowned. "Take a look at this e-mail. It arrived about an hour ago." He handed a printed document to Grey, "From Rome. Read it."

Grey took the document and began reading. It was the fourth sentence that made him suck in his breath. Alarmed, he continued reading.

Dear Mr Grey

My name is Franco di Paulo. I am 92 years old and live in the Via Conte Rosso in Rome, not far from the Colosseum. I have written you this e-mail as I consider it vital that I meet you at your earliest convenience. As I cannot divulge what this is about, may I simply mention the name Kobus Botha.

I do hope that I have caught your attention and pray that you will consider my request, as the consequences of not doing so may be dire indeed. My contact details are in the separate attachment.

Yours sincerely

F. di Paulo

"How the hell does he know my real name?" Grey sat down, downed a quarter of his pint and read the e-mail again. "There's no way on this planet this di Paulo character would mention a name like Kobus Botha in an e-mail addressed to Michael Grey unless he knows who I am."

"Pretty much what I thought. What now?"

Grey swilled the beer in his glass, watched the swirling foam remnants and took another look at the e-mail. "Whoever he is, this di Paulo knows about me and has something he'll only talk about face to face. He wouldn't ask me to go to Rome for a social chit-chat, plus he's 92 years old."

"Going to Italy then?"

"I think I will. The man's got me intrigued. Can you find out more about him for me?"

"Sure, I'll have whatever I can find ready by tomorrow midday. When are you planning to leave?" asked McLaughlin.

"Let's see." Grey took his smart phone and checked his diary. "Monday looks good. The appointments I've made can be handled by someone else. If I catch the early flight out I'll probably make it back the same day. Don't think it'll take much longer. If di Paulo can't tell me what's bothering him in two or three hours, I suppose it'll all have been a waste of time anyway. What interests me is how the hell he got hold of my real name!"

"Me too." McLaughlin folded his arms, sat back and gave Grey the look. "You think I need to reorganise my life for the next week or so?"

"Could be, Billy, could be." Grey smiled. "I suppose we'll know by Monday night, won't we?"

The following morning Michael Grey woke as usual at 05:00, got up, changed into his running gear and hit the road for his daily 10 kilometre run. It was the best time of the day, considering he lived in a flat in Kensington, later than that and the traffic and pedestrians would have prevented a free run. That morning – he always used the same route so he could time himself – he completed the run in precisely 41 minutes, a touch better than his average, but still over a minute slower than his best time. Not bad for someone approaching 50. He unlocked the door to his flat and headed for the shower. On the way he noticed his cell phone blinking. He picked up the phone, noted the number and immediately called back. His call was answered within seconds.

"Hey Michael! Been out for your run?"

"As always." Grey walked into the kitchen, opened the fridge and grabbed a bottle of fresh orange juice. "What's up? Didn't you get any sleep last night or did you wet your bed?"

"Nah, I slept for two hours then it got the better of me. This di Paulo was working on my tits so I decided to check him out. You know what I'm like; can't help it."

"Yeah, you're a lunatic when it comes to this kind of stuff. So what'd you find?"

"Not much," said McLaughlin. "One thing though, the guy's got a history so squeaky clean I reckon it's a crock!"

"You're sure?"

"About as sure as the Pope's a Catholic. Apparently he owned a bakery until he sold it and retired. No offences of any sort; tax totally up to date, and so it goes. Doesn't draw a state pension either, seems to have sorted out his retirement privately. Basically he's a borderline saint. Until late 1994. Then, within the space of four months he gets himself seven parking tickets and three speeding fines. Like the man's been in Rome for all his life and suddenly loses the plot? On top of that he pays them all immediately. Do me a favour, will you?"

"Hmm." Grey paused. "You're saying we might have a fake here?"

"I am. Then I had another look at the e-mail. The contents were damn near perfect as far as the English goes. And that from an Italian baker who's lived in Rome all his life? Then we have Kobus Botha thrown into the mix. Come on, Mike, who the hell does di Paulo think he's trying to fool?"

"No idea Billy, but all the more reason I need to see him. The whole thing's starting to stink just a tad."

"I agree," said McLaughlin. "Get to Italy, my boy, your flight's arranged. I've also sent di Paulo an e-mail telling him you'll be there on Monday morning. Guess what? He responded within an hour, around 04:00. The man clearly doesn't sleep much."

Rome, Italy

At 10:32 the following Monday morning the scheduled British Airways fight touched down at Rome's Fiumicino airport. One of the first passengers to disembark was Michael Grey, who made his way through customs and immigration without much fuss or bother. Less than 30 minutes after landing he was in a taxi on the way to Via Conte Rosso where he arrived just after 11:30. Grey paid the taxi-driver and made his way to the front door of a multi-storey apartment building typical of that area of Rome. To the left of the main entrance were a series of name tags. Grey studied the tags for a few seconds, found the name he was looking for, and pressed the intercom button next to the flat number. The buzzer indicating that the door could be opened sounded almost immediately. Grey walked into a short corridor, entered a small lift and pressed the button for the sixth floor. Not much later he knocked on the door to apartment 6A. The door, as had the main entrance door to the apartment block, opened instantly, as though someone had been watching him. Facing Grey was a tall, yet frail man, a halo of fine, white hair around his otherwise completely bald head. He looked at Grey over the top of a pair of large, horn-rimmed glasses perched on his nose. In his right hand he held a walking cane.

"Mr Grey?"

"Yes, that's me. You must be Mr di Paulo?" replied Grey, immediately noting the strange, yet familiar accent of the old man in front of him. Di Paulo definitely wasn't Italian.

"Please, do come in," said di Paulo, ushering Grey into the apartment. "Tea or coffee?"

"No, thank you. Perhaps later. I must say your English is excellent."

"Thank you," said di Paulo as he shuffled into the lounge of the open plan apartment, Grey close behind him.

The apartment, Grey noted, was very well furnished; certainly not what he would have expected when he first entered the building. Grey sat down in on a black leather settee and waited as di Paulo took his place in a recliner opposite him.

"Well, Mr Grey, I appreciate you having come here." He took a handkerchief from his pocket and blew his nose. "Pardon me. The colder weather at this time of the year does get to me."

"No problem, Mr di Paulo, I live in London and do understand." Grey took a brief moment to look around. "I must say, you have a very neat apartment, very impressive. Not quite what I'd have expected from a retired baker." Di Paulo looked up. So, as expected, they'd carried out a back ground check on him.

Grey continued, "But, maybe we should dispense with the small talk. You sent an e-mail to Grey & Mc Laughlin. Listening to you talk, you clearly aren't Italian, nor are you English. In fact, I'd say you're South African. And who's this Kobus Botha you mentioned in your e-mail?"

"Very observant, Mr Grey. You are, of course, correct, I'm not really Italian. Nor for that matter are you really English. So why don't we stop pretending and continue our discussion in Afrikaans... *Kaptein* Botha?"

"Fine," replied Grey, switching to Afrikaans. "Who the hell are you and how do you know who I am?"

"I see I have your attention. Who am I? Clearly not Franco di Paulo," di Paulo smiled and continued, also in Afrikaans, "my real name is Francois Labuschagne, and like you, I am a South

African. How do I know about you? That's easy. At the same time you, Captain Botha of 1 Reconnaissance Battalion, became famous because of the Angola incident, I was one of an inner circle of men who, at the time, shaped events in South Africa. In fact I was so close to the military and political leadership I called the President by his first name. I wasn't one of those who had their names and pictures splattered all over the press; I was very much in the background. Call me a powerbroker if you wish. It might, however, interest you to know that I was also one of a handful of people who decided and agreed that you needed a future and let you become Michael Grey. Would that explain it?"

"I don't believe I'm hearing this." Grey sat on the settee, incredulous. "Now I do need a drink. You don't happen to have a whisky handy, do you?"

"Yes, in the cabinet behind you. Help yourself. And a small one for me as well, if you would. No ice, but do add some water."

Grey got up, went to the cabinet and found a bottle of Johnny Walker Black. He poured himself a double, fixed the old man's drink, handed it to him and sat down once more.

"All right, Mr Labuschagne. What is it you want to tell me?"

"How much time have you got?"

"Three hours. Then I need to head back to the airport."

"Good, very good." Labuschagne took a sip of his drink. "I've spent a lot of time thinking about the best way to go about this, and have concluded the only way is to give you the full story.

Let me take you back all the way to 1957. I was 33 at the time, a young physicist working for the South African Atomic Energy Corporation as it was known in those days. I was also an ardent supporter of the National Party, assisting wherever I could when it came to party political functions, election campaigns and the like. Someone must've noticed how zealous I was, and it didn't take long before I was introduced to a Herman Marais. If I recall correctly it was in 1961. He introduced me to Dr PJ Meyer, who, at the time, was the chairman of the *Afrikaner Broederbond.* Not much later, young as I was, I became a part of the inner sanctum."

"The *Broederbond?* Interesting.

"Oh yes, it was. You have no idea how powerful we were. The decisions taken by us were considered sacrosanct, the gospel for the National Party. The President was part of this group. Not that we took spontaneous decisions. Far from it; we deliberated at length, especially when it came to important issues. Opinions were canvassed, doctrine had to be considered, and so it went. Which is also why I know about you and your past. As I mentioned earlier, I was one of the people who made the decision to allow you to become Michael Grey."

"I suppose you've also been keeping an eye on me. As to you sitting here, let me guess, when South Africa finally went democratic in 1994 you left the country under a false identity and came here as Franco di Paulo?" asked Grey.

"Obviously. Unfortunately, most of our covert activities were shut down just prior to the 1994 elections, especially those activities we ran outside the country. Up until then we kept a close eye on you and your progress. After 1994 and the shutdown of our networks, what you were doing became a matter of conjecture rather than fact. Only snippets of reliable information related to your activities reached me from time to time, from a London-based colleague who unfortunately passed away two years ago. Anyway, back to my story; what we did for you back in 1987, we did for ourselves in later years. Some of us simply couldn't stay in South Africa, we had to leave. I am one of those who had to leave and I chose Italy. It could've been America or any other country, but Italy had the right climate and I have always liked Italians, particularly the food. But, I digress. Now you know who I am, let's go back to 1957 and the South African Atomic Energy Corporation. Does the Atoms for Peace programme mean anything to you?"

"No, can't say it does, but I'm sure you're about to enlighten me."

"The Atoms for Peace programme was an American initiative that came about as a result of the atomic bombings of Hiroshima and Nagasaki. Ever since then, the world had been living in dread, watching helplessly as one atomic test was conducted after the other. It was Eisenhower who started the Atoms for Peace programme. His basic idea was to show the world that nuclear energy could be used for peaceful purposes, with mankind able to derive great benefit from the power of the atom. Until then it had all been about annihilation; who could build the biggest bomb. Sure, there were other, deeper-seated reasons for the programme, but that is not our concern. What did happen was that South Africa signed a 50-year collaboration agreement with the United States under the Atoms for Peace mantle in 1957. In 1965, the Americans delivered, as per the treaty, a 20 megawatt nuclear research reactor, together with the enriched uranium to run it. We called the reactor Safari 1 and installed it at the purpose-built site at Pelindaba."

"So far it's all a very interesting history lesson. What's the real point?"

"Bear with me. You also know South Africa possessed atomic devices?"

"Yes; at least there was speculation about atomic devices stored at Pelindaba when I left the country. From what I know, we did have them."

"Correct. The devices did exist. We merely dismantled them before the country was handed over to the African National Congress and Nelson Mandela. What we wanted to avoid, at all costs, was a black government with access to atomic weapons. We also signed the Nuclear Non-Proliferation Treaty. Damn, did we look good in the eyes of the world!" He chuckled, "Just imagine. We, the apartheid state, the first nation to voluntarily disclose its weapons programme, dismantle the devices and give the International Atomic Energy Agency full access to our nuclear installations. It was a brilliant move."

"If you know all of this, then maybe you can fill me in on something that's never been confirmed. You'll surely recall the incident where that satellite picked up a flash somewhere off Antarctica. It was near the Prince Edward Islands if I remember correctly. Myth has it that we tested a device. Did we?"

"Of course I remember. The Vela incident; September 1979. I'll neither confirm nor deny that it was an atomic test," Labuschagne grinned ever so slightly, "but we're getting a bit ahead of ourselves. Late in 1971 the decision was taken, in order to safeguard the country, to manufacture our own nuclear weapons. Not to attack anyone with, but rather to use as a political deterrent. By then sanctions had been imposed on us, and the first indications of increasing black militancy were being observed. We knew it would only get worse, and history tells us we weren't wrong in our assumptions. With sanctions in place, there was no further need to stick to the terms of the Atoms for Peace treaty. What for? We were being unjustly treated and our country was increasingly at risk of being taken over by the blacks. The idea was to use the atomic devices as a threat, along the lines of 'don't push us too far as we have the ability to annihilate you'. So we embarked on the process of building the atomic bomb. We had the technology, the scientific brains, and, most of all, access to vast amounts of uranium. You may ask how I know all of this. Well, I was one of the people involved in the decision to build the bomb. I was also part of the team responsible for designing and building the devices."

Grey got up and went to pour himself another double whisky. "Okay, Mr Labuschagne. I assume you didn't ask me to come to Rome to tell me all of this. What is it you really want?"

"I'm getting there. Between 1979 and 1989 we built a total of eight devices, all of them of the gun-triggered type..."

"Pardon," interrupted Grey, "gun-triggered? What's that?"

"A type of nuclear device. We deemed them easiest to manufacture and they needed highly-enriched uranium to function, which we could produce and had access to at the time. You see, we had the facilities to manufacture highly-enriched uranium, which took place at what we called the Y Plant at Pelindaba. We also built facilities at Pelindaba, the 5000 series buildings, for the various tests that had to be carried out. The actual assembly then happened at Kentron Circle, in the middle of the Armscor Girotek vehicle testing facility. In total, we built eight devices. The first one was a prototype fitted with a depleted uranium core only and no fissile material. Then we manufactured a further six complete, functional devices, ready for use. The last and eighth device was in the process of being manufactured when we killed off the project. "

"And?"

"Patience, Mr Botha. In August 1981, five of the most influential men within the *Broederbond* got together. I was one of them. We had a top-secret meeting on a farm near Zeerust. It was there that we made a decision I have now come to regret."

"What decision was that?"

"It was decided to build a bomb outside of the official channels. Call it the ninth device."

"What?"

"You heard me. We decided to build a clandestine device. That was, however, never disclosed; the device was never declared. As it stands, I am the only living person who knows about it. Now you do as well. All the other people involved have since died, some in untimely fashion and the others from natural causes."

"Hold it for a second," said Grey, "are you telling me there's an atomic weapon built by South Africans that no-one knows anything about?"

"Yes, I am."

"How the hell did you do it?"

"It took years. What we did was manufacture the parts of the ninth device as part of the process of building the others. Each completed part was smuggled out of the Kentron Circle facility and taken to a safe place north of Pretoria. By 1986 we had all the parts, all that needed to be done was to assemble the unit."

"And over all the years no one leaked any information as to what was happening?"

"No. It was a really complex operation, designed not to attract any attention. Every time parts were smuggled out and delivered, the courier was terminated. An unfortunate loss of life, I agree, but it was deemed a necessity."

"But why did you do it? What were you hoping to achieve?"

"We knew it would be a matter of time before what we termed the 'liberal' faction within the National Party, which was growing in strength by the day, would cave in and hand over power. In the event of that happening, we were going to assemble the device and plant it in a rented flat in the heart of Pretoria. We would then have threatened to detonate the device unless the party leadership stood down and let the conservative faction within the National Party take control."

"Isn't that exactly what happened?" asked Grey. "I mean when de Klerk unbanned the ANC and let Mandela out of prison, why didn't you execute your plans?"

Labuschagne took another sip of his whisky. "It was too late. By then the National Party was badly damaged internally, there was no longer the mass conservative nor the ideological support needed to successfully take over the leadership. On top of that, de Klerk had done the one thing nobody had expected; he had released Nelson Mandela. Can you imagine what would have happened to South Africa if we had detonated the bomb with Nelson Mandela a free man? The country was riding the crest of the wave of change; the liberals were in the ascendancy and our power was eroding faster than a heap of sand in a raging torrent. Had we gone ahead the country would have been plunged into full-scale civil war. We would possibly have killed a few hundred thousand in Pretoria, but what would have followed would have meant the death of millions; certainly the entire white population would have been decimated. We couldn't allow that, so we pulled back at the last minute. Also, and perhaps it is a good thing, we were still busy designing and building the triggering mechanism."

"You didn't have a triggering mechanism? You mentioned you were planning to use the device in Pretoria?"

"The design of the triggering mechanism had been completed, but not the actual construction. You see, the mechanism used to activate the official devices could not be used. Those mechanisms were designed to trigger the devices during flight. Ours was a stationary device."

"Thank God you didn't succeed. Where's the device now? What happened to it?"

"That, Mr Grey, or Kobus Botha," sighed Labuschagne, "is the real reason you are here today. As mentioned before, we - and here I refer to my four colleagues and I - left the country. The unassembled bomb, minus the triggering mechanism, remained in South Africa, very well hidden. Unfortunately we eventually ran out of money and there was only one way of obtaining enough cash to allow us to live comfortably to the end of our days."

"Christ Almighty, Labuschagne! Please tell me you didn't..."

"Yes, we did. Two years ago we sold the device and spirited all the components out of South Africa."

Grey sat on the settee, staring in utter wonder at the old man opposite him, not knowing whether to scream or to feel sorry for him. "Can you at least tell me who you sold the device to? And who's we?"

"Yes, I can. I have cancer, you know. The doctors have given me less than two weeks to live. I have lived with what we have done for the past two years, never mind the years spent in Italy remembering all the other atrocities I've been party to in the name of a political system. I need to atone for those sins. Oh, my colleague, who was still alive when we sold it? It was Pieter van Zyl. He lived in London at the time."

"Listen, Labuschagne. Right now I don't give a rat's ass for you or your sins. Who the hell did the two of you sell the nuke to?"

"I only know him by the name of Udo. We believe he bought the device on behalf of an organisation called the Meinhof Kollaboration. We were paid US $50 million for the device, deposited into a Swiss bank account."

This time Grey did scream. "Do YOU realise what the FUCK you have done?!! DO YOU??!! You know what the Meinhof Kollaboration is? No? A bunch of fucking maniacs, that's what they are!! And you sold them a goddamned nuke?!!!" He grabbed Labuschagne by the lapels of his jacket, shaking the frail old man, "What else can you tell me? WHAT ELSE?!!"

"Nothing. I swear it. You know all I do!"

Grey dropped the old man back into his chair and made for the door.

"Mr Grey!"

Grey stopped and turned. "What?"

"Please! Stay!"

"What the fuck for? You make me want to puke!"

"Then please, find the device; I implore you!"

"Yeah," snarled Grey, "I'll try. I'm out of here." He opened the door to leave, then stopped and turned, "One last thing, Labuschagne."

"Yes?" The old man was trembling.

"I hope you rot in hell!"

Minutes later Grey had left the building, found a taxi and told the driver to take him to the airport. As the taxi reached the first intersection, the Termini railway station visible in the distance to his left, he was on the phone to Billy McLaughlin.

"Billy. I reckon the two weeks you were talking about for our next escapade start right now."

McLaughlin, although sitting in London, could sense there was something very wrong. "Big problem?"

"Bigger than you think. I didn't need the three hours; I'm on the way back to the airport. I need to get back. Tonight."

"That bad?"

"Worse. Listen, I can't talk right now, but find out whatever you can about a German organisation called the Meinhof Kollaboration. With what this grandfather's just told me we need to get a proper handle on them sooner rather than later. I'm cutting the call now. See you in a couple of hours in Wimbledon. Make sure you're there."

London, United Kingdom

By the time Grey arrived at Grey & McLaughlin's IT and electronic intelligence-gathering headquarters it was well past 22:00. Based in South Wimbledon, just outside London, it was housed in Billy McLaughlin's old student flat. Not that it was anything like a student flat any longer. Compared to what had been a small, yet neat set-up in a typical bachelor's flat when they had first met all those years ago, it was now so state-of-the-art that the heads of most global intelligence agencies would have given their left testicles to be able to call it their own. Built, run and managed by Billy McLaughlin alone, Grey & McLaughlin plc had the ability to establish if someone was sneezing elsewhere on the planet if they so wished. Nor was it obvious what the flat housed, since, from the road, the building was as nondescript as it could get and the entrance was just another entrance to a flat. The location of the set-up was not something advertised by Grey & McLaughlin plc.

Grey let himself in and headed for the nerve-centre of the operation. Billy McLaughlin, seated behind a veritable bank of screens, was so engrossed in what he was doing that he never even noticed Grey enter the room.

"Hey, Billy!"

"Mike!" McLaughlin spun around in his chair. "Didn't hear you coming in! What the hell's going down? Never heard you so sombre in my life."

"I'll get there now. What'd you manage to find out about the

Meinhof Kollaboration?"

"Rabid crowd's the best way to describe them. Kind of make your average terrorist organisation look like a kiddies' picnic; very much into anti-fascism, anti-imperialism, the usual bit of anarchy and decidedly anti-Semitic. Not big; probably a handful of people. Run by a character called Jens Keller. Highly intelligent bastard, yet from all accounts he's a complete lunatic. They're banned in Germany. Keep moving from place to place; no one knows where they are at any given point in time. The German police have been trying to run down Keller and his cohorts - one Anne Biedermann and a Karl Stegemann - for the past few years, but they're just too elusive. Seem to use a couple of aliases and must have access to some top-class forgers. The group's allegedly been involved in a number of bank robberies and other extortion activities. There was an instance where they kidnapped the son of a wealthy industrialist, were paid a million Euros ransom, then dropped the kid off next to a freeway in the middle of the night. The boy was carrying a plastic bag. You won't believe what was in it."

"What?"

"His right hand. The bastards had chopped it off, just for the hell of it."

"Jesus!"

"Yeah, right royal evil swines! Then there're a couple of deaths they claimed to be responsible for. One of those occurred in an accident on the A1 Autobahn outside Muenster in Northern

Germany where a high-profile CDU politician came to grief, something to do with a tyre bursting at high speed. Then a house fire in Munich, where a high-ranking police officer burnt to a crisp. Last, and it's the cherry on cake, the assassination of US Senator Golding in Berlin. There're also a number of other incidents the German authorities believe were orchestrated by the Meinhof Kollaboration, but couldn't conclusively link them to the events. One other thing; they frequently come up with You-Tube video clips, which are usually removed by the authorities just as quickly as they are posted; the content's simply too extreme. The last few displayed an alarming degree of Jew-baiting. For whatever reason, they hate Israel with an absolute passion. Don't ask me why, but they do. Strange thing is that they've gone very quiet over the past year or so. That's it from my side. So, what about this di Paulo?"

"The miserable old fucker sold them a nuke."

"Ahh... stop... What did you say?"

"He... sold... them ... a... nuke."

"You're crazy, right?"

"No. 100 percent sane. And di Paulo? Italian my ass! The bugger's a bloody South African. Skipped the country and hid away in Italy. Not only did he sell the bloody thing, he was involved in designing and building it."

"But I thought they'd destroyed them all!"

"So did I. Until today. They built one nobody knew about and ended up stashing it away in South Africa, somewhere outside

Pretoria. When the National Party's wheels fell off many of the party diehards left the country. Di Paulo – crap, his name's really Francois Labuschagne – and a couple of his mates had to get out as well. Two years ago they ran out of money. So what did they do? They smuggled the unassembled, but otherwise complete nuke out of the country and sold it to the Meinhof Kollaboration for US $50 million."

"They what? Are they mad?"

"As mad as a convention of goddamned Hatters! Labuschagne's the last of the merry lot; his mates have all passed on. He told me he's only got two weeks left to live. Cancer. Which is why he got hold of us. The geriatric old fart knows exactly who I am; he was one of the men who allowed me to become Michael Grey. Now he's dying and says he wants to atone for his sins."

"Atone for his sins?" spluttered McLaughlin. "Fuck me! Anything else he wants?"

"Absolutely. He wants us to find the bomb."

"Wonderful! Bloody marvellous! I'm so happy I could shit! They sell a nuke to the Meinhof Kollaboration and now this Labuschagne wants us to find the bloody thing? Did he give you a name?"

"Someone called Udo. That's it." Grey shrugged. "Maybe I should've stayed longer. He says he told me everything, but you know what these types are like. Interrogate them properly and watch what else comes out in the wash. Might still have to do that."

"With someone who's over 90 and dying of cancer? You'd probably kill him in two seconds flat."

"Depends on how you do it."

"All right," said McLaughlin. "Give me a sec to get my head around this little lot. We've got a pseudo-Italian pensioner who sold a nuke to an organisation that models itself on the defunct Red Army Faction and who happen to hate Israel. Does that sum it up?"

"Kind of," answered Grey.

"So where in hell did the Meinhof Kollaboration get US $50 million from? A couple of bank robberies? Not likely. And what do they want to do with bomb? You don't go around shelling out 50 million for a nuke unless you know what to do with the thing. You got any idea?"

"I don't Billy. I really don't. I just can't see them using the nuke to blow up part of Germany, it makes no sense. It's the Israel part that worries me."

"Israel? You think they'd do that?"

"Why not? Imagine the scene. A nuke detonates in Israel and flattens Jerusalem. Or Haifa. Maybe Tel Aviv. Hundreds of thousands of civilians dead. Who do you think the Israeli's would immediately blame?"

"That's obvious. Iran."

"Ten out of ten. And what do you think the Israelis would do?"

"Retaliate?"

"Damn right they would! Next thing Tehran disappears in a cloud of radioactive dust. But we know that Iran didn't do it; the Israeli's don't! What we don't know is if Iran has the bomb or not. Assume they do. In next to no time the second nuke explodes in Israel because Iran thinks the Israelis started it. What happens then?"

"Shit. Complete Middle East meltdown; nukes all over the place, millions of deaths and it could spill over to God-only-knows-where. Mike, we've got to try and stop this thing."

"You got that right," muttered Grey. "I'm trying to figure out how."

"What about telling the Yanks? We could always call one of our contacts there. Or we could get hold of the Israelis and warn them?"

"I think we need to warn the Israelis first before we get anyone else involved. They've got their feelers out all over the place. Thing is we've never dealt with them before, so who do we call?" Grey sat back and thought for a few minutes, McLaughlin watching him quietly. "Here's what we do. We contact the Israeli Mossad HQ in Israel. Unless I'm badly mistaken we'll hear from them very quickly. "

"I'm on it." McLaughlin turned his chair and began typing on his keyboard. "I remember seeing their website... aah, here it is - www.mossad.gov.il. Believe it or not, you can send them information via the net. You want to see what they say they do on their home page? Not exactly subtle! I'll give them your contact number. What else do you want me to write?"

Grey got up and looked over McLaughlin's shoulder at the screen. "Just write - *Require immediate response. Please call number given. Possible threat against Israel involving WMD. This is no hoax* - That should do it. It wouldn't surprise me one little bit either if they know who we are." Grey watched as McLaughlin typed and then hit the send button. "Now we wait."

It didn't take long. Less than five minutes later Grey's cell phone began to ring. "Hmm. Unknown number. I bet it's them." He slid his finger across the green answer icon on the screen of his phone. "Michael Grey speaking."

"Mr Grey. I am responding to a message received from you. We would like to send someone to talk to you," said an anonymous voice.

"Is that the Mossad?"

"Yes. Where are you?"

"London."

"Wait a second please." The caller went off the line and Grey could hear voices in the background. He was back seconds later. "Can you write?"

"Yes."

"Take down this address." The caller gave Grey an address in Tottenham. "Go there as soon as you can. Someone will be there waiting for you."

"Will do. Any contact number?" asked Grey.

"No. It is not needed. And Mr Grey, thank you for calling." The caller hung up.

By the time Grey arrived at the address given to him, not far from the home of Tottenham FC at White Hart Lane, it was close to midnight. He looked about to see if someone was watching him or if he had been followed. Noting nothing out of the ordinary, he knocked on the door. He didn't have to wait long. The door opened and a dark, curly-haired man of medium build, wearing jeans, a sweater and a brown leather jacket appeared in the doorway. His dark olive skin tone indicated that he did not come from the UK. Grey, at first glance, judged him to be approximately 30 years old.

"Mr Grey?"

"Yes."

I'm Ronnie Kreyzer. Glad you could make it. Come in."

Grey entered the house. If he hadn't known any different, he would have thought he'd entered the home of the average family living in the area. Waiting in the lounge was another man. As Grey entered, he got up and held out his hand. Unlike his colleague, he was far older, Grey estimated him to be over 60 years of age. Although also dressed casually, he was clearly the more senior of the two. Grey took the offered hand and shook it, noting the firm, strong grip.

"Good evening, Mr Grey. My name's Gideon Scholl. Please,"

he indicated the lounge suite, "take a seat. Something to drink?"

Grey sat took off his coat, sat down, and made himself comfortable. "A cup of coffee would be great if you've got."

Scholl nodded at the younger Kreyzer who made his way to the kitchen. As he left the room Scholl continued, "Thanks for coming. I know it's late, but then I suppose people in my line of work don't keep regular hours. You strike me as having the same predicament. Maybe we should start by you telling me a bit more about yourself."

"Sure," answered Grey. "Before I do that, can you confirm who you're with?"

"Good. I like cautious people." Scholl took a passport out of his jacket pocket and handed it to Grey. It was a diplomatic passport issued by the State of Israel, made out to a Gideon Scholl, date of birth 26 July 1957, born in Haifa.

"Diplomatic passport. Good enough for me. You're with the Mossad, right?" Scholl nodded and Grey gave him a brief outline as to who he was and what Grey & McLaughlin plc did, particularly the more discreet activities of their operation. As he spoke, Kreyzer walked in carrying a tray with three cups of coffee, milk, sugar and teaspoons. He placed the tray on the small lounge table and sat down. It took Grey, who was acutely aware he was sitting opposite a professional in his field, a few minutes to finish.

"Interesting," said Scholl, "it ties in nicely with the little we know about you. You've just filled in a few of the gaps. You'll appreciate we obviously checked our databases to see if we had anything on you before we arrived here. Can't be too careful, not in our game, and definitely not as an Israeli. Anyway, I'm Head of Station here in London. Your message set off all sorts of alarm bells in Israel and we were sent out here immediately. Not surprising, since you mentioned a weapon of mass destruction. Can you elaborate?"

"Yeah. I'll try to stick as far as possible to the chronological order. Feel free to interrupt and ask questions. Let me start with this." Grey handed a folded copy of di Paulo's e-mail to Scholl. "Read it. That's what got all this started."

Scholl read the e-mail and handed it to Kreyzer. "Cryptic. I suppose you went and saw him?"

"Yes; today." Grey spooned two sugars into his cup, added milk and began to stir. "Flew to Rome this morning and arrived back just over two hours ago. Now I'm here."

"So it's a real problem in your eyes. Okay, go ahead. We'll try not to interrupt," said Scholl.

It took Grey ten minutes to relate the events of the day. Every now and again Scholl and Kreyzer looked at each other, the expression on Scholl's face grimmer and grimmer with each minute that passed. Neither of the two said anything, not interrupting Grey as he spoke. "And that, gentlemen," ended Grey, "is why I called you."

"Mike – you don't mind me calling you that? – We've had a couple of threats of this nature over the past years, most of them from crack-pot organisations that don't know how to spell the word nuke. All of them have turned out to be fictitious so far; false alarms. This is different! If this is real – and I emphasise if - then it's possibly the biggest threat our nation's faced in the last three decades."

"Mike's fine." For a brief moment Grey paused, contemplating his response. "I agree with you. Sure, there's an outside chance it's all bogus, but I personally feel that what Labuschagne told me is the truth. What vexes me, is if the nuke was sold two years ago, why haven't the Meinhof Kollaboration done anything with it yet?"

"There's an answer to that. Tell me," asked Scholl, "does anyone else know about this?"

"Only Billy McLaughlin."

"Good. I'd like it to stay that way. Back to the Meinhof Kollaboration and why they haven't done anything yet. We know them; they're very much on our radar when they expose themselves from time to time. Our name for them is simply MK. We had a chance to remove Jens Keller a few years ago but had to pull back at the last minute. Pity! Tell me, what do you know about nukes, Mike?"

"Enough that when they blow up they cause a huge amount of damage and other misery."

Scholl glanced across at Kreyzer. "Ronnie."

"Let me give you a bit of my background, Mike," said Kreyzer. "Eight years ago I joined the Mossad. Before that I studied mechanical engineering at the Weizmann Institute of Science, ended up with a doctorate. Why I joined the Mossad isn't important; let's say it was a calling. Because of my background, the Mossad exposed me to the intricacies of nuclear devices, with specific emphasis on suitcase nukes. We've always believed that one day someone might try it, so, all the better to know how to deal with them if it ever did happen. What you've just told us about is the South African gun-triggered device. We know about the design details of what used to be the South African bombs until they were dismantled. Years ago, and you'll know better than most, our links to South Africa were very strong, so strong in fact that we collaborated on delivery systems for atomic devices and so on. Most nuclear warheads are designed to be detonated during flight, either on a delivery system such as a rocket, being lobbed from an aircraft, or, in the case of many tactical nukes designed to be used on battlefields, fired from a cannon. The triggering systems usually involve complicated pressure-sensitive and velocity-linked technology, which prevents them from blowing up when they're stored or being handled on the ground. Many of them only arm themselves once a certain velocity or altitude has been reached. In short, there are a whole lot of safety mechanisms built into these devices. I'll leave it there. Thing is, it's not all that easy to convert a velocity or altitude-triggered device to a stationary land-based device and get it to explode. Sure, it can be done, but you need the expertise to do that. As an example, you could take any intercontinental ballistic missile-based device, give it to a terrorist organisation and ask them to arm it. They wouldn't even know where to begin. My guess is MK bought the device – which was stripped down to its individual components and, thank God, without the triggering mechanism – and had to find someone to do the conversion, build the trigger and assemble it. What scares me is that they've had a two year head-start."

Grey pondered that for a while. "Scares me too. You don't go and buy a nuke if you don't know what you're going to do with it and my gut tells me you're the target."

"I think you may be right. We can assume, whatever the timeframe, it's probably targeted at us and it's close to happening," said Scholl. "We've got to find it."

"Why don't you give your American counterparts a call and ask them for help? Or the BfV in Germany? That'd give you plenty of resources. Surely you'd find this Jens Keller and his cohorts?"

"Unfortunately, it's not as simple as it seems," replied Scholl. "The Germans? Maybe they'll help. But they typically don't like the fact that we have assets in their country. Our methods are, shall we say, a bit too direct for them? Not that they're bad at what they do, far from it. But first we have to convince them that they might have a rogue nuke lurking about in their country. Unless we can prove it, they won't really believe us. If they're convinced, they'll want to handle it themselves. We can't risk that, not if what you said is real, and I believe it is."

"And the Americans?" asked Grey.

"What I tell you now you never heard. We can't use the

Americans, not for this one. We found out about three years ago that there's a highly placed, very influential and extremely wealthy group in the USA that quietly advocates – no, actively encourages – military activity in crisis spots around the world."

"Oh? Who's that?"

"We don't know them by name, but we do know they - or he or she - exist. As far as we can tell, it can't be more than a handful of men or women who make the real decisions, but they seem to have a widespread network and support base. We believe they're part of the arms manufacturing cluster in America and benefit from military activity of any kind."

"Okay. So it's not nice, but not particularly unusual. Why's this group such a problem?"

"One of their particular objectives appears to be creating a situation where armed conflict between Iran and Israel becomes a reality. Imagine what would happen if we went to war with Iran. The entire Middle East would go up in flames with only one beneficiary..."

"I get it. The arms industry! But how do you know about this group?"

"How do we know?" This time Scholl took time to answer. "Without going into the detail, we ran a covert joint operation with the CIA a few years back in the USA. Four Iranian fundamentalists had entered the US with the intent to blow up the Israeli Embassy in Washington and three of our consulates, Atlanta, Miami and Los Angeles. We were about to close in on them before they did any damage when a newspaper article appeared in the Jerusalem Post. It revealed the entire plot, our plan of action, even gave the names of the four Iranians involved. Even worse, the article called on the Israeli government to launch an immediate counter-strike against Iran. It blew the entire operation, not only from our side. The four Iranians vanished; we certainly never caught them."

"How the hell did that happen?"

"We don't know. The article was sent in by an anonymous person from America; a letter couriered to the *Jerusalem Post* by FedEx from Boston. The shit-storm it caused in Israel was severe to say the least. Safe to say, someone had leaked highly classified information and it wasn't the Mossad, so it can only have been someone in the CIA. We never found out who, but it forced us to concede that working with the CIA on future projects of this nature was something to be avoided at all costs. For whatever reason, someone out there was protecting the Iranians and let them know – publicly – that we were onto them! As to the Israeli reaction? Well, the Israeli government sent a clear message to the Iranians that any further activities against Israel would result in an immediate military response. We had to. You have no idea how close it was to full-scale armed conflict."

"Just because of one newspaper article?"

"It was the way it was written that did the trick. You need to understand the Israeli psyche to appreciate the effect it had," said Scholl. "Sure, we Israelis have different views on how to deal with the Palestine issue and a host of other internal matters. But don't, whatever you do, attack us as a nation. We know most of the Arab world would love to see us disappear as a State. To them, the sooner we cease to exist the better, but it's not going to happen. Threaten Israel as a whole and we will fight, to the death, if necessary. And fight we can, as the Arabs have found out to their detriment on at least three occasions. Ask the Syrians what happened to them during the Yom Kippur War in '73; they'll tell you a thing or two. In short, you can piss us off, but don't take it too far. Which is precisely what the newspaper article did. It was written in such a way that the average man on the street understood it to be Iran declaring open war on Israel. The nation felt threatened and, as a result, the nation, as a collective, demanded a response."

"A response that may well have been hugely rewarding for the American military-industrial complex, not so?"

"Yes, and in no small measure, irrespective of the outcome of such a conflict. Perhaps we would win, who knows? But let's assume for one minute we were annihilated. The destruction of Israel would create a situation in the Middle East where the Western World, particularly America, had very little, if any, influence. The mooted Great Islamic State could become a reality. Most Arabs, certainly the fundamentalist Muslim faction, view America as the Great Satan. At best, it would be the Cold War all over again, except this time it would be the Western World versus the Great Islamic State or Federation of Islamic States, or whatever. Safe to say, billions upon billions of dollars would be spent on military hardware and ramping up military readiness. And once again, who benefits most? The arms industry, in particular, American arms manufacturers."

"So you think this person or group of people in the USA could well be trying to orchestrate a situation for which there can be only one outcome?"

"Exactly. And they came close; real close." Scholl put down his cup of coffee and lit a cigarette. "Someone out there is attempting to convince either Israel or Iran to start a war. They've tried once and failed, but only just. I think they're trying it again, this time with the help of a nuke."

"Yet Iran, as much as they hate you, would be innocent."

"Innocent or not, no one will care, certainly not in Israel. Iran *will* be blamed and Israel *will* react in kind. The result *will* be inevitable disaster. I'll tell you this much, MK alone wouldn't have hatched a plot of this nature. Even if they'd robbed enough banks to get hold of US $50 million, they'd have spent it on creating all sorts of other mayhem, not the purchase of a disassembled nuclear device minus a triggering system."

"So you really believe this group in the USA is behind this?"

"I do. As I said, it's a recipe for complete disaster."

"And the Meinhof Kollaboration?"

"If anything, a pawn; someone to blame afterwards. I may be wrong, but it's unlikely they're the brains behind this."

"Shit."

"Very much so." Scholl sighed. "So we can't use the Americans because of the danger of this group finding out we know what's going down, they seem to be too highly placed not to find out. If they are using MK, which right now seems to be a given, and have funded them, they'll make damn sure MK either goes to ground and we don't find them at all, or, if they find out someone's onto them, they'll accelerate the process. What we need now is absolute secrecy, speed of execution and whatever help we can get that doesn't involve Germany or the USA. Which brings me to a question," Scholl paused and looked straight into Grey's eyes, "will your company assist us?"

There was a moment of silence. "I don't make those decisions myself. I need to discuss this with Billy first, but, knowing Billy, I'd say, in principle, the answer would be yes. I'll give you a definite answer tomorrow."

"I understand." Scholl took a pen from his shirt pocket, found a scrap of paper and wrote down a number. "Here. My telephone number," he said, handing the paper to Grey. "If I haven't heard from you by midday, I'll assume you can't help. In that case I'd like to thank you for informing us, wish you all the best and ask you to forget we ever met. We'll go ahead by ourselves anyway. I do, however, hope I'll hear from you."

"What about di Paulo?"

"Him? Unless he expires tonight, he certainly won't die in Italy."

The following morning an ambulance stopped outside the

building housing di Paulo's apartment in the Via Conte Rosso in Rome. Two men, dressed as paramedics, climbed out, went to the front door, expertly picked the lock and let themselves in. Minutes later they knocked on the door to di Paulo's apartment. Di Paulo, not expecting anyone, opened the door to find out who was there. A split second later he had a hand clamped over his mouth and was being frogmarched back into the apartment. He tried to struggle, but it was useless, the man holding him was far too strong. The second paramedic closed the door quietly, took a syringe from the top pocket of his overall and grabbed di Paulo's arm. Di Paulo, trying to scream, but not able to because of the hand clamped over his mouth, felt the prick as the needle went into his arm. Two seconds later he was unconscious. Soon after, two other paramedics, who had been waiting in the ambulance, made their way into the apartment. They had a stretcher with them. Less than eight minutes after the first two paramedics entered the apartment block, the unconscious di Paulo was in the back of the ambulance. Sirens blaring, the vehicle raced through Rome towards Ciampino, the older of Rome's two main airports. Pre-declared a medical emergency requiring a Jewish tourist to be taken back to Israel due to a heart attack – arranged in advance by the Mossad – the ambulance came to a halt at the open door of a waiting chartered Bombardier Challenger 604 jet in the livery of Orange Aviation, an airline based in Ben Shemen at Ben Gurion International Airport in Israel. Three hours later, the aircraft landed at the Palmachim Airbase, not far from Tel Aviv. By the time di Paulo came to his senses, he was in an isolated ward in an Israeli military hospital, where a series of not entirely friendly men began to ask their questions.

Just before midday, Gideon Scholl received the call he had been hoping and waiting for.

CHAPTER 2
ORGANISED EVIL

The Meinhof Kollaboration

Jens Keller closed the *Der Spiegel* magazine he'd been reading and got up. The article he'd finished reading dealt with the German government plans to – once more – pump massive funds into a new assistance programme for the German *Mittelstand* industries, the highly-vaunted heart of German economic success. The *Mittelstand*. One word that described everything Jens Keller hated, one word driving him on with a passion that had long since turned into overt fanaticism. The *Mittelstand*. It had to be destroyed, together with the bourgeois pigs who owned the industries and controlled the wealth of Germany. And how much of it was once again in the hands of the Jews? He watched Anne Biedermann sitting at the other end of the dining-room table, writing a script for their next video-clip. At the other end of the table sat Karl Stegemann, the components of a Glock handgun spread around in front of him. *He never stops cleaning his weapons, does he*, mused Keller. They had been idle for too long now.

Boredom had long since set in and he knew it was dangerous; it caused them to drop their guard. Keller walked across to the window and looked out, his mind wandering back to the days it had all started. Ah yes, Andreas Baader... what a man, what a martyr, what an inspiration! And Gudrun, Ulrike, Horst... had they succeeded in what they'd set out to do, how different Germany would be! Free of the shackles of the *Mittelstand* swine, of Jewish influence. Baader, the visionary! And yet it had all ended; Baader's work destroyed by the German State. In his mind, Keller owed it to Andreas Baader to continue where he had left off so many years ago...

Andreas Baader. What history had he created to spawn someone of the calibre of Jens Keller?

Together with Gudrun Ensslin, Ulrike Meinhof and Horst Mahler, they were the founders of the Baader Meinhof Group, which, in 1970, became the Red Army Faction, or the RAF. Professing to be a communist, anti-imperialist, urban guerrilla group engaged in armed resistance against what they perceived to be the fascist German state, the RAF conducted a series of operations resulting in the assassinations of politicians, highly-placed government functionaries, bankers, media group owners and the like.

It all culminated in the latter part of 1977, subsequently termed the *German Autumn*. By then, three of the founding members, Andreas Baader, Ulrike Meinhof and Gudrun Ensslin, had been arrested and imprisoned in a purpose-built, ultra high-security block at Stammheim Prison in the north of Stuttgart, southern Germany. Also arrested and imprisoned were Holger Meins and Jan-Carl Raspe, both of whom had joined the RAF at a later point in time.

By the end of the *German Autumn* four of the five were dead. The first to die was Holger Meins, who perished in prison in November 1974, the result of a protracted hunger strike. Then, in 1975, the infamous Stammheim trials against the remaining four began. It was perhaps one of the darkest times in post-war Germany's legislative history. Laws were changed to help the German State prosecute the accused, allowing the State to exclude several defence attorneys with possible RAF allegiances from the trial, in order to prevent sensitive information from being leaked to the accused, as well as preventing any possibility of second generation RAF involvement. In a nutshell, the German authorities had decided, irrespective of legal or constitutional ramifications, that if the RAF was capable of playing hardball and dirty, then so could they. During the course of the highly publicised and sensational trial, Ulrike Meinhof was found dead in her cell in May 1976, allegedly a suicide, questionable at best. At the end of April 1977, the remaining defendants were sentenced to life imprisonment.

Not that the attacks stopped during the trial period, if anything, they intensified. In early April 1977, Siegfried Buback, German Federal Prosecutor – who had gone on record saying that people like Baader didn't deserve a free trial - was assassinated along with his bodyguard and driver. The RAF claimed responsibility.

In July 1977, Juergen Ponto, head of the Dresdner Bank, was shot and killed in front of his home in a botched kidnapping. Again the RAF claimed responsibility.

Shortly after the Ponto assassination, Hanns-Martin Schleyer, a former officer in the Nazi SS and by then President of the German Employers' Association - hence one of the most powerful industrialists in West Germany – was taken hostage; the kidnapping by RAF members resulting in the deaths of three policemen as well as one of the drivers in Schleyer's convoy.

Then, on 13 October 1977, Lufthansa flight 181, a Boeing 737-200 called Landshut, en route from Palma de Mallorca to Frankfurt, was hijacked by four Palestine Liberation Organisation terrorists. Eventually landing in Mogadishu, Somalia (after flying to Rome, then Lanarca in Cyprus, the Kingdom of Bahrain, Dubai and Aden in South Yemen) the demands made by the PLO terrorists, calling themselves Commando Martyr Halime, were largely the same as the demands made by the Schleyer kidnappers – the release of the RAF detainees in Stammheim. On the way to Mogadishu, during the short stop in Aden and after a landing on a sand airstrip, the pilot of the aircraft, Juergen Schumann, was murdered by the terrorists. He had been allowed to leave the aircraft to inspect the airworthiness of the Boeing 737 and had allegedly used the opportunity to speak to ground authorities. He returned to the aircraft he was in charge of and was shot though the head in full view of the passengers. The body was later dumped from the aircraft onto the tarmac of the airport in Mogadishu.

On 18 October 1977, in the early morning hours, German Special Forces of the Grenzschutzgruppe 9 – or GSG 9 - stormed the aircraft. The operation, called *Feuerzauber* – Magic Fire – resulted in the deaths of three of the terrorists with none of the passengers suffering serious injury. The highly successful operation would forever change the way the international community dealt with acts of terrorism. The GSG 9, up until then an entity most Germans knew nothing about, was catapulted into the realms of super-stardom, becoming a name known in nearly all German households. Within half an hour of the successful storming of the aircraft the news of the rescue was broadcast in Germany.

The very same night the imprisoned members of the RAF allegedly committed suicide in Stammheim Prison. But was it suicide?

Andreas Baader was found dead in his cell with a gunshot wound in the back of his head. Gudrun Ensslin was found hanged in her cell. Jan-Carl Raspe, with a gunshot wound to the head, was taken to hospital where he died the following day. Irmgard Moeller, a further detainee, had several stab wounds in her chest. She survived and was ultimately released from prison in 1994. The circumstances under which the inmates died were highly suspect to say the least. How on earth did the most heavily guarded prisoners in Germany, in a purpose built prison, die of gunshot wounds, hanging and stabbing themselves? How did guns find their way into the cells of Baader and Raspe? How had Ensslin managed to hang herself? And how did Moeller manage to stab herself in the chest, not only once, but several times, never mind where the knife had come from? To this day there are those who argue that the deaths were not suicides, but murders carried out by the German State.

On 19 October 1977, only hours after the deaths of Baader, Ensslin and Raspe, the body of kidnapped Hanns-Martin Schleyer was recovered in the trunk of a green Audi 100 motor vehicle in Mulhouse, France, by French police after the French authorities had been informed where to find him. He had been executed. The French newspaper Liberation received a letter stating the following:

After 43 days we have ended Hanns-Martin Schleyer's pitiful and corrupt existence... His death is meaningless to our pain and our rage... The struggle has only begun. Freedom through armed, anti-imperialist struggle.

As much as the terror acts of the RAF and aligned groups attracted widespread condemnation, there was a significant part of the German population who quietly sympathised with the RAF, particularly the more liberal sector. Germany had come out of World War II damaged beyond belief. Twenty years later, the physical damage had been repaired, but not the psychological damage, ex-Nazi's were once again amongst the most influential of people in German society. Hanns-Martin Schleyer was a point in case, as were men such as Kurt Georg Kiesinger, a proven member of the NSDAP, the Nazi Party, who became Chancellor in 1966. Also, the German government had banned the Communist Party in 1956, which did not go down well in all quarters. Hence many of the younger generation in the early 70s, particularly the more left-aligned, took the view that the German State was still fascist - unsurprising - considering who was running the government, the economy and how many of the key role-players had a Nazi past.

Added to the mix was the notion of many Germans that absolute authority was dangerous and to be avoided at all costs. God forbid something akin to the Third Reich would manifest itself again. In short, Germany in the late 60s and 70s was a hotbed of political activism and extremism, spawning not only the RAF, but also organisations such as the Revolutionary Cells, Movement 2 June, the Socialist Patients' Collective, Kommune 1 and the Situationists. As a last point, the notion that the main protagonists in these organisations were mere rabble-rousers needs to be dispelled - most were highly intelligent, intellectual young men and woman, misguided perhaps, but far from stupid.

Of all the people mentioned above, one of the founding members of the RAF, Horst Mahler, is still very much alive and currently serving a 12 year prison sentence for Holocaust denial and banalisation, as well as other pro-Nazi utterances, which is surprising, coming from a man who had been involved in the formation of the leftist, communist RAF.

Not that it really mattered to Jens Keller. Who cared whether or not Mahler had switched from one extreme to the other? He was still a founding member of the RAF, wasn't he? And if he could embrace right wing extremism, then why not Jens Keller?

Born in 1980 in the town of Böblingen, just outside Stuttgart,

Jens Keller was the only son of Maria and Lutz Keller. The first years of his life were spent in happy ignorance. His parents did, however, notice that their child was possibly gifted, and, at the age of four they took him to a clinical psychologist who confirmed their suspicions. From there on, Jens Keller's life changed. By the time he was six he had mastered the piano, played chess at a level that would have allowed him to take part in the German National Chess Championships, was dealing with university entry level mathematics and devouring every possible book he could read.

It was between the ages of six and twelve that he showed where his real interest lay, history and current affairs. His private tutor, a 69-year-old Professor named Roland Probst, who had been his mentor from the day Jens's parents had discovered what abilities their child had, had taken quiet notice and begun the process of forming the opinion of the child.

Had Maria and Lutz Keller known who Professor Roland Probst really was, they would, in all likelihood, have had the man arrested. The portly, semi-bald, grey-haired man, a bachelor by choice, came across as quiet, gentle and extremely articulate. Not that he was homosexual; he could simply never quite understand the opposite sex. While he wasn't exactly authoritative, he certainly commanded respect. When Professor Probst spoke, people listened, not because they had to; they wanted to. The CV he had handed the Kellers during his interview was, to say the least, impressive; it was certainly more than good enough for Lutz Keller. Keller, an orthopaedic surgeon at the Klinikum Stuttgart, employed the Professor on the spot. He could, after all, afford it.

What Probst, whose parents had died at the hands of the Nazi's, did not disclose during the interview with Lutz Keller, were his political affiliations. Probst believed deeply in communism, the very ideology that had cost his parents their lives. For as long as Probst could remember he had been a supporter of the banned DKP, the German Communist Party, although never publicly acknowledging it. In addition, he had, in his youth, been one of the many who sympathised with the RAF and what it stood for, pro-communism and anti-fascism.

Three days after Jens Keller's 16th birthday, on one of their regular educational excursions to the city of Stuttgart, Probst took Keller to Stammheim Prison. It would be the culmination of Probst's efforts in shaping the young man's future. They spent an hour there, looking at the building from the outside from various vantage points, followed by a further two hours in a small Italian pizza restaurant. In those three hours Professor Probst gave Jens Keller a brief history of the RAF, its founding members and what had happened at Stammheim. Jens Keller was hooked. Gently guided by Professor Probst, he began researching the history of the RAF. By the time he was 18, a degree in history already under his belt, he knew more about the RAF, as an individual, than most other experts combined.

Then Professor Probst died. Jens Keller lost not only his mentor, but also his grip on reality. His parents didn't understand at the best of times what he was talking about, it was simply too advanced; nor did most of the other people he had contact with. There was, however, one character at the University of

Mannheim, not far from Stuttgart, where the young Jens Keller had embarked on his second degree - political science - who did. An equally gifted student, Marius Berger, took a liking to Jens Keller and the two began to spend time together. Keller, not entirely communist, but definitely anti-fascist, and Berger, not entirely fascist, but decidedly anti-communist, should have been at loggerheads. They weren't; their superior intellect did not permit silly notions such as differences of opinion to trouble them. Rather, they looked for ways to accommodate each other's diverse opinions.

By the time he had completed his degree and Marius Berger had moved to Berlin, Jens Keller had developed his own theories about the rights and wrongs of the world; somehow blending parts of communism and socialism with elements of nationalism and right-wing extremism. The history of the imprisoned RAF founding member, Horst Mahler, hadn't escaped him either, nor had Mahler's teachings, both from the early RAF days as well as the recent right-wing oriented years. If Mahler had gone from one extreme to the other, then Jens Keller had managed to combine them. Above all, the perceived heroism of the Baader Meinhof Group, the activities of the Red Army Faction and the deaths of most of the founders in Stammheim Prison inspired him. To him they were akin to modern-day martyrs.

At some point in 2003, at the age of 23, Jens Keller began to think about forming his own organisation. In his mind, the ideals of the RAF, combined with a few ideas of his own, had to live on. That same year Jens Keller sat down and wrote the manifesto for the Meinhof Kollaboration, finally completing the document in the summer of 2003. In August 2003, with no direct link to Jens Keller, the first Meinhof Kollaboration post hit the internet.

In October 2003, as a result of the Internet post, he had his first recruit, the 22-year-old Anne Biedermann. Less than a month later, 24-year-old Karl Stegemann joined the two, and the Meinhof Kollaboration became a small, fully-fledged, operational terrorist entity.

Anne Biedermann, a mousy, nondescript, flat-chested closet lesbian, had suffered years of sexual abuse at the hands of her father, the owner of a successful engineering company in the small town of Gronau, a few kilometres away from the Dutch border in the German Münsterland. Her mother, although she denied all knowledge of the abuse, had had an inkling of what was going on, but had done nothing. At the age of 16, Anne Biedermann ran away from home, crossed the border and settled in a commune in Enschede in the Netherlands. Most of the commune members, drop-outs with political convictions ranging across the spectrum, had one thing in common – in one way or another they were all radical. Biedermann, with her past, fitted in perfectly. She hated her parents, considering her father, in particular, to be a bourgeois pig and a sexual pervert to boot, someone she would quite happily see dead, and her mother to be a spineless, self-absorbed socialite bitch. Both of them, as far as she was concerned, had no right to exist.

Unlike her parents, the members of the commune treated

her with respect, and she felt more at home in the commune environment than she ever had in her past life. There was, however, a side-effect to living with such a motley assortment of young men and women. From day one she was exposed on a daily basis to the extreme and often obscure views of her co-inhabitants. In as much as most of them were spaced-out for the better part of their waking hours - the drug of choice being hashish - they were all intellectuals in their own right. It did not take long for Biedermann to form her own views on a number of contentious issues. Discussions in the commune often centred around topics such as American imperialism, global economic injustice, the role of Al Qaeda in society, the effect of Zionism on the Middle East and so on. Being a member of the commune meant taking part in these hashish-fuelled discussions and debates which often lasted for hours on end.

Biedermann found out very quickly that the trick was to have a view on everything; all the better if such a view could be substantiated. She absorbed everything she heard and began to research the entire spectrum of political issues affecting the planet, so as to be able to take part in the daily discussions from a position of strength. Within a year, the young woman had been elevated to some sort of hero status within the commune. Able to counter-argue convincingly when the need arose, her opinions were not only listened to with interest, they were often taken as gospel.

When, in 2003, Anne Biedermann stumbled across the Meinhof Kollaboration post, she knew she had found her particular niche in life. Getting hold of the brain behind the Meinhof Kollaboration was not easy; the post had no links. She did the only thing she could think of that would possibly result in contact being established, she put out her own post, a far less contentious one, but succinct enough to attract attention. It also included an e-mail address. One month later she received the e-mail she had been hoping for. A week later she met Jens Keller in Hamburg.

Karl Stegemann, the third son of very wealthy parents, was not cast in the mould his father and mother would have liked him to be. The family wealth had, for over two generations, been generated by the manufacture of an exclusive range of snow-skis, and more recently, snow boards. Not surprisingly, it was expected of all family members to excel at winter sports, and, in the main, they did. Not Karl Stegemann, however. He hated anything to do with sport and was, unlike his brothers, of very small build with a penchant for the performing arts. Whereas his brothers got their kicks out of acrobatic performances in the half-pipes of some freezing winter sport resort, he got his kicks out of opera, ballet and reading. As a result he was shunned by his family. Even his parents, who had tried to change him, decided eventually that every family unfortunately had a black sheep and Karl Stegemann would be it - tolerated, but not entirely accepted.

It did not do the young Karl, who was also highly intelligent, any good. As the years went by the young man developed a dislike for what society perceived to be a successful person, turning ultimately to sheer hatred. It was just after his 16th birthday that

Karl Stegemann's future was determined. Although he had been bullied throughout most of his school life, it had never been serious until the day one of the so-called popular kids, a good-looking, well-built student, who excelled at soccer and very little else, decided to humiliate Karl Stegemann in front of his friends. Stegemann had tried to retaliate without success. In the end, he was weeping quietly, minus his trousers, as a group of girls sniggered and his tormentor and friends laughed. When he told his parents later that day they simply told him to get over it, and that he had probably provoked the incident in the first place.

Something snapped. Seething with rage he told his father to fuck off and stormed out of the house. For the first time in his life he started feeling the need to destroy the society responsible for his humiliation. Then in 2003, he was studying accounting at the time – not by choice, but rather at the insistence of his parents, who had determined what he should study and that his studies should take place as far away from home as possible – he came across an internet post of the Meinhof Kollaboration. What it said appealed to him to such a degree that he too, as had Anne Biedermann, decided he needed to make contact. Just as Biedermann did, he posted his own details with succinct commentary, except that he used The Student Room website as contact point, not an e-mail account. Less than a week after uploading his post he received a message on the same website. This time the meeting was held in Cologne, where he met Jens Keller and Anne Biedermann. They hit it off so well that less than five minutes into the meeting they agreed to join forces and take the Meinhof Kollaboration to new levels.

All three were far from stupid; they had the political will and all had been radicalised, while each was able to contribute in his/her own way. Keller had the organisational skills and money, Biedermann the planning skills and contacts, and Stegemann – also with money - the absolute willingness to execute. Biedermann, through one of her commune connections, made contact with a rather dubious gentleman in the Dutch town of Amersfoort, who provided them, at a cost, with false German papers. Rudimentary at best, they were however good enough to cater for basic necessities such as signing for rentals and opening a bank account. Two weeks later Anne Biedermann left the commune for good, while Jens Keller and Karl Stegemann dropped out of university. Under their new identities they shacked up together in a small flat in Hamburg.

In the first year of operation, the Meinhof Kollaboration concentrated largely on rhetoric, posting article after article on whatever forum they could. Most of the posts never made it past the site editor phase, and those that did were invariably removed within days of going public. Two physical activities did, however, take place. In 2004, the factories owned by both the Stegemann and Biedermann families burnt to the ground. Police investigations quickly established arson as the cause of both fires. In both cases, oxy-acetylene bottles had mysteriously exploded in the workshops of the two companies in the early hours of a Sunday morning, the one incident in May, and the other in June, 2004. There was no one around at the time of the explosions, hence there were no casualties; but it was found that the gas bottles had been opened, with a small, timed incendiary device taking care of the rest.

While the Stegemann factory re-opened four months later, the Biedermann operation never recovered. Anne's father, Reinhold Biedermann, succumbed to a heart attack within a month of the fire. As a result of the arson attack, he had been unable to deliver on a massive contract and the contract had been cancelled, ruining the small, yet prosperous engineering firm. Her mother, Marion Biedermann, re-married a short while later. Unbeknown to her husband, she had been having an affair with a younger businessman in the town for the past three years. For her, life continued as though nothing had happened, other than the fact that her partner and source of income (there had after all been a handsome insurance payout) had changed. Unbeknown to Anne Biedermann, her father, the one man she had hated more than anything in the world, had also provided for her in his will.

Within two months of her father's death, much to her surprise, a sum of just over 500 000 Euro was deposited into Anne Biedermann's private account, the one thing she had kept intact from her youth. The three members of the Meinhof Kollaboration discussed at length what to do with the unexpected windfall and decided to quietly withdraw the money and deposit it into a different account. It took them the better part of 18 months as they did not want to raise suspicion by withdrawing the full amount in one transaction. When the last cent had been withdrawn, Anne Biedermann closed the account, erasing the last trace of her official existence. As far as the German authorities were concerned she had simply vanished. There was, after all, no death certificate to say otherwise. The same applied to Jens Keller and Karl Stegemann. They too disappeared off the radar of the German authorities. In late 2005, shrouded in anonymity, the Meinhof Kollaboration took their activities to the next level.

It was by a mere quirk of fate and carelessness that the German police and the Federal Office for the Protection of the Constitution, the *Bundesamt für Verfassungsschutz* or BfV – which is the internal intelligence organ of the German State - finally established who was behind the Meinhof Kollaboration. In 2008, the Meinhof Kollaboration posted a video-clip on You-Tube. In it, the three masked members of the organisation, dressed in combat fatigues and wearing black balaclavas, were sitting behind a trestle-table covered with the Meinhof Kollaboration flag, a hand-sewn affair incorporating parts of the old Baader Meinhof / RAF emblem. Also on the table were three automatic rifles. The three masked persons went on and on about their particular vision, the cleansing of society of Jews, the removal by force of the German *Mittelstand* – what they considered to be the bourgeois middle-class who owned the means of production and controlled a large part of German capital – as well as the nationalisation of the large German multi-national corporations, all in favour of creating a nationalist, socialist, communist state. The rambling discourse of the three was difficult to follow at best, but it was the first time all three had spoken, two of the voices clearly male and the other female.

The one serious error the Meinhof Kollaboration had made before posting the clip on You-Tube, was not editing the recording thoroughly enough. Hardly visible on the right of the clip was a window. The curtains had, however, not been drawn, and, barely visible through the window, was the sliver of a church steeple in the background. The German authorities did notice, however, and it did not take too long to establish the identity of the town which boasted that particular steeple. What they did not know was the exact location of the flat. They sent in a number of plain clothes agents who began pinpointing the location as best as they could without attracting too much attention. By the time they had the exact location, Keller, Stegemann and Biedermann, as part of their operational planning, had moved on. The German authorities did, however, manage to establish - via identikits created with the help of the building's janitor - who was behind the Meinhof Kollaboration.

Yet the random and frequent movements of the three terrorists made them extremely difficult to trace. Although the German BfV - via the department responsible for foreign intelligence, the BND or *Bundesnachrichtendienst* - made the identikits available to the intelligence agencies of friendly foreign countries, they did not make them public in Germany; rather hoping that the three, without an inkling they had been identified, would be found by German authorities, which, of course, did not happen. Keller, Stegemann and Biedermann had been acutely aware all along that the German authorities would be after them, and had spent an inordinate amount of time changing their appearances; be this their hairstyles, the wearing of coloured contact lenses, beard growth or the use of theatrical make-up, to name but a few of the measures they took. Biedermann, as much as she resented it, even went as far as wearing padded bras from time to time.

The Israeli Mossad, who had been keeping an eye on the Meinhof Kollaboration Internet posts and had also been sent the identikits, took matters a little more seriously than most other intelligence agencies; after all, anything anti-Jewish was considered a direct threat to Israel. They alerted their agents and sources in Germany to be extra vigilant, very nearly apprehending Jens Keller in 2010 after a tip-off, but missing the target by less than an hour.

The American CIA and NSA also received the identikits. Within a week the identikits had been leaked by a junior CIA employee to an individual who paid him a small monthly retainer for passing on any information related to Middle East activities. The activities of the Meinhof Kollaboration fitted the bill, and the identikits were passed on, ending up at a meeting held by a group of men in Washington DC. With that, the Meinhof Kollaboration gained a silent follower, every new internet post being watched and dissected.

The group, calling themselves The Patriots, had a single objective – to ensure that the arms industry and military complex of the United States of America would continue to flourish for decades to come. Hence, instability in the Middle East, as well as in certain other parts of the planet, was of great value to The

Patriots. Ensuring that this instability remained – or even increased – was a key consideration in the long term plans of The Patriots. For that purpose, they would do anything and everything, never mind how unorthodox the methods. At some point in 2010, one of the group's members made a proposal. Devious, cunning and completely out of the ordinary, the proposal, after some debate, was unanimously accepted. With money being no stumbling-block – The Patriots had a combined worth in excess of US $10 billion – they went to work.

CHAPTER 3
SALE OF DESTRUCTION

Europe / USA, 2013

Francois Labuschagne sat in his flat looking out of the window. The heat outside was unbearable; the sellers of the famed Italian *gelato* making a killing off the multitudes of tourists who inundated the city during the summer. Not that the sales of *gelato* or the heat were of any concern to Labuschagne; he had a problem far greater than any of the mundane issues the thousands of ice-cream merchants in Rome would ever be faced with in their lives. Labuschagne, with no pension to rely on, was fast running out of money. At the age of 89 he knew he could not rely on the Italian welfare system; he had, after all, never contributed to it, and he was about as Italian as Kenneth Kaunda of Zambia was American. Yes, he was "officially" Franco di Paulo as far as the Italians were concerned, but there it stopped.

Ever since arriving in Rome late in 1994, he had kept to himself, shopping alone, not saying anything to anyone. The only thing the Italian authorities had on him as far as records were concerned, were a number of fines for a variety of traffic offences, all of them issued between 1994 and 1995. He had always paid them on time, making sure not to attract any attention. Life, for what it was worth, was as good as it could get. But now, with the money required to sustain his lifestyle running out, he needed to do something drastic. He picked up the telephone and dialled a London number. His call was answered a short while later.

"Paul Gillings speaking."

"Pieter! How are you?" Labuschagne started in Afrikaans, the man he was speaking to not Paul Gillings, but rather Pieter van Zyl.

"Francois! How are you? Haven't heard from you for a while!" responded van Zyl, also in Afrikaans.

"Not bad, thank you. Listen, we have a bit of a problem."

"Let me guess," answered van Zyl, "we're running out of money?"

"Yes," sighed Labuschagne, "I suppose you've figured it out as well. On my side I can manage another six months at best, I don't know about you."

"Similar, Francois, similar."

"So what do we do about it? Any ideas?"

There was silence for a few moments. "Yes, I have an idea," said van Zyl. "I don't know if you'll like it."

"Well, why don't you surprise me?"

"The article."

"What about the article?" asked Labuschagne.

"We've got it, don't we? And it's only the two of us, the others are all dead. Why don't we sell it?"

"You must be joking!"

"No Francois, I'm not." Van Zyl's voice came across as gentle, soothing. "You and I are both old, we don't have much time left. We both need money. If we sell the article, we'll be sorted out for the rest of our days."

"And the ramifications? What if it is used? Dead or not, we would be responsible. It would be us! I don't know if I could stomach that."

"Come on, Francois. You know very well that what we did all those years ago was not always entirely humane, so let's not start having scruples now! We have something very expensive to sell, and I'm sure there's a willing buyer out there. Tell you what. Let me come to Rome and we can discuss this in more detail."

"Fine. Arrange it, sooner rather than later."

Francois Labuschagne ended the call. Nothing had been said that could possibly trigger European or American electronic surveillance systems, no key words had been spoken that they knew of. Two days later Pieter van Zyl arrived in Rome. By the time he left the decision had been taken. The unassembled nuclear device would be sold. The question was how.

A week later van Zyl had managed to contact Ben Khalid, an

arms dealer he had had contact with during his years in South Africa. Khalid, unscrupulous to the extreme, had the reputation of selling anything military to anyone capable of the purchase. When Khalid heard what van Zyl had to offer he very nearly came in his pants. This was big; bigger than anything he had ever come across. All he had to do was find a client. Ben Khalid, who knew how to shut up, sent out the very discreet word. He had something out of the ordinary to sell.

It took some time - twenty-three days to be precise - until he had the bite he had been hoping for. On the 27th of July, late in the evening, one of his cell phones rang. The number of that particular phone was known only to a few select people scattered across the globe. One of those people was Rudi Schultz, an American who specialised in sourcing anything and everything for anyone who could afford it, acting as a middle- man between purchaser and seller. That the seller and purchaser were, more often than not, unsavoury characters who were up to no good, did not bother him in the least. His religion was money, and the God he prayed to did not differentiate between the good, the bad and the downright ugly.

Schultz knew the rules of the game. He mentioned nothing over the phone apart from wanting to meet with Khalid to discuss the possible purchase of the rather unusual artefact on offer. Schultz, understanding the language used, had a very good idea of what the unusual artefact could be. He also had a client who had indicated a very special requirement and, with a bit of luck, Khalid would have exactly what was wanted.

The meeting was set up, and four days later Rudi Schultz met Ben Khalid in a small, upmarket restaurant in Lisbon. Schultz was not disappointed. They haggled for hours, finally settling on a price. In as much as Khalid had wanted a hell of a lot more than the price ultimately agreed upon, Schultz did present the rather convincing argument that, although Khalid had a nuclear device for sale, the customers for such a device would be, to say the least, very limited. In addition, Khalid, as Schultz had succinctly pointed out, needed to consider the effect of the sale of a nuclear device to the wrong persons.

Khalid - not that he cared what the device would be used for, as long as he was nowhere around when it did go off – was afraid of one thing. Selling various small arms, mortars and ammunition to all sorts of rebel and terrorist organisations was one thing; if it leaked out who the seller was no one would really care. Selling a nuke was a different matter entirely. Unfortunately, most of the organisations he considered to be his clients, had the rather nasty habit of being riddled with in-fighting and leaking like sieves. If it ever came out that he, Ben Khalid, had sold a nuke, it would be the end of his career; if not removed permanently by some or other intelligence agency, he would, in all likelihood, spend the rest of his life in a prison in one of any number of nations, top of the list, America. This limited the clients he could sell the device to rather severely. Just as Khalid knew this was an unfortunate reality, so did Schultz. Both knew that they had to protect themselves. They found the solution to their predicament during their next meeting the following day. It would take some time to arrange and they agreed that Khalid would not sell the device to anyone else for the next two months while Schultz did the necessary. The next morning Khalid was on the way back to his luxury apartment in Monaco and Schultz made his way back to the USA.

Back in the USA, Rudi Schultz arranged for a hasty meeting with his client which took place a day after he had landed. Schultz, schemer of note, advised his client regarding what he had to offer and that he could deliver. However, since it would be delivered in individual components, minus a triggering mechanism, the price would be pegged at US $80 million. For a complete device he would have demanded at least a further US $20 million. His client agreed. The second part of the negotiation was more difficult. Schultz would only supply the device if he knew who it was for, explaining to his client the subtleties of international arms trading and the dangers of being linked to the sale of an atomic device. His client understood very well, and it did not take too long to reach principle agreement. Schultz would be paid US $30 million which he would split with his contact in Europe; the balance would be paid directly to the actual supplier. Neither Schultz nor Khalid would be implicated. Twenty-five percent of the amount would be paid as soon as the first components arrived at a destination still to be advised, a further twenty-five percent once the fissile material was received, and the last fifty percent when all components were safely in the hands of the new owners. Schultz agreed and left the meeting.

Within two hours he was back on a plane to Lisbon where he

met Ben Khalid at the same restaurant for a third time. There he advised Khalid of the plan. Khalid was only too happy, US $15 million more than he had hoped for. All he had to do was to advise van Zyl that he would be contacted by the purchaser, who would state that he was interested in acquiring a religious artefact van Zyl had for sale. The deal was effectively done.

The next move was for The Patriots to make contact with the delivery vehicle they had in mind, the Meinhof Kollaboration. It proved to be a touch more than just difficult. The US $80 million for the device was considered small change; each member of the group contributing an equal share within 24 hours. Finding Jens Keller, however, was a different kettle of fish altogether. They knew, thanks to the identikits, who they were looking for, but not where to find them. Even the German police and the BfV didn't have a clue.

It was one of the youngest members of The Patriot leadership, a 38-year-old billionaire and techno whiz-kid, who came up with the solution - to use bait the Meinhof Kollaboration would not be able to resist. He knew of just the right bait; Senator Marty Golding. An Oklahoma-based, prolific, pro-Israeli politician, Golding had the habit of defending the actions of the Jewish State wherever and whenever he could. In addition, he had a penchant for appearing in public, thriving on his own popularity and public adulation. The Patriots knew he was a primary target of the Meinhof Kollaboration, since that much had been made clear in two recent Internet posts. With more than enough clout and influence, The Patriots arranged for Senator Golding to be invited as key-note speaker to a series of three hastily organised, pro-Israel day conferences in Germany.

Needless to say, the Senator jumped at the chance; not only would he be flying first-class with his wife accompanying him, he would stay in the best hotels Germany had to offer - and be paid US $50 000 for his efforts. What Senator Golding did not know was how highly publicised the three conferences - one in Munich, one in Frankfurt and one in Berlin – were in Germany. The degree of publicity was unusual, but had the desired effect. The pending arrival in Germany of Senator Marty Golding was duly noted by Keller, Biedermann and Stegemann. One of their top ten targets was on the way to Germany; his exact movements, including the hotels he was to be staying at, as well as dates, were openly cited by the German press, much to the consternation of both the German authorities, as well as Senator Golding's security detail.

Senator Golding and his entourage departed for Europe on schedule. Ten days before the departure of Golding, 60 men and women, the watchers, all with copies of the identikits of Keller, Biedermann and Stegemann, had also left the USA en route to Germany on separate flights. So, too, had three senior members of The Patriots, who would be the contacts for the watchers. None of the 60 watchers knew of each other, they merely had the identikits and a contact number. Nor did the three members connected to The Patriots know of each other. Twenty of the group went to Munich, the next twenty to Frankfurt and the remainder to Berlin. Each one of them had been given the same task –to hang around in the vicinity of the hotels Senator Golding had been booked into, looking for anyone resembling one of the three persons in the identikits, and, if they could identify them, to call the contact number given.

For the first four days nothing happened. It was late afternoon on the fifth day when one of the watchers, a middle-aged woman observing the five-star Hotel Adlon Kempinski at Unter den Linden 77 in Berlin, noted a young female vaguely resembling the identikit of Anne Biedermann walk towards the hotel. The watcher followed from a distance and immediately called the contact number she had been given. Three minutes later a young man approached her and mentioned the code word he had given her when she called. She pointed at the entrance to a building on the other side of the road, opposite the main entrance of the hotel, and described what the person she had been following was wearing. The young man nodded and told her to leave; then sat down on a bench at a nearby bus-stop and waited.

When Anne Biedermann left the building he got up and followed her from a distance. She was about to board a bus, waiting in a throng of people, when he made his move. He closed in rapidly, bumped into her and she turned to face him. It was the first close-up view he had had of her. He knew immediately that the young woman glaring at him was the person he had come to find and he thrust an envelope into her hand.

"Don't do anything stupid, Ms Biedermann," he said in English. "Take the envelope; open it when you get to wherever you stay. Follow the instructions. We are your friends." Without saying anything else he turned and walked away.

Biedermann, perplexed and acutely aware that someone had somehow found her, made her way back to the flat where Keller and Stegemann were waiting, changing buses six times on the way to make sure she was not being followed. When she got to the flat she did not enter it immediately, waiting for a further ten minutes to see if anyone out of the ordinary appeared on the scene. Noting no one, she decided it was safe and made her way up to the tenth floor of the building. There again she waited for five minutes in the corridor, only then entering the flat. Keller and Stegemann were sitting in the small dining-room going over their plans and she tossed the note onto the dining-room table.

"What's this?" demanded Keller.

"Don't know," answered Biedermann. "Someone knows who I am or who we are."

"What!"

"You heard me." She told them what had happened.

"*Scheisse!* Were you followed here?" asked Stegemann.

"No, I made sure. But we need to get out of here. Now."

Jens Keller sat back, took the note and looked at it. "No. Wait. Whoever identified you and called you by name wasn't one of the pigs. If it had been, he wouldn't have exposed himself, he would've followed you. They'd be all over us by now. He said 'they', not 'him', were our friends." He stopped talking, carefully opened the note and read it. "Listen to this. It's in English."

We are your friends. We have a proposal to make for which we will pay US $5 million. We have not followed you and do not know where you are. We trust that this demonstrates our sincerity. Contact us on the number below and ask for Jerome. We are waiting for your call.

"Who the fuck are they? And how the hell did they find us?" Biedermann was agitated.

"We'll find out," said Keller, "when I've met with this Jerome character. In the meantime pack your bags, we're leaving. Is the next place arranged?"

"Yes," replied Stegemann. "I've got the keys. It's not far from here. We can get going right now."

"Good. I'm going to meet with this Jerome. Don't tell me where the next flat is, I'll call you when I'm done and you can give me the location then. If it's the pigs I don't want to know where you are, nor do I want to be able to tell them if they pump me full of chemicals."

"What about Golding? Do we proceed?" asked Stegemann.

"If I don't come back, abort," replied Keller. "If I do, we go ahead."

Packing up did not take long and they left the rented flat, individually, five minutes apart. Keller was last to leave. As Biedermann and Stegemann made their way to their new address, Keller climbed onto a bus for the short trip to the place he had been told to meet Jerome; a dingy Lebanese cafeteria in the suburb of Kreuzberg. Waiting for him at a table in the far corner of the establishment was a young man, dressed in sneakers, jeans and a black leather jacket. The conversation lasted for over an hour. Not much later, the watchers in Munich, Frankfurt and Berlin were called and told to cease all activities. As the watchers were being called back, Jens Keller contacted his comrades and made his way to their new hideout.

Days later, Senator Golding arrived in Germany for the start of his tour. His first stop was Frankfurt, followed by Berlin and Munich. Frankfurt went very well, and the following day, a Sunday, he made his way to Berlin, where he arrived in the early evening. It was still light and, as he got out of the chauffeur-driven limousine at the entrance to the Hotel Adlon Kempinski, his wife close behind him, he stood up to wave to a small crowd gathered there. Next thing he was lying on the floor, half of his head blown away, blood and brains leaking onto the pavement.

As the crowd screamed, many running away in a mad panic, Golding's security detail desperately trying to ram a hysterical Mrs Golding back into the limousine, Karl Stegemann quietly closed the window of the room on the third floor of the building he had occupied for the past two hours; a small office he had broken into, knowing in advance that there was no one about, some 150 metres away from the hotel entrance. He disassembled the silenced sniper rifle and packed it into his backpack, left the office and walked out of the back entrance of the building. There, he climbed onto a scooter and left the scene, the piercing sound of wailing sirens of fast-approaching police vehicles muffled by the helmet he was wearing. The Meinhof Kollaboration had to include a new target in their top ten list.

Four days later, Udo Greiner, aka Jens Keller, flew to London on easyJet. He was heavily disguised; the chances of anyone figuring out who he really was were extremely remote. Brown eyes instead of blue, long, neatly combed hair, business suit and tie, theatrical make-up – the application of which Anne Biedermann had become an expert in over the years - distorting any otherwise recognisable features, he sailed through passport control in both Düsseldorf and Gatwick using a forged passport. From Gatwick he caught the train into London, switched to a tube that took him to Morden and walked the short distance to a small, yet well-appointed residence less than a kilometre away from the tube station, with no idea that the ELINT gathering set-up of Grey & McLaughlin plc was a stone's throw away. There he met Pieter van Zyl.

He returned to Germany unnoticed after a very successful meeting and having spent some unheard of time for rest and recreation in the British capital. The one mistake he had made during his discussions with van Zyl was to mention he was acting on behalf of the Meinhof Kollaboration.

Rustenburg, South Africa

At the end of August, Pieter van Zyl, undertaking the last trip he would ever make, touched down at what had by then been renamed OR Tambo International Airport in Johannesburg, South Africa. Entering the country as Paul Gillings, he too got through passport control without a problem and made his way to the Gautrain terminal (a trans-rapid-rail system connecting the airport to South Africa's commercial hub, Sandton and terminating in Pretoria) located on the top floor of the airport building. He got out in Pretoria, caught a taxi and arrived at the farm half-way between Pretoria and Rustenberg over an hour and a half later, where he was met by Johannes. There Pieter van Zyl went to work.

The following morning he walked across to the barn he had locked all those years ago. Johannes had kept his word, the potential curse of the *sangoma* no doubt having a lot to do with it. The barn hadn't been opened, and he had to break the padlock they had locked the barn doors with since the mechanics had rusted to pieces. He opened the doors and walked into the gloomy interior. There was dust everywhere, myriads of spider-webs hanging from the nooks and crannies of the rafters. The floor was still covered with the layer of straw, brittle, and was bone dry. He walked into the middle of the barn and moved the straw away with his feet. It took him a while to find what he was looking for, the dirt filled indentation in the floor. He cleared the straw and dirt away from the indentations exposing the trap-door. Opening the trap-door was not easy. It took over an hour and the use of a rope slung over a wooden beam directly above the door latch, but eventually he managed, the hinges creaking as the heavy trap-door swung slowly upward.

Van Zyl took a torch he had with him and shone the beam into the darkness below the trap-door. He took a deep breath and made his way down a series of steps, looking for the light switch he knew was somewhere on the wall to his left. It did not take long to find and he flicked the switch. Against all odds, most of the ceiling-mounted fluorescent tubes still worked, lighting up the chamber in front of him. Van Zyl looked around and heaved a sigh of relief. As far as he could make out it was all still there, hundreds of crates and boxes stacked neatly along the concrete walls of the chamber. He went across to the first box on his left and opened it. It contained a series of files, one of them an inventory list of what was supposed to be in the chamber. He took the list and began methodically checking that nothing was missing. A few hours later he had completed the task, left the chamber, put off the lights and closed the trap-door. From then on he immersed himself in the complex task of arranging the logistics of moving the components of the device to Europe.

It took him the better part of two months. At least three shipments were considered to be a minimum requirement; all would be via sea freight from three South African ports, with entry into Europe via three European ports. The parts concerning him most were the explosive materials, in particular, the highly-enriched uranium. What van Zyl did have was a very specific set of instructions as to how he needed to go about the shipments.

The first container would contain an old 1958 Austin Healy in need of restoration, ostensibly bought by a collector in Germany at a very good price. The vehicle arrived on the farm a week after van Zyl. For the next couple of days, a number of the parts making up the atomic device were concealed in the sump of the engine, under the tappet covers, inside the piston chambers and a number of other places no one would bother to look unless suspicion was raised.

The second container was filled with catalytic convertors which had been removed from late model motor vehicles, all of which had been scrapped after being involved in major accidents. The convertors had been bought by a German scrap metal merchant, who would sell them on to a number of clients specialising in the removal of the precious metals found in the catalytic convertors. Of the 1000 odd convertors in the container, 70 had been tampered with. Those 70 units contained the balance of the parts of the nuclear device, bar the highly-enriched uranium.

The highly-enriched uranium components left South Africa in the third container, loaded with South African manufactured solar geysers and destined for Croatia. Of the 200 units stacked in the container, 8 had pressure vessels containing a little more than just fresh air. Lead-lined, they contained the machined uranium parts.

Europe

In the month of October, the three containers left South Africa, one via Durban, one via Cape Town and the last via Port Elizabeth. The export paperwork was perfectly in order; customs inspections had been circumvented by quietly paying a substantial sum of cash to a number of officials within the customs departments of the three ports – money was, after all, not a problem.

The first container, the one with the Austin Healy, entered Europe via Rotterdam. Pre-cleared, the container was scanned, nothing untoward was found, and it was released for transit to Germany. The final destination was an automotive workshop in Gelsenkirchen, where the container was unloaded, the contents packed into a small warehouse and locked up.

The second container, with the catalytic convertors, came in via Salerno in southern Italy. Whether acknowledged or not, the Italian Mafia still had influence in the area, and, if paid well enough, could ensure that certain import procedures were ignored. The container went straight through customs without any inspections and was on the road to Germany within hours of discharge. A day later the container arrived at the premises of the scrap metal merchant in Duisburg where the contents were unloaded and stacked into a second small warehouse, which was then also locked.

The ship with the third container docked in the port of Split in Croatia in mid-November. Here too, a number of officials had been suitably paid, the container cleared port without any trouble and was sent to the delivery address in Zagreb. The contents, as was case in Gelsenkirchen and Duisburg, were locked away in a small warehouse.

Within days of the arrival of the containers in Europe,

the three warehouses were visited by mechanically-minded gentlemen, who stripped the components of the atomic device out of the miscellaneous parts that had concealed them. At the end of November, the parts of the device were safely stored in the basement of an old villa in the small German town of Schopfheim, in the southern part of the Black Forest. The villa, originally the home of a textile industrialist in the early 20th century, had been rented in September for an initial three year period for one specific reason – the basement rooms. One of the vast underground rooms, originally a wine cellar, measured some 75 square metres of open space. The wine racks had long since been removed, and, over a period of two months, the interior had been renovated. The contractors employed to do the job had been made to understand that they were building a sound studio. A purpose-built, five ton goods-hoist formed part of the extensive modifications. They did not know that the only sound ever to emanate from the converted wine cellar would be one of electric drills and other mechanical engineering tools. The contractors had long since departed the scene when the goods destined to be stored in the renovated cellar arrived. Now, stacked against the far wall of the basement, were the parts of the nuclear device from South Africa, neatly labelled. Four large steel safes, one in each corner, contained the weapons' grade uranium components.

Two weeks prior to the arrival of the device components, the new occupants of the villa moved in: Jens Keller, Karl Stegemann and Anne Biedermann. Three weeks later they were joined by a further individual, a 52-year-old Iranian scientist, Dr Amir Asadi.

He had entered Germany illegally using false papers provided by The Patriots and was a highly skilled designer of atomic weapons. By the end of November, the Meinhof Kollaboration had gone to ground, and the painstaking process of assembling the device began in earnest.

The one missing physical component, the bomb casing, was on order. Disguised as a stainless steel air-receiver for a high pressure compressor, it would contain the various parts of the device. The Meinhof Kollaboration thought they had embarked on a project guaranteed to give them a permanent place in the terrorism Hall of Fame. The Patriots, on the other hand, were well on their way to orchestrating the single most radical change in the balance of power in the Middle East since the Crusades, and all for personal gain.

As for Pieter van Zyl? At the end of the year a neighbour noted a persistent odour coming from the house van Zyl rented in Wimbledon, London. He knocked on the door on frequent occasions for a number of days. Since there was no answer, he assumed van Zyl was not in town. Eventually the odour became so bad that the neighbour called the police. One of the officers knew exactly what the smell was. They broke open the door and found his body, decomposition already at an advanced stage. An hour later the body was removed and the forensic squad moved in. They found nothing untoward, and a day later an autopsy confirmed the suspicions of the police. Van Zyl had died of a massive heart attack.

CHAPTER 4
HUNTING SEASON

Europe

By mid-October 2016, the world, and in particular, Europe, had fully recovered from the gas and oil catastrophe of November and December 2015. The energy crisis over, the European economy was once again in full swing, largely on the back of the liberalisation of the Chinese markets. Never before had so much been manufactured and exported to that vast country in the East. At the same time, Chinese exports to western economies doubled. With GDP growth well above five percent for most countries, the world was, generally-speaking, a very happy place.

This would not have been so, had the powers that be been privy to two particular meetings that took place within days of one another, one in Washington DC and the other in Tel Aviv. The first meeting, a closed session of the small leadership group of The Patriots, took place in a private suite in the Fairfax at Embassy Row hotel in Dupont Circle, Washington DC. The second meeting took place in a small, modest flat in downtown

Tel Aviv maintained by the Israeli Mossad.

Washington, USA

The meeting at the Fairfax in Embassy Row was a rather upbeat affair. Everything had so far gone to plan perfectly; the feedback from Europe was highly satisfactory. The three members of the Meinhof Kollaboration, apart from posting the odd video-clip on the various public forums of the Internet, had kept to their word and refrained from any activities for close on two years. The assassination of Senator Marty Golding had been the last operation they had conducted, resulting in a nationwide, yet highly unsuccessful, manhunt, lasting for six months. News received a day earlier was that Dr Amir Asadi was in the final testing phase of the device. It had taken him the better part of eight months to construct the triggering mechanism. The actual assembly of the device had proven relatively uncomplicated, although it too had taken time. The assembly was now nestled in the stainless steel cylinder, the end-cap welded into place, with three USB cables running out of a small opening on the top. The cables were connected to three different laptops, all high-powered Sony Vaio Pro 13 units. The final configuration would need only one of the laptops, but it would still take a day or two to get there. Dr Asadi, who had kept largely to himself during his long stay in the villa in Schopfheim, with little time spent doing anything else but work, was exhausted, yet satisfied. All he had to do now was explain to Jens Keller how to arm the device, a simple task involving setting a timer.

The five men of The Patriot leadership group knew exactly what the state of progress was. Over a sumptuous dinner of excellent Maine lobster, all washed down with 2006 Corton Charlemagne white wine from France, the decision was taken to move on to the execution phase of the plan they had hatched. A day later the necessary instructions were given.

Tel Aviv, Israel

The meeting in the flat in Tel Aviv was decidedly more sombre. Four men were present: Michael Grey, Moshe Immelmann – Head of Station of the Mossad in Germany, Abel Sharon – at that time heading up the Mossad, and 40-year-old Aaron Cohen, one of a select group of men the Mossad used for a variety of clandestine operations. It was Sharon who summed it up.

"We know MK has a bomb. Probability is high they'll use it against us, we don't where they are and we don't know how to find them. That right?"

"That's about it," replied Immelmann. "Question is what do we do? And how?"

"If I knew, we wouldn't be sitting here." Sharon was agitated, unsurprisingly so. Tasked with keeping Israel out of harm's way he was faced with a nightmare of note. "Any clever ideas?"

"We find the people or person who facilitated the sale." Grey had been listening to the discourse of the conversation for a while without saying much. "There's no way Labuschagne or van Zyl would've been able to get hold of the Meinhof Kollaboration themselves, they must have gone via a dealer. Might just point us in the right direction."

"Let's assume they did. We can't exactly go questioning every arms dealer around. One: there's too many of them; secondly, they're not exactly cooperative when it comes to this kind of thing. What've you got in mind?"

Grey noted the level of scrutiny he was being subjected to. "For either van Zyl or Labuschagne to have gotten this right, they, or at least one of them, must have had some sort of contact. Remember, I was down in South Africa for long enough. In those years we needed whatever we could get, and a lot of what came in was via brokers who didn't give a shit about sanctions. They'll have had their contacts. I assume they used one of them, even though it's years later."

"And?" Sharon probed. "If they did have contacts, any idea who? Our friend Labuschagne didn't know; truth be told he didn't know much of anything. Kept on telling us that van Zyl was the one who arranged for the sale and that he doesn't know anything. Interviewing him was a complete waste of time. There's also no point in asking him again, his brain's fried."

"Shit. So the only person who could have told us was this Pieter van Zyl and he's dead. Pity he didn't tell his mate Labuschagne more of the detail. But," Grey smiled, "there may just be a way of finding out. I'll deal with it."

"Good. I suggest we get started. If you don't find anything tangible within the next 48 hours, we reconvene. No, screw that; we reconvene anyway. Mike, Aaron's your side-kick, whatever you say he'll do. Understood, Aaron? Moshe will assist wherever he has to when it comes to anything in Germany." He turned slightly and spoke to Moshe Immelmann directly. "Arrange the necessary papers for Mike to get in and out of Israel without any problems, can't have him subjected to the usual measures. You might as well arrange a set of papers for Billy McLaughlin at the same time; can't hurt and we'll never know if we suddenly need him here as well. Anything else?" asked Sharon. The assembled men shook their heads.

"Okay then, we'll leave it there for now. Gentleman, let's find these bastards and the bloody device!"

An hour later Grey had made two phone calls, first to Billy McLaughlin and then to Jaco van Rensburgh, his ex-colleague and chief go-to guy when it came to extra, trustworthy manpower. As McLaughlin began compiling a list of every arms dealer known on the planet, Grey was speaking to van Rensburgh, who ran a successful private security business in Durban, South Africa, and who, as usual, addressed Grey by his real name.

"Kobus! Been a while! What's up?"

"I was wondering if you could do me a favour."

"For you anything. What do you need?"

"I'm looking for an arms dealer who had good connections with the South African Defence Force and government between

1980 and 1990. Any idea?"

There was a short pause before van Rensburgh answered, "No, I don't. But I think I know someone who just might."

"Oh? Who's that?"

"Our mutual friend in Umlazi, James Sithole. He's always supplied what we needed, like part of the kit we used a couple of months back in Namibia. He might just have an idea."

"Can you get hold of him? It's pretty urgent."

"If he knows he'll tell us. Might cost a bit. How much are you prepared to spend?" asked van Rensburgh.

"Offer him US $2 000; should be enough. If he's got the answer I'll transfer the money through to you."

"No worries. I'll lay it out. Give me an hour or so and I'll call you back. Anything else?"

"Yeah. I might just need you. Can you be on standby?"

"Was wondering if you'd ever ask. You can make that an affirmative."

Less than an hour later Grey's telephone rang, the display showing the +27 prefix for South Africa.

"Jaco?"

"Yeah, it's me. Listen, I spoke to James. Took him about two seconds to come up with an answer. Ben Khalid."

"Who the fuck's that?"

"Don't ask me. James reckons he was involved with the SA government and supplied all sorts of stuff, not only weapons. How does he know? Says he's been in the game for so long nothing happens in SA without him finding out. Remember, in those days the ANC also needed arms. Khalid was one of James's competitors; he reckons the bastard cost him a lot in terms of lost deals. Looks like this Khalid played both sides. Doesn't surprise me."

"Thanks. Helps me a lot."

"No problem." Van Rensburgh hung up and Grey turned to speak to Aaron Cohen who had been hanging around in the background in the small bar on the Tel Aviv beachfront.

"Ben Khalid, Aaron. That's where we'll start. I'll find out from Billy where he is. Can you arrange a plane? We'll probably need one, I doubt this Khalid's based in Isreal."

Cohen took his own telephone and dialled a number. The conversation was short, all of it conducted in Hebrew. "Done. Ready to leave as soon as you say so. You think this Khalid might put us on the right track?"

"Possibly, Aaron. It's certainly worth a shot."

"Can I make a suggestion?"

"Sure, go ahead."

"If it was this Khalid character, he'd have been paid; he certainly won't have done it for nothing. Which means it would have been some sort of transfer into an account, not so?" ventured Cohen.

"I suppose it would have." Grey replied. "You're suggesting Billy starts checking Khalid's bank accounts in the meantime?"

"I'd definitely consider it. No one walks around with US $50 million cash. You try and withdraw half a million in cash from a bank and see what happens, never mind 50 million! You'd have all sorts of alarm bells ringing all over the show. If the Meinhof Kollaboration's got the bomb there must have been some serious financial transactions, which would be traceable. If your man Billy can check out Khalid's accounts, all he has to do is look for a substantial amount that came in around two years ago. It had to have come from somewhere. If such transactions do exist, maybe he can establish the source?"

"Good point," grinned Grey and called McLaughlin. The call was answered within seconds.

"You again?"

"Someone's got to keep you busy. Listen, have you stumbled across a Ben Khalid?"

"Sure have. He's about seventh on my list."

"There's a strong probability he may be involved. Any idea where he lives?"

"Somewhere in Monaco. Exact location unknown; haven't gotten to that level yet but I can find out pretty quickly."

"Great," said Grey. "We'll be making our way to Monaco. One more thing. Once you've found out where he lives, see if you can get hold of any bank accounts he has, doesn't matter where. Check them out and see if sometime, two years ago, a large amount was transferred into one of them, or possibly a few payments of split amounts. I'm talking of a couple of million. If so, from where and from whom. Do the same with Labuschagne's accounts, especially the one in Switzerland."

"I'm onto it," answered McLaughlin. "Anything else?"

"No. That's it. Call me back once you've got something." Grey hung up.

Monaco

The chartered Bombardier Challenger 300 landed at Cote d'Azur Airport in Nice, France, some 30 kilometres away from the small principality of Monaco at 16:00. Grey and Cohen left the aircraft and made their way through the airport. As they walked out of the airport building a black Ferrari 458 Spider pulled up at the curb, the driver waving at Cohen.

"And this?" exclaimed Grey, giving the sleek, black machine an appreciative look.

"Our ride," grinned Cohen. "We're in Monaco, remember? Can't exactly arrive in a VW Beetle. Don't worry, there's so many of these exotics driving around here they don't even attract attention any more. Thing is, if you want to do business in Monaco, it's always a good idea to make a small impression; means you're the real deal. You want to drive?"

"Absolutely. I love these things. What about the driver?"

"Don't worry, he'll make his own way back."

Cohen got into the vehicle and Grey climbed in on the driver's side, adjusted the seat and mirrors and slipped the car into gear. They left the airport on the La Provencale A8 main road and headed towards the French Italian border. As soon as they hit the open road, Grey pushed harder on the accelerator and the Ferrari surged forward, the V8 engine growling as the vehicle surged forwards. Not much later they left the A8, turned right down the A500, through the Tunnel de Monaco, and down towards the small principality.

Monaco, all of 2.02 square kilometres, is considered the second smallest, yet most densely populated country in the world. With the highest number of millionaires and billionaires per capita, and an average real estate price of over US $58 000 per square metre, it is also a place of unheard of business deals, many entirely legitimate and some more dubious in nature. With such a concentration of wealth, power and potentially shady characters, many intelligence agencies keep some form of presence in or near the principality. The Mossad was no exception, at the time operating out of a small flat just outside the borders of the principality, in a place called Saint-Antoine. Seven hours after the meeting in Tel Aviv, Michael Grey was back on the telephone talking to Billy McLaughlin, this time on speaker for Aaron Cohen to listen in.

"Found anything on Ben Khalid?"

"Yeah. He lives in Monaco all right, in Rue des Geraniums.

Couldn't find a contact number so I've sent you a recent photo of the man, should be on your e-mail by now. I know he's in Monaco at the moment, he seems to travel using his real name. Flies in and out of Nice. The departure and arrival records only show only one Ben Khalid and he moves around a lot. Anyway, he arrived back two days ago and hasn't left since, so I assume he's in town. Shouldn't be too difficult to find him. If he's anything like the rest of the well-to-do, he won't bother eating at home, he'll eat out. If you watch his flat between say 19:00 and 22:00; chances are good you'll spot him either leaving or arriving. That's what I'd do if I were you."

Cohen nodded at Grey. "What about the bank accounts?"

"Khalid keeps an account with the Credit Foncier de Monaco. Strange thing with Monaco, although they have all sorts of laws protecting the rich and famous, the House of Grimaldi has a distinct aversion to money-laundering and things like financing of terror-related activities. They'll look after you, but then it's by their rules. One of those rules is that a bank account holder, no matter how wealthy and no matter what type of account is held, must identify him or herself to the bank. There's a lot of regular movement into and out of his account, but nothing like a couple of million at a time though. So I checked on where the bulk of the money had come from. One account ticked all the boxes, a Swiss account in Khalid's name held with Landolt & Cie, a family-owned bank. Difficult to get in, but I managed. Between October 2014 and December 2014 there were three deposits, two of US $3.75 million and one of US $7.5 million. Nothing before and nothing after that was anywhere near as big. Nor did anything that size occur in any of his four other accounts."

"Might just be what we're looking for. Any idea where it came from?

"Sitting down? You might just want to."

"I'm sitting."

"America. From the Bank of America of all places. Account holder, one Rudi Schultz. I had a look at this Schultz and, guess what? He's also an arms dealer, had him on my list. It gets better still. That account had three deposits totalling US $30 million between..."

"October and December 2014?"

"You got it. Also from an account held with the Bank of America. When I checked, absolutely nothing came up. I couldn't access anything. The account's there all right, but when I try to access it, it says the account doesn't exist. No idea how that works, it's kind of like there's a bank within the bank with layered accounts. Someone's gone to great lengths to make sure the account's very nicely hidden away. Question is why? Anyway, two days after each deposit was made, Schultz transferred exactly half the amount out of his account and into Khalid's account in Switzerland."

"Which connects Khalid and Schultz pretty nicely. What about Labuschagne's Swiss bank account?"

"That's a problem. I know what bank it is and how much was

transferred out of the account into van Zyl and Labuschagne's personal accounts in London and Rome, but only because I could access the history of both van Zyl and Labuschagne's accounts at their respective banks in the UK and Italy. Unfortunately, the bank in question in Switzerland, the one that the money came from, is very obscure, very old school and more secure than Fort Knox. They only deal with select hand-picked clients. Their internal database isn't linked to anything; it's completely inaccessible from outside. So while I can tell you what went into their personal accounts in London and Rome and that it came from Switzerland, I can't tell you what went into the Swiss account and from where."

"Can't we tell the bank we need to make a payment into Labuschagne's account? Then they'll have to tell us where to transfer the money to. Won't it open a door for you?"

"It possibly would and I tried. Never been stone-walled so quickly. The Swiss gentleman I spoke to was rather taken aback at my request. He told me that only the account-holder could give such an instruction, in person, at the bank. It would then be the banker who would personally contact the party due to make the payment and give the necessary instructions. He was very surprised I hadn't been told, which is as far as I got. I suggest you go and find Khalid. Have a chat to him. Then this Schultz. Personally, I guess he's the better bet of the two. For now it's the best I can give you. Only other thing you could do is get Labuschagne to Switzerland and let him give the instruction to make the account details available to you."

"No longer possible, I'm afraid. Labuschagne's brain's gone. The interrogation by the Israelis did more damage than even they thought, and they took it easy. You were right, a 92-year-old on the verge of death couldn't handle it. All we've got left is a living vegetable, so he's no good to us whatsoever."

"Damn! So I suppose it'll have to be Khalid to start with?"

"That's about the size of it." Grey ended the call and Cohen spoke up.

"How the hell did he do all of that so quickly?"

Grey grinned. "Let me tell you something about Billy McLaughlin. There're probably two other people on this planet with his particular skill set and both of those are mates of his. I don't think there's anything he doesn't know about encryption software and how to get into other people's systems without being noticed. On top of that, he's an absolutely brilliant programmer, and he's the most pig-headed individual I've ever come across. If you tell him something's impossible he'll go out of his way to prove you wrong. He's done it to me a couple of times. I know he'll figure out a way of finding out how that bank in Switzerland works, but it'll take him time, which is something we don't have." He looked at his watch. "17:30. Let's get going."

The two men left the building and twenty minutes later the black Ferrari pulled up not far from the apartment block in the narrow Rue des Geraniums. Grey and Cohen remained in the car watching from a distance. Billy McLaughlin was right. At precisely 20:34 Ben Khalid left his apartment, walked up the road to his parked car and climbed in. He did not notice the two men sitting in the black Ferrari, and, even if he had, it would not have attracted his attention, Ferraris were after all a dime a dozen in the principality. He himself drove a Maserati Grancabrio. He had barely turned the corner at the end of Rue des Geraniums en route to the Le Vistamar and Terrace restaurant in the Hotel Hermitage when the black Ferrari pulled away from the curb, following him. It did not take long; the Hermitage was just over a kilometre away from Khalid's residence.

As Khalid settled down for a quiet supper, Grey and Cohen made their way back to Rue des Geraniums and parked the car. Not knowing what security measures were in place – and there were bound to be a whole number - they waited for Khalid to return, which happened two hours later. As Khalid got out of his Maserati he suddenly noted the presence of two men, one on either side of him. Sensing trouble, he bent down and was about to reach for the small Beretta 3032 Tomcat he kept concealed in a calf-holster, when he felt the tell-tale nudge of a muzzle against his spine.

"Don't do anything stupid, Mr Khalid." The voice was cold, English and deliberate. "One wrong move and you'll be a cripple for the rest of your life. Now, if you'd be so kind, please take your weapon and place it on the ground in front of you."

Khalid knew he was not dealing with just another thug. This was different; there was real, palpable, cold menace. He slowly removed the Beretta from the holster and did as he had been told.

"Who the hell are you? What do you want?"

"A quiet chat, Mr Khalid." This time the second person was speaking. "Your apartment would be most suitable. I suggest you lead the way. Oh, and by the way," the man gave him a brief glimpse of a large calibre silenced handgun, "we do suggest you cooperate."

Khalid, flanked by the two men, made his way to the entrance to the apartment block, unlocked the front door and entered the dark entrance foyer. His apartment was on the second floor. He was about to press the button on the panel next to door leading into a small elevator when he was stopped by the older of the two men.

"No elevator. Take the stairs. And keep the lights off."

At that point Khalid knew he was dealing with real professionals. The lights in the elevator would have been on and a small security camera would have recorded Khalid and the two men with him. Unfortunately for Khalid there was no camera covering the staircase. They walked up the dark flight of stairs and came to the door leading to Khalid's apartment. He unlocked it and was about to walk in, when he received the next instruction.

"Stop right there, Khalid," the younger of the two men spoke again. Khalid stopped. "The control panel of the security system, the one on the wall to your left. Switch everything off, alarm system, beams, pressure sensors and whatever else you have installed here." By then both Grey and Cohen had pulled black balaclavas over their heads. "I will follow you. Then go to wherever you have your own CCTV system set up. Turn it off. If you have a backup system, turn it off as well. Don't try and trick us. It would be very unwise and very unhealthy."

Khalid shuddered. There were pressure sensors, and his idea had been to step onto them, a silent alarm alerting the staff in the control room of the security company he paid a substantial amount of money to every month. But to activate the alarm he would have had to move forward, the first series pressure sensors under the carpet over a metre away from the control panel, and he'd been told not to. If he did, he had no doubt that it would probably be the last move he ever made. He had no option, and switched the system off.

"Done. And there's no CCTV set-up in here. Now can I put the lights on?"

"No," replied Grey. "Where's your study?"

"Down the passage to the left."

"Go." Grey pushed Khalid along and they entered the dark study. "Sit." Khalid sat down on the high-backed leather executive chair. Grey repositioned a halogen reading lamp on the desk, pointed it towards Khalid and switched it on. Khalid blinked rapidly, the light blinding him. As he blinked, he felt his hands being tied behind the back of the chair.

"Right, Khalid. Let's get started." Khalid could not see Grey, only hear the voice behind the glare of the lamp. "Why don't you tell us about a Mr Pieter van Zyl? Or Rudi Schultz? And all you know about the Meinhof Kollaboration."

"Who?" The fear in Khalid's voice was evident. *What was this? How did they know?*

"Listen, my friend," said Grey quietly, "we have all night. And the next day if need be. We can do this in one of two ways. Either you talk voluntarily, or we make you talk. One way is easy and painless; the other will take longer and involve a lot of pain. Your choice. The result will be the same, you'll talk, I assure you. Now, let's start again. Pieter Van Zyl, Rudi Schultz and Meinhof Kollaboration. And we know it's a nuke you sold."

Khalid knew there was no way out. Two hours later, everything meticulously recorded, Cohen made a call. Within minutes three further gentlemen entered the apartment. They had been called by Cohen four hours earlier and had been waiting in a closed panel van not far from the Rue des Geraniums. Khalid would shortly be joining Francois Labuschagne in Israel. As the panel van with the three men and Ben Khalid left Monaco for the Cote d'Azur Airport in Nice and the waiting aircraft, Grey and Cohen proceeded to take the apartment apart, bit by bit.

By the time Ben Khalid arrived in Israel, Grey and Cohen were locking up the apartment. It had been ransacked. Anyone entering would immediately conclude that a robbery had taken place. A few discreetly placed pieces of evidence would link Ben Khalid to a drug deal. The police would surmise what had happened; a narcotics deal had gone sour, the apartment had been trashed by enforcers of the purchaser and Khalid, clearly the seller based on the evidence they found, had been removed. That would be it.

The authorities in Monaco would not be at all unhappy to see a drug dealer removed from their area of jurisdiction.

Grey and Cohen, on the other hand, had what they wanted - written records of Khalid's dealings taken from a concealed safe to which Khalid had reluctantly given the combination, full copies of the hard-drives – which had subsequently been wiped clean - taken from two desk-top computers, as well as Khalid's laptop.

Grey and Cohen slipped unnoticed out of the apartment, made their way to the airport and landed at London's Heathrow Airport five hours later. As they made their way to Billy McLaughlin's private IT empire in South Wimbledon, Ben Khalid was into the third hour of a rather unpleasant interrogation session in a basement room under a nondescript building on the outskirts of Tel Aviv. The following day - Billy McLaughlin had ripped the hard-drives and laptop apart and extracted whatever information there was to be gleaned - Grey and Cohen were on the way back to Tel Aviv where they arrived late at night. After a few short hours of sleep, Grey, Cohen, Sharon and Immelmann reconvened in the same flat in Tel Aviv. The first 48 hours had passed.

Abel Sharon was the last to arrive and wasted no time. It had just gone 06:00.

"Morning gentlemen. I see we're all present. I briefed the Prime Minister yesterday. To say he's concerned is an understatement. I told him Grey & McLaughlin have been roped in to help. He told me to use whatever resources the State has at its disposal and to get rid of this impeding disaster. He's got enough on his plate with the latest shit going down in the West Bank. His exact words were – "Make this thing go away, Abel. I can deal with the West Bank and whatever other Palestinian issue any day, I can't deal with the threat of a nuke. If that thing goes off here, it's the end of Israel". Rather direct and pretty much the truth. He did ask me if it was a hoax. We've had a couple of those in the past. I told him it wasn't." He sat down. "Over to you, Mike. What did you find out in Monaco?"

Grey took four slim folders and handed one to each person present, keeping the last one for himself. "I'll sum up what's happened so far, the file has the detail. Van Zyl got hold of Khalid and offered him the bomb. Khalid then put out the word to anyone he thought might be interested. Enter Rudi Schultz, an American arms dealer as bad as Khalid. He had a party interested in buying the nuke. Sales price ends up being US $80 million, of which 30 million goes to Schultz who then pays Khalid 15 million. The actual purchaser is an unknown entity, we assume American. The other 50 million was then paid directly to van Zyl and Labuschagne, probably by the same unknown entity who paid Schultz. We know they received the money because Labuschagne told us so. We have a contact number for Rudi Schultz. I've taken the liberty of sending one of my men there to hook up a fictitious arms deal, he's on his way to the USA as I speak. Once he's tied Schultz down he'll arrange a meeting at which Aaron and I will also be present. I expect that'll happen in the next day or so. Aaron and I need to get going by this evening at the latest. It would be good if we could use that Challenger again. At which point we'll have Labuschagne, Khalid and hopefully Schultz out of the way. What we need to do now is find out who Schultz's contact was. Once we know, we'll be able to dig deeper; with a bit of luck find a link to the Meinhof Kollaboration."

"Agreed; you two get going. We'll make a different plane available, the Challenger doesn't have the legs. We've got direct access to a Bombardier Global Express, that'll do very nicely. Gets you to just about anywhere on the east coast of the USA non-stop."

"Just one small problem."

"What's that?"

"I need a different set of papers. The Americans know me far too well. The minute I arrive there they'll know about it and be all over me like a bad rash. Not that they don't like me, they'll just be very curious to know what I'm doing in their country. It'll have to be something I haven't used before."

"We figured as much," replied Sharon. "Here," he tossed an envelope across the table at Grey, "your new identity for this mission. Until this is over you are Benjamin Sachs, American citizen. You said your man is on the way there. How's he getting into the States? Using his real name?"

"No, he's using a different passport. We arranged some a while back for two or three of my key men down there, and that's something the Americans don't know about. He'll be travelling as a British national so he doesn't need a visa. One last thing. What about Khalid? Anything from him yet?"

Sharon shook his head. "No, not much else other than what you've said. He confirms the Rudi Schultz connection, knows the end client was apparently the Meinhof Kollaboration but not who paid for the device. Could have been anyone. Schultz needs to talk and I don't care what you do to make it happen."

Schopfheim, Germany

As the four men dispersed, Dr Amir Asadi was showing Jens Keller how to arm the atomic device in the villa in Schopfheim. Keller, watched by Anne Biedermann and Karl Stegemann, did not take long to understand, taking notes as Asadi spoke. When Asadi came to the end of his explanation he asked if Keller had understood everything. Keller nodded; his gesture was, at the same time, a signal for Karl Stegemann. He pulled out a 9mm CZ Star Parabellum he had stuck behind his back into the waistband of the Levi jeans he was wearing and shot Asadi through the right side of the head, killing him instantly. Four hours later the body of Dr Amir Asadi had vanished, buried under a 50 cm thick layer of concrete covering a hole in one of the other rooms in the basement of the villa in Schopfheim. The device was ready. All that remained was the delivery.

CHAPTER 5
THE PATRIOT LINK

New York, USA

Jaco van Rensburgh had left OR Tambo airport in Johannesburg on the scheduled South African Airways flight direct to New York a day earlier. One of the longest ultra long-haul commercial flights by any airline, he disembarked at JFK International Airport after a marathon 16 hour and 15 minute flight. Prior to his departure he had called Rudi Schultz on the number provided by Grey. He gave his name as Gerald Pearson, stating that he was a mercenary with a contract to assist and provide arms to a prominent war-lord in the Central African Republic and asked for an urgent meeting. At first Schultz had played his cards close to his chest, wondering who this Pearson was and how he had obtained his number. When van Rensburgh told him he had US $10 million to spend in cash, not the usual payment in the form of blood diamonds or other suspect methods, Schultz took the bait. Smelling quick money - a sale of the nature this Pearson character was talking about usually involved inferior arms and even more suspect ammunition, (Africa, particularly the parts run by war-lords, was considered a dumping-ground for equipment the rest of the world no longer wanted) he agreed to meet Pearson in New York.

Van Rensburgh, using his assumed name, entered the USA and made his way to Manhattan, where had booked a suite for three nights in The Towers of the Waldorf Astoria at 100 East 50th Street. Rudi Schultz was suitably impressed. Many of his clients preferred using dodgy downtown hotels in obscure cities, paranoid about being seen by anyone. This was different; the man he met in the opulent suite was dressed in a suit and tie, the only hint of his real profession a tanned, leathered face and a handshake akin to a vice-grip. That evening they had supper together. Schultz, assuming his capacity for drink would surpass that of his potential customer; inebriated men, after all, tend to talk too much, began to order one round of alcohol after the next. Instead, it was Schultz who did the talking. He couldn't have known that van Rensburgh had a capacity for drink legendary in the South African Defence Force. They agreed to conclude the following afternoon and Schultz left the hotel, drunk as a Lord, yet delighted with his progress. The following day at 14:00 he arrived back at The Towers and made his way straight up to van Rensburgh's suite.

This time the meeting turned out to be a nightmare. He had hardly sat down when van Rensburgh, a smile on his face, told him two further people would be joining the meeting. Schultz was about to protest when the door to the bedroom opened and two men emerged, Michael Grey and Aaron Cohen. Cohen immediately moved across to the entrance door of the suite, blocking the exit, as Grey sat down in an armchair. Schultz, primed to recognise danger, knew he was looking at trouble but was unable to do much about it - three against one were not odds he considered to be favourable, unless he was armed. He wasn't, yet the man sitting opposite him was; a silenced Glock 17 on his lap.

"Good afternoon Mr Schultz. Have a seat." The man in the chair spoke as though he was talking to an underling.

Schultz decided to take matters head-on. "I don't know who the fuck you are, and you clearly have no fucking idea who you're dealing with. This conversations ends, right here, right now." He got up to leave. "Then I suggest the three of you get the fuck out of town. No, make that the country. Cause, when I find you, and I will, you're fucking dead. Got it?"

"Rudi, Rudi. Please." Grey smiled gently and got up. "Why don't you rather shut the fuck up and stop embarrassing yourself? Now sit down. I'm not here to play games, nor are my two colleagues. And before you carry on bleating, remember one thing. The shit you sell? The weapons? We have been known to use them. You haven't."

Schultz didn't have a choice. He sat down. "What do you want?" He turned to look up at van Rensburgh, who had a strange grin on his face. "Pearson, right? You set me up, didn't you, you bastard?"

"Perhaps," said van Rensburgh. "I suggest you listen to my friend here, otherwise I might just have to rip your head off your shoulders."

"Who paid you the $30 million?" asked Grey softly.

At which point Schultz knew he was in deeper trouble than he could handle. "I don't know what you're talking about."

Grey stopped smiling. "Schultz. You've got two options here. I gave your friend Ben Khalid the same choices. He was clever; I don't know if you are. Talk and you'll be okay. Don't talk and we'll take you to the top of the building and throw you off. Rather high from up there, isn't it?"

Van Rensburgh nodded. "Should leave a rather nasty mess on the pavement."

"You can't do that!"

"Oh? Damn!" said Grey, sarcasm evident in his voice. "You're right. Of course we can't, we'd be breaking the law. Sounds pretty rich coming from the man who arranged the sale of a nuke to a terrorist organisation, doesn't it? Tell me, who the fuck was breaking the law then? Wasn't me, was it? I'll ask again. Who paid you?"

"You know what you're getting yourself into?"

"Yeah, we do. The evil machinations of the lunatics you sold an atomic bomb to."

Schultz didn't know what to say, wondering if it was better to commit involuntary suicide by trying to take out the three men, at least one of them armed, or to talk. He knew the risks of exposing his client; it wouldn't be viewed in too kindly a manner if he leaked his name. On the other hand, he didn't want to end his life prematurely, and definitely not on a New York sidewalk. If he talked, he could at least still run, to where he didn't know. If he didn't, he had no reason to believe he wouldn't be departing from this world before the end of the afternoon. He made his decision whatever the consequences, but he'd make it as difficult as possible.

"Pierre Morgan."

"Pierre Morgan? Who's that?"

"My client. You asked, remember?"

"How do you contact him?"

"I fucking call him, you dummy. How else?"

"I suggest you don't get clever with me, Schultz. Is there a code word or something you use when you talk to Morgan?"

Schultz paused. "Go fuck yourself. I'm not telling you."

Grey stopped smiling and gave Cohen a hardly noticeable nod. Schultz didn't see it coming. Next thing he was being held down by van Rensburgh as Cohen took his left hand and snapped the middle finger. Schultz shrieked briefly, then vomited onto the carpet. "You bastards..." he muttered, wiping a dribble of puke from his chin with his good hand.

Grey sat there, unmoved. "Consider that to be a little appetiser." He leaned forward. "Next we'll break all the other fingers, one by one. Then we'll move on to the other hand. If that doesn't help, I'll put a bullet through each of your elbows, then your kneecaps. If by then you haven't told me what I want to know we'll take you to the top of the building."

Schultz talked after a further two of his fingers had been broken. Half an hour later Grey had the name of the person he was looking for, the contact method, as well as a code word. As Rudi Schultz left the hotel, his damaged hand covered with his jacket, wondering why he had been allowed to go, a young man fell in behind him, keeping his distance. Schultz arrived at his parked car, climbed in and started the engine, thanking the Gods he was driving an automatic and not a stick shift. He didn't notice a young man following him climb into a conveniently waiting taxi. Nor could he know that his smart phone was being monitored by Mossad agents, three men working out of the back of a highly modified delivery van the Mossad operated when the need arose.

Grey knew exactly what Schultz was going to do. There was no way he would not warn his client, it was his only shot at remaining alive, never mind remaining in business. The entire exercise of getting a name, contact number and code word had been a game. Sure, it had given them some interesting information, but Grey was smart enough to know that if he, Michael Grey, called the number, mentioned the person by name and gave the code word, the call would more than likely be terminated and the telephone number would never be answered again. Letting Rudi Schultz go had always been the ultimate objective.

Schultz did not disappoint. Less than an hour after leaving The Towers of the Waldorf Astoria he pulled into a parking space outside the hotel he was staying at, the New York Marriot Downtown at 85 West Street. As he made his way into the hotel the young man following him got out of the taxi, walked quickly through the lobby and joined him in the elevator. Schultz pushed the button to the seventh floor, not bothering about the man next to him, the throbbing pain from his broken fingers so acute he wouldn't have noticed if Beyonce Knowles had walked into the elevator without any clothes on. Both men left the elevator on the seventh floor, the young man continuing down the corridor as Schultz opened the door to room 710. By the time Schultz was holding his damaged fingers under cold water in the bathroom of his hotel room, the young man was back on the ground floor, making his way through the lobby, out of the hotel and across the road to the parked panel van. Half an hour later, his hand in a plastic bag filled with slowly melting ice cubes, Rudi Schultz made the call Grey had been waiting for, all of it recorded by the three men in the panel van.

" Pierre. Rudi here. There's a problem."

"What problem?"

"Someone found out what I sold you. They set me up and got me into a meeting. Broke three of my fingers."

For a brief moment Pierre Morgan, a commodity trader living in Stamford, Connecticut, said nothing. "What did you tell them? Who are they?"

"Fuck, Pierre, everything. They threatened to kill me. One of them's a Brit with a funny accent, calls himself Gerald Pearson. I don't know if it's his real name. There were two others, no idea who they are. I'm trying to warn you. They know your contact number, your name, the code we use and they know about the nuke. If anyone calls, don't answer..."

"Where are you?"

"The Marriot Downtown at 85 West. Room 710."

"Don't move. Speak to no one. Don't answer any calls. I'll be there in three hours." The line went dead.

It took Pierre Morgan a little less than three hours to get to the hotel from his home in Stamford; the traffic en route to lower Manhattan as congested as always. Half an hour before he arrived two Mossad agents made their way into the hotel, one of them to a hastily-booked room on the seventh floor, two rooms away from room 710, the other remaining in the lobby. The agent in the lobby found a seat where he could keep an eye on the elevators. He sat there and waited, pretending to read the daily edition of the New York Post. Kitted out with a hardly noticeable earpiece and a match-sized microphone attached to the lapel of his jacket, the agent was able to communicate with the men in the delivery-van, who were in constant contact with the agent in the room on the seventh floor. The minute the agent in the lobby noticed the elevator stopping at the seventh floor he informed the men in the van, who promptly informed their colleague two doors away from room 710, who in turn pretended he was leaving the room, noting if anyone went to Schultz's room. Fourteen times it was a false alarm.

When Pierre Morgan arrived he didn't notice he was being watched. Nor did it seem at all unusual when a middle-aged man left his room two doors away from room 710, closed the door and walked to the elevator Morgan had just stepped out of. Morgan knocked on the door of room 710 and Schultz opened it. As Morgan entered, closing the door behind him, the man waiting at the elevator turned and headed back to the room he had come from. Moments later the men in the delivery-van had an exact description of Pierre Morgan. Morgan eventually left the hotel, climbed into his car and made his way back to Stamford. Only this time he was followed by Michael Grey and Aaron Cohen, the delivery-van with the communication monitoring gear not far behind.

Back in room 710 in the New York Marriot Downtown Rudi Schultz lay on his bed, the sheets soaked in blood. Killing Schultz – Morgan hadn't had a choice in the matter, the order to eliminate him coming from his own contact - had involved using a Tazer to incapacitate him, dragging him onto the bed and then slitting his throat with a carpet knife. It had been messy, the first attempt not finding the jugular vein. Schultz, a mixture of sheer terror and pleading in his eyes, tried to scream but could not. The second cut found the right spot and Schultz mercifully expired. But, had anyone seen him? Would the police suddenly come knocking on his door? Morgan didn't know.

Stamford, Connecticut, USA

Pierre Morgan arrived back in Stamford, stopping his Mercedes Benz CL63 AMG Coupé outside the entrance to 111 Harbour Point, and made his way to his luxury apartment on the third floor. The drive back from New York had passed in a blurry haze; if anyone had asked him how long it had taken he would not have been able to answer. The first thing he did when he entered the flat was to get rid of the bloody latex gloves he had used during the killing, first washing them as best he could before popping them into the waste disposal unit.

For over four years everything had been just fine, Morgan's personal wealth growing to more than US $300 million. Within the space of one afternoon and a single telephone call, the situation had changed significantly. He had turned into a reluctant murderer, the police no doubt already investigating who could have committed the crime. Never before had he been called upon to do something even remotely close; the most difficult task given to him by the leadership of The Patriots up until then the purchase of the atomic device. Morgan shuddered. It had been so good for such a long time, the occasional call from his contact giving him inside information on certain lucrative deals about to materialise, information without which he would never have become as rich as he was. That most of the deals were linked directly or indirectly to the arms industry escaped him, as far as he was concerned he was dealing with commodities, no matter what the commodities were. He had always known the day would come when he would be called upon to return the favours; it was part of the arrangement. It happened the day he had told his contact of the nuclear device Rudi Schultz had on offer. Within an hour he had been called back and told to commence negotiations, a task he had carried out to the full satisfaction of his contact.

Now he had been obliged to tell his contact, two years after the purchase of the device, that Schultz had been found and had leaked. The response had been immediate; get rid of Schultz and wait for further instructions. All he could do now was to wait for his contact, who had also curtly advised him not to mention him by name going forwards in case any of their calls were monitored, to call.

How Morgan and Schultz had come to know of each other in the first place was by chance more than anything else. Morgan had been on a two week vacation to Cancun in Mexico. It was there that he had met Schultz. Schultz, also on vacation, started the conversation with the man sitting next to him at the bar counter, watching a few skimpily-clad ladies gyrating on a raised dance floor just beyond the bar area. They hit it off well and, before the end of the vacation, Morgan had a good idea of what Schultz did, whereas Schultz, by way of a veiled hint from Morgan, knew that if he ever had something "special" to offer he should contact Morgan. The something "special" finally came about the day Pieter van Zyl had contacted Ben Khalid who, in turn, had sent out the word to a select number of his clients, amongst them Schultz. When Morgan, courtesy of a paid-for trip to Orlando for an urgent meeting with Schultz, heard about it he could not believe his ears. He left the meeting, called his own contact and advised him what was on offer. Within an hour the call came back advising him to start negotiations. Three days later the purchase of the nuclear device had been concluded.

To understand the predicament Morgan found himself in one needs to appreciate the command and control structure of The Patriots. A decidedly top-down driven affair, it was designed to protect the identities of those who wielded the real power. It was akin to a series of lengths of chain hanging from a small main body, with each link in a particular chain knowing only the link above it and below it. Each chain, comprising up to 75 individuals, finally linked to one of the men who constituted the main body, an entity consisting of five individuals. They were the founders and core members of The Patriots. In the event of an individual or a link in a particular chain being compromised, that link was removed. The remaining chain, still attached to the body, could then be re-grown, the discarded length of chain simply left to fall apart. In total, The Patriot network comprised just on 7396 individuals, each one selected for a specific skill set and looked after, commensurate to the respective position the individual held in the chain. Hence, if the leadership of The Patriots needed something to be done, the skill to do so was inevitably available somewhere within the network. It simply meant sending out the order via the individual who controlled the particular chain containing the required skill, and then cascading it down to the targeted link. The entire network was very well looked after, but it came with a price - when it came to payback time, no matter in what shape or form, delivery was expected.

Morgan thus had no idea who the actual leaders of the movement were; all he had was the name and telephone number of his contact, one link above him in the chain, and the name and telephone number of the contact one link below him. Where exactly he was positioned in the chain he did not know, he had always assumed it was reasonably high up. He couldn't know, and never would, that he was eight links away from the very top. As it went, the link Pierre Morgan represented had been compromised and had to be removed. He was a dead man. At precisely 22:34 Morgan's cell phone rang.

"Morgan?" The caller's tone of voice was detached, clinical.

"Yes."

"Is it done?"

"Yes, Schultz is dead."

"What did he say?"

Morgan took four minutes to relay the detail of what Schultz had told him.

"Stay where you are. I'll call back in a few hours." Once more the line went dead.

Down on the street, not far from Morgan's parked AMG Mercedes, Grey and Cohen sat in their parked Buick Enclave, watching the entrance to 111 Harbour Point. Morgan, they guessed, if he were to leave the building, would again come out of the main entrance, unless he had a second car, which was unlikely. Parked a little further behind them was the converted delivery-van with the three Mossad agents. They had picked up the incoming call, noted the number and what the call was about. Within a minute Grey was talking to Billy McLaughlin in London.

"Billy. I've got an American number. Can you find out who it belongs to?"

"Give it to me," said McLaughlin.

Grey gave him the number. "Will it take long?"

"No, shouldn't really. Problem with American numbers is you can't tell if it's landline or cellular, they all look the same. I'll call back."

It did not take McLaughlin long to find what he was looking for and call back. By then Grey had already advised van Rensburgh, who was still in the Marriot Downtown in New York, that Rudi Schultz had been eliminated.

"Mike. It's an AT & T mobile number. Washington DC area code, 202. Guess what? The number belongs to a dead person."

"Run that by me again, will you?"

"A dead person," said McLaughlin. "Some 95-year-old man. Died two-and-a-half years ago. Lived in an old age home in a suburb in Washington."

"Why the hell's it still operating?"

"Someone out there's clearly still paying the account. As long as the account's being paid, AT & T wouldn't care, would they? I don't think they'd even know the owner had passed on."

"Then who's using the phone now? Any idea?" asked Grey.

"No. I suggest you stay where you are; give me an hour or so. By then I'll be able to tell you a lot more."

Grey and Cohen sat back and waited, not much being said between the two of them. Just before 23:00 a white panel van pulled up across the road from where they were parked, the decals on the side identifying it as belonging to *Ted's Emergency Appliance Repairs – 24/7*. A man in a blue overall got out, took a tool-box from the back of the van and entered the building. Neither Grey nor Cohen thought much about it. The people who were wealthy enough to stay at 111 Harbour Point would be able to afford to pay someone to come and fix a broken appliance in the middle of the night. Fifteen minutes later the repairman left the building, packed away the tool-box and drove off. Another fifteen minutes went by when suddenly the windows of an apartment on the third floor blew out in a deafening roar of orange flame. At the same time the lights on the second, third and fourth floors of 111 Harbour Point went out.

"What the fuck?!" yelled Grey, his ears ringing from the blast less than 50 metres away from them, the sound of glass shards falling on the roof of the Buick sounding like mini hailstones.

Cohen was already pulling away from the curb, tyres squealing, shouting at the driver of the panel van parked further behind them via a hand-held two-way radio. "Ben, get the hell out of here! NOW! Head for the Connecticut Turnpike and drive in the direction of New York. We'll catch up with you. GO!" Cohen tossed the two-way radio onto the back seat of the Buick and turned to Grey. "This place will be crawling with cops and firemen in about a minute from now! If you ask me, someone's just removed our friend Morgan from the scene!"

"The guy in the panel van! The repair service. It must've been him!" Grey looked out of the back window as Cohen left the scene, smoke and flames billowing from the destroyed apartment. In the distance they heard the first sound of wailing sirens.

"Fucking right it was!" spat Cohen. "Who else? Morgan receives a single phone call. We know the number, what was said, but we don't know who called. Then this van arrives; departs 15 minutes later and next thing the apartment blows up! What the hell are we dealing with here?"

"No idea, but they don't play games... Jesus! Jaco van Rensburgh! He's in the Marriot Downtown! I hope they didn't blow up Schultz's room as well!" He grabbed his phone and punched in van Rensburgh's number hoping it would be answered. It didn't take long.

"Mike! Glad you called. Get a load of this. After you called I made my way up to Schultz's room and let myself in; wasn't difficult. Schultz is dead all right, Morgan cut his throat. Christ, what a mess, there's blood all over the show! I'm still in the lobby. Can't stay here much longer, the staff here's starting to look at me funny. What do you want me to do now?"

"Did you notice anything unusual, any possibly suspicious persons making their way to the seventh floor?"

"Unusual yes, suspicious no, not as far as I can tell. A guy carrying a tool-box from a crowd called *Ted's Emergency Appliance Repairs – 24/7,* that's what it said on the back of the guy's jacket, went up there about 20 minutes ago and left again just before..."

"Christ! Jaco, get the fuck out of there, quickly!"

"You okay?" Van Rensburgh, already getting up to leave, knew Grey better than most, and the tone of his voice told him something was very wrong.

"*Ted's Emergency Appliance Repairs – 24/7!* It's not a repair service – it's a goddamned hit squad! The same crowd just went and blew up an apartment in the building Morgan was staying, more than likely with Morgan in it!"

"Shit!" Van Rensburgh walked out of the main entrance of the Marriot and hailed a taxi. "This is getting a touch serious, isn't it?"

"Yeah, it is. You out of there?"

"Getting into a taxi. I'll see you back at The Towers."

New York, USA

Grey kept looking out of the back window of the fast-moving Buick to check if they were being followed. There was nothing, but that could change any minute. If the people Morgan had been in contact with had the kind of clout to send out hit squads, then what else were their capabilities? *Never, ever, underestimate your enemy,* thought Grey, as Cohen turned onto the Connecticut Turnpike and slowed down, cruising along a notch above the speed limit. By the time Grey and Cohen arrived back at The Towers it was well past 02:00. Van Rensburgh, who had long since arrived, was nursing a cold beer and watching television as Grey and Cohen walked in.

"Get a load of this, guys! Breaking news! One and a half hours ago there was a massive explosion on the seventh floor of the Marriot Downtown. Jesus, do those boys know what they're doing or what? Teds fucking Emergency Repairs... my ass!"

Grey and Cohen stopped in their tracks, staring at the screen. Flame and smoke were billowing out of five windows on the seventh floor of the hotel, debris all over the road. Police, reporters and a National Guard unit were on the scene, milling about everywhere. Eight fire engines were dousing the flames with high-pressure water cannons, while thousands of bystanders gaped at the destruction. It looked like a war zone. A reporter from CNN was already speculating about a possible terrorist attack, drawing comparisons to the bombing of the World Trade Centre prior to the events of 9/11.

Grey made his way across to the drinks cabinet, his eyes glued to the scene unfolding on the screen. "Christ! We've really started something, haven't we? Morgan's history and now any chance of someone finding out Schultz was murdered before the explosion's gone up in smoke as well; there won't be enough left of him."

"You got that right," remarked Cohen as he sat down. "If I didn't know any better I'd say we exposed someone's nerve and then went and stood on it."

"What now?" queried van Rensburgh.

"Back to reality," said Grey. "Whoever ran Morgan has the ability to send out hit squads. We know it's a man because we've got the transcript of the telephone call, but we have no idea who he is. The people who control the setup are ruthless, won't stop at anything and, more importantly, they're highly bloody efficient." He put down his drink, removed his laptop from its bag and set it up on the lounge table. "Skype call. Billy's waiting in London."

"Secure enough? Can't someone listen in?"

"Suppose they could, but then they'd really have to be geared up for it. Skype uses Advanced Encryption Standard –called Rijndael – works on 256 bit encryption. Better than cell phones. Aah... here he is."

Cohen and van Rensburgh grouped behind Grey as McLaughlin's face came up on the video stream.

"Morning gents. Or evening. Whatever. How's things going?"

"It's a mess. Go and check out CNN America. Someone just went and blew up Pierre Morgan in his apartment in Connecticut and then Rudi Schultz – make that Schultz's body, 'cause they'd murdered the fucker before then - in the Marriot Downtown in New York. The Marriot explosion's on TV right now."

"God almighty!" exclaimed McLaughlin, who had switched on his TV and changed to the 24-hour CNN channel. "You've really gone and pissed on someone's battery, haven't you?" The three men watched as McLaughlin ran his fingers through his long hair. Typically dressed in jeans and a T-shirt, McLaughlin wasn't quite the epitome of a successful executive. Computer geek maybe, and he really was; albeit one of the best in the business. "Gotta say my stuff's a bit more mundane. That number you gave me? The one belonging to this dead grandad? I had a closer look at the phone records, payment records and so on. Believe it or not the monthly bill is paid from the same account used to pay Schultz! Problem is we don't know who owns the account because it can't be accessed. Then there's a detailed listing of the numbers dialled. This gets real strange. It's only ever been used to dial two numbers; incoming numbers I can't trace as they aren't listed. Anyway, I had a look at the two numbers Morgan called. Guess what?"

"No idea. What?"

"It's the same all over again. Both numbers belong to dead people, also paid from the same account, and also only used to dial two numbers, Morgan's number and one other unknown number. And so it carries on. At one end I got to level eight and there it stops. The phone at level eight has outgoing calls to a whole series of different numbers. On the other end I haven't finished yet, I'm at level 22. No idea where it ends. Whatever it is, using Morgan's phone as the baseline, what I call level eight seems to be the top of a contact chain and level 22 heading towards the bottom end. Irrespective of the level, the phones belong to people who aren't alive any longer, and the billing for every one of them is paid from the same unknown bank account."

"How many outgoing numbers at the last level?"

"Level eight or level twenty-two?"

"Level eight."

"Thirty-eight different numbers."

"Let me get this straight," Grey breathed deeply, "the chain ends at what you call level eight. The level eight phone, unlike all the others that call two numbers, calls thirty-eight different numbers. Incoming calls you can't track as they're not part of the billing. The monthly billing for all phones is paid from the same account, the one we can't trace because it doesn't appear to exist. All the phones belong to dead people. That right?"

"Pretty much so. I then started to trace back one of the other 38 phone numbers and followed the chain. Same thing all over again. All the phones in that chain also belong to dead people, all billings paid again from the same account. If you ask me, the phones used to dial two numbers only belong to people who have one contact they report to and one contact who reports to them. Nicely set up. The level eight phone would be the main man, or one of them."

"Any idea of the size of this network?" asked Grey.

"No, not yet," replied McLaughlin, "but you can assume it's massive. Take the chain we discovered as standard. Then take level eight going up and level twenty-two going down, again using Morgan as the baseline. Makes 31 levels in my book. Now multiply 30 levels - assuming each chain has 31 levels - by 38 chains, and you get 1140 people. We know how far up it goes, but not how far down. Starting right at the top, say the lowest level is 50 in all cases. Take 38 and multiply by 50 and you get 1900. The lower the levels go and the greater the number of chains, the larger the network. Whoever set this up is a real clever bastard, I'll give him that much!"

" Any good news?" asked Cohen.

"Don't know if it's good news. One of the 38 numbers is not an American number. It has a 0049 prefix, which means it's Germany."

"Germany? A link to the Meinhof Kollaboration?"

"I don't know," said McLaughlin. "The number has been dialled on 32 occasions and is a landline number in a small town in southern Germany near the Swiss and French borders."

"What town?" asked Grey.

"A place called Schopfheim, about 30 odd kilometres from Basel up a valley called the Wiesental. The number, according to German Telekom data, is registered to an old villa in the town. There's a twist. The Telekom contract was cancelled three days ago."

"Time to go."

Grey shut down the lap top and he and Cohen left the hotel,

heading out to La Guardia airport and the waiting Bombardier Global Express jet. Van Rensburgh remained in New York. He would be joined two days later by Gert van Tonder, who, as were van Rensburgh and Grey, was also an ex-South African Reconnaissance Force operator. The two, assisted by American-based Mossad agents, would form the American leg of the operation.

Schopfheim, Germany

As van Tonder, also using an assumed identity, boarded the SAA flight in Johannesburg for the long trip to New York, Grey and Cohen landed at the small regional airport serving the Swiss town of Basel - Euro Airport Basel Mulhouse Freiburg. Waiting for them was Moshe Immelmann, who had been briefed on the latest developments and had already sent five other Mossad agents to Schopfheim. He had also established that the occupants of the villa had cancelled the three year lease for the villa two months earlier and had handed back the keys a few days ago. At least someone had, the owner of the rental agency had not recognised the identikits of Jens Keller, Anne Biedermann or Karl Stegemann which Moshe Immelmann had showed him.

The villa was a huge, rambling, three-storey rectangular building, set in the middle of a property Grey guessed must have been well over 10 000 square metres in size. Well away from the town, it was so isolated that even Osama bin Ladin would - had he been alive - have been happy to use it as a hide out. Completely lacking any modern building features such as Thermopane windows, inner wall insulation or a high-tech heating system, the villa must have cost a small fortune to run. Immelmann took a set of keys from his pocket and unlocked the front door.

"Nice!" said Grey. "How'd you get hold of the keys?"

Immelmann grinned. "I rented the place for three months." The hinges of the massive solid wooden double door creaked as Immelmann pushed it open and stepped into the frigid interior. "Here it is. If we have to, we can spend the next three months turning this place on its head. I suggest we get started."

Immelmann, Grey, Cohen and the five other Mossad agents split up, two men to each floor. Cohen, together with one of the other agents, headed down into the basement. Grey had barely finished with the first room when he heard Cohen shouting for them to come down. He left the second floor and bounded down the stairs, two steps at a time.

"Found something?"

"Not sure," said Cohen, leading the way. "Check this out." They entered the basement room modified by the three previous occupants of the villa. There was nothing left except a few planks standing forlornly in a corner and the modern goods hoist at the far end of the room. "Somebody sure spent some money on renovations. And a goods hoist going up to the garages? What the hell for? But that's not all. Come." He walked into the room furthest away from the staircase leading into the cellar. A single light-bulb glowed dimly high above them. "Look at this," said

Cohen, pointing at the floor.

Grey looked down and got on his haunches. "Concrete," he murmured, and scratched the surface with his finger nail. It was cold and slightly moist. "Not even properly set yet."

"Exactly," said Cohen. "Roughly one metre by two metres. As though something's buried under there."

"Only one way to find out," muttered Grey. By then Immelmann and the others had joined them. "We need a jack-hammer. Can we get one here somewhere?"

"Leave it to me," said Immelmann. Not much later a delivery vehicle from a local plant hire company pulled up in the courtyard. Immelmann signed the delivery note and paid cash for the hire of the jack hammer, advising the driver to come back the next day to collect the equipment. Shortly afterwards, one of the Mossad agents, ear-muffs on to drown out the staccato noise of the jack-hammer and wearing safety goggles to protect his eyes from flying mortar fragments, went to work. He had been at it for the better part of ten minutes when he suddenly stopped.

"Moshe! I've found something!"

Grey, Immelmann and Cohen, who had moved to the far side of the basement to avoid going deaf, went back to where the agent had been digging up the floor.

"Look there," said the agent, wiping sweat from his brow and pointing at the hole. "If you ask me, it's a bloody foot."

Grey bent forward to take a closer look. Sure enough, the

jack-hammer had unearthed what looked like the top half of a shoe. "You're right. It's a shoe." He looked up at Immelmann. "Looks like we've got a corpse on our hands."

It took over an hour for the Mossad agent with the jack-hammer to break away enough concrete. Grey stared down onto the shallow hole. It was a corpse, remarkably well-preserved in the concrete, the stench of putrefying flesh not as bad as he would have expected. A further half hour later, three of the Mossad agents removed the corpse from the opened concrete tomb, wrapped it in a sheet and carried it up the stairs to an oversized kitchen on the ground floor. There, they dumped it into a large chest-deep freezer they had switched on as soon as it became evident what was concealed by the fresh concrete. By then Immelmann had already sent a whole series of photographs of the corpse to Israel. The Israelis didn't take long to establish the identity of the deceased, their databases full of pictures and details of those they considered to be enemies of the state, both verified and potential.

Immelmann, noting the number as his secure phone rang, answered immediately. "That was quick. What've you got?"

"You solved one small mystery, Moshe." It was Sharon. "Your dead man is none other than Dr Amir Asadi."

"Asadi?"

"Iranian nuclear scientist. He vanished about two years ago. Had him on our list of potential elements to remove. Suppose we don't have to worry about him any longer."

"I remember," replied Immelmann. "He specialised in nuclear weapon design, didn't he?"

"That's the one." Sharon was silent for a brief moment. "He obviously went to Germany to work and was eliminated when he'd finished the job."

"And the nuke, which we have to assume is now operational, is gone... Shit, Abel," breathed Immelmann, a cold shiver running down his spine, "the bastards really are going to do this?"

"Right now I'd have to say yes. Find out as much as you can, question whoever you need to. I'm off to brief the Prime Minister; it's crucial that he knows what's happening. This is no longer just a threat, it's very real." He hung up.

Immelmann turned to Grey and Cohen.

"Our corpse has been positively identified. Dr Amir Asadi, Iranian nuclear scientist and weapons designer. From what I've just been told he was probably here for a period of around two years. Kind of explains the renovated basement and the goods hoist; they must've assembled the bomb here. They certainly wouldn't have carried the complete device up the stairs, so they put in the hoist. We're three days too late, gents. Where the hell did they take the device? Somebody must've seen something."

"Maybe we should talk to the neighbours."

"Hah?"

"The neighbours," said Grey. "Can't really think about anyone else."

"Yeah, right. Neighbours. Come on, Grey. Look at this place. There aren't any neighbours, are there?" muttered Cohen.

"Yes there are."

"And where would they be?"

"There." Grey walked across to the window and pointed. "The front of this place faces a whole number of houses on the other side of the valley. We need to talk to the people who live there. Maybe one of them noticed something unusual or saw someone. Look, I know those houses out there are a long way away, and chances are we'll draw a fat blank, but it's the best I can come up with. Unless anyone's got a better plan, 'cause I haven't."

There was no other option, and an hour later, Grey, accompanied by a Mossad agent who spoke fluent German, knocked on the door of the first house on the other side of the valley, the villa clearly visible some 400 metres away. Claiming to be with the *Bundesamt für Verfassungsschutz* – the Mossad agent had the appropriate identification – he asked the owner of the house if he had noted anything suspicious going on at the villa. No, he hadn't seen anything. They got the same response at the second house, the third, the fourth, and so it went. Immelmann, Cohen and the other agents, using the same *modus operandi,* were not having any luck either. By the time Grey and his colleague rang the door-bell of the 29th house, a neat double-storey building, they had come to the conclusion that they were conducting an exercise in futility. They waited for a minute for someone to answer the door-bell and were about to walk away when a middle-aged woman opened the door, wiping her hands on an apron tied around her waist.

"Ja? Kann ich Ihnen helfen?" she asked in German.

The Mossad agent introduced himself and Grey, explained in German what they wanted and then translated it into English for Grey's benefit.

"It is fine," interrupted the woman, switching to heavily accentuated English. "I speak English well. Would you like to come in? I may be able to help you."

Grey looked at the agent accompanying him and then at the woman. "Thank you, Ma'am. We would appreciate it."

They walked into the house and the woman took them through to the lounge. As the two men sat down she went back to the stairway in the small foyer and called out.

"Fabian! Come down please! We have visitors!" A short while later a young boy, Grey estimated him to be around 11 years old, appeared in the lounge. Grey noticed immediately that there was something wrong with the boy. The expression on his face was blank, the pallid skin on his slight, bony frame a tell-tale sign he had last been in the sun ages ago. He was drooling slightly, standing in front of the two men and his mother, staring vacantly.

"Fabian!" She spoke in German. "Say *Hallo*."

He looked at her as though he didn't understand what she had said.

"Say *Hallo*, Fabian!" she said, this time more forcefully. This time the boy seemed to understand.

"*Hallo.*"

"Hello Fabian. How are you?" asked Grey gently.

"Unfortunately he won't answer; he does not speak English at all and only a little bit of German. Nor can he speak properly. He only knows a few words, *Hallo* is one of them." Fabian's mother smiled wryly, a fleeting hint of bitterness in her eyes. Fabian simply stood there, glued to the spot, not saying anything else. "My apologies," she explained, "You asked if I had noticed anything going on at the villa. The answer is no, I did not. But," she pointed at her son, "he definitely will have."

"Ma'am, I really don't want to be rude or ungrateful, but what will he be able to tell us? You just mentioned he cannot really talk."

"I need to explain. Fabian has been handicapped since birth. He is what you call an autistic *savant*. He does not go to school and I stay at home to care for him."

"I'm sorry," replied Grey, puzzled, "it must be very difficult for you. Please, carry on."

"Yes, it can be very difficult. But there is also a bright side. You see, Fabian has this incredible gift. He cannot look after himself, cannot talk, cannot read or write and cannot even do basic sums. But... he can draw. He draws everything he sees."

"Oh?"

"I call it a gift from God. At least I like to see it that way, it does help me find some acceptance for my son's handicap." She paused. "You see, Fabian," she smiled at her son, "spends his entire day sitting at the window in his bedroom, drawing and painting the same picture over and over again, yet no picture is ever the same as the other."

"Interesting. But what does it have to do with our question?"

"The window of his room faces the villa."

"Oh? Are you telling me he, ah... monitors the villa?"

"Yes, except he does not know it. And he draws whatever he sees."

"Is there any way we could have a look at his drawings? Do you have any? Especially recent ones?" asked Grey.

"Oh yes!" exclaimed Mrs Gruber. "Because they are so good, it has become a habit for me to take his drawings - and Fabian creates at least six every day - date them and then file them. By now I must have thousands. Perhaps it will be of assistance?"

"Ma'am, you have no idea how much this may help."

"Then I think we should go and have a look." Mrs Gruber got up and beckoned Grey, Cohen and her son to follow.

Fabian's room was unlike any boy's room Grey had ever seen. Yes, there was the obligatory bed, small desk and chair. But there it stopped. On the far side of the room, next to the window, stood an artist's easel and a technical drawing-board, not the norm for a young boy's room. A large, sophisticated telescope stood just beyond the window, the aperture facing outward, focusing on what lay in the distance. Yet it was the walls that made the room so unique. They were covered in drawings, all of the same scene, but with slight variations. They were pictures of the villa, identical in all aspects to the view from the window, each different only in the sense that they took into account the weather, as well as whatever was different at the villa at the precise time the work was created. Some were watercolours, some oil paintings and others could best be described as technical drawings. There was one common trait throughout - they were exquisite to the point that a photograph could not have captured more detail.

"Wow! And these are all your son's drawings?" Grey was astounded. Fabian, who was standing next to him, beamed at his own work.

"Yes, he painted or drew them all. Beautiful, aren't they?"

"Beautiful? They're amazing! And you say he draws at least six of these every day?"

"Yes, sometimes as many as ten."

"And you keep them on file?"

"Yes, I do. I think one day they may be valuable."

"Not one day, Mrs Gruber. For us they have more value now than you can imagine. Could we have a look at what he drew over the past two weeks?"

An hour later - Moshe Immelmann and the others had arrived as well - they left the home of Mrs Gruber, each man carrying 5 Lever-arch files, 40 in total, containing 2000 drawings. They would be returned within a week. When Mrs Gruber eventually queried what it was all about, Moshe Immelmann explained to the woman that the *BfV* were conducting a joint operation with the British Security Service, the details of which he could not divulge. Hence the English, and yes, it was a matter of state security. Mrs Gruber was intrigued and flattered. Helping the State in an investigation was the most exciting thing that had ever happened to her. A pity that Immelmann had told her she was not allowed to talk about it to anyone – she would have loved to tell her neighbour, Mrs Gehlen. Although she did not know it yet, she would never have to worry about the welfare of her son again. She and her son would be looked after forever, courtesy of the Israeli government.

For the next eight hours Immelmann, Grey and Cohen went though the files of pictures. By the end of the exercise they knew the members of the Meinhof Kollaboration had indeed been residents of the villa for the past two years. Analyses of the pictures drawn over the past six days also revealed how the weapon must have left the villa, yet this created more of a headache than anything else. Within the space of twenty-four hours, five days previously, vehicles from three different transport organisations had arrived at the villa, all depicted beautifully in Fabian Gruber's drawings. All had, Grey and Immelmann estimated, load capacities of between five and eight tons. One vehicle was from a company called Fiege, one was from GKN Freight Services and the other from a company called Kaufmann Spedition. One of them must have carried the nuclear device. But which one?

Tel Aviv, Israel

Back in Israel, Abel Sharon's meeting with the Israeli Prime Minister had been a tense affair. He had listened for exactly two minutes to what Sharon had to say when he stopped him in mid-sentence, pressed the button of the intercom on his desk connecting him to his PA and told her to come through. A few seconds later the door opened and she walked in, note pad and pencil in hand.

"Yes, Prime Minister?

"Get hold of General Scholl and Samuel Goldberg. I want them here. Now. And arrange some coffee for four people. That'll be all." She left the room and Ezra continued speaking to Sharon. "It's time to get Scholl and Goldberg involved. This whole thing's getting a bit too hot."

Roni Ezra's PA had barely bought in the tray with the requested coffee when the door opened and General Chaim Scholl, IDF Chief of Staff, entered the Prime Minister's office, Samuel Goldberg, Head of the Ministry of Public Security, hot on his heels.

"Thanks for getting here so quickly." Prime Minister Roni Ezra motioned the men to take a seat. "You want to listen to this. Abel, go ahead."

Abel Sharon stood up and spoke for a full ten minutes, not interrupted once by the three men in the office. When he had finished he sat down, the air-conditioner in the office humming quietly. General Scholl, who had started tapping the end of a pencil on the table five minutes into Sharon's briefing, broke the silence.

"I need to get my head around this. Somewhere around two years ago, two South Africans sold an unassembled rogue nuke to the Meinhof Kollaboration. One of them died shortly afterward of natural causes, and the other's been picked up and brought to Israel a couple of days ago. Only thing missing on the nuke was the triggering mechanism. The money to buy the nuke came from some crowd in America, identity unknown. Then this Iranian scientist Asadi arrives on the scene, assembles the nuke, builds the triggering mechanism - all of it in some villa in a small town in southern Germany - and then gets taken out. Our men get to the villa three days too late; the occupants and the bomb have vanished. The bomb's in all likelihood on the way here. The Mossad got involved only a few days ago when the initial alert of what was happening came in from a Michael Grey, who was subsequently roped in to help." He glared at Sharon, fuming. "I don't believe this! Never mind that we seem to be faced with a real cock-up here, I'd like to know who the hell this Michael Grey is and how come he knows so much and we knew nothing?"

"I'll start with Grey. Ever heard of Grey & McLaughlin plc?... No?" Goldberg and Scholl shook their heads. "The mess at the end of last year that nearly took out Europe? They fixed it."

"You're taking the piss!"

"No, I'm not. We all think it was the Yanks who once again saved the planet. At least that's what it looks like on the surface, what the public knows. Well, it wasn't the Yanks, it was Michael Grey, working on behalf of the Americans. Truth is Grey's an ex-South African Special Forces operator, was a Captain in 1 Reconnaissance Battalion of the old SADF in the late 1980s." He stopped for a moment, waiting for what he had said to sink in. Noting the scepticism, he addressed General Scholl directly. "Chaim, you remember the Kobus Botha incident that was all over the South African press around that time?"

"I do, even made the news here. Apparently this Botha survived for a couple of weeks in the Angolan bush after a botched mission. From what I recall, they eliminated their objective, but only he made it back. You telling me Botha and Grey are one and the same person?"

"I am. Right now he's working with us. If he hadn't found out about this, we'd never have known. The only reason Grey knows is because this Labuschagne character knew him from years back. When Labuschagne found out he had advanced stage four cancer and was living on borrowed time, he decided to come clean. He knew about Grey and had no one else to confess to who'd be able to do anything about it, so he contacted him. Back to Grey. What he and his partner, Billy McLaughlin, have achieved, together with a few of our men, in just over four days borders on the impossible."

"McLaughlin?" asked Goldberg.

"Billy Mclaughlin. The man's an absolute genius when it comes to ELINT gathering."

"Whatever... so we have Michael Grey and Billy McLaughlin. My question is why the hell no one bothered to tell us about this pending fiasco earlier?"

"You know the drill, Samuel. Verify the data, determine the threat validity and then talk." He noted the sarcastic look on Goldberg's face and pressed on. "Tell me, how many threats of this type do we get every year?"

"How the hell should I know? One? Two?"

"Last year alone we had 12. Reason you don't hear about them is because the minute we stick our noses into the threats, and we do it each time it happens, they turn out to be hoaxes. The reason you're hearing about this one is because we believe it's the real deal."

"But surely we should've known about this sooner?" Goldberg was clearly exasperated.

"No, there was no way! Within hours of Grey finding out, he'd told us. In my book it speaks volumes for the man. From there on it happened too quickly. Right now it seems obvious there's a nuke on the way here and we don't know how it's going to be delivered. Nor do we have any idea of the actual target."

"What about the Iranians?" ventured Scholl.

"What about them? What the hell have they got to do with it?" shouted Goldberg.

"Jesus, Samuel! Get a bloody grip on yourself!" Roni Ezra was starting to get a touch annoyed. "Has it ever occurred to you who we'd normally blame immediately if a nuke went off over our territory?"

"Obviously the Iranians," muttered Goldberg.

"Damn right we would! Now you tell me, if this thing does blow up in one of our cities, how the hell we'd convince our population it wasn't the Iranians? Sure, 40 percent might just believe us and that's the upside! The remainder, by far the larger part, wouldn't; regardless of what we said. They'd think it was Iran. What do you think they'd expect us to do?"

"Retaliate?"

"Right. Retaliate. And if we don't, we'd have a full-blown civil war on our hands in next to no time. So, do YOU want to give the order to start nuking a country we know has nothing to do with this mess? Because I certainly won't."

"No," said Goldberg, barely audibly. He realised he hadn't thought it through, something you didn't do when Roni Ezra was around. "I apologise. It's just that... you see... this fucking thing could mean the end of us as a nation!" he blurted out.

"Don't I know it? We've got to find this thing before it's too late. Then, somehow or other, we've got to let the Iranians know what's happening. Sure, they hate us with a passion; probably more than we hate them. But someone meddling in our mutual differences and sparking off an unintentional, uncalled for nuclear exchange in the process just won't do. Nor will it do for the Iranians, especially when it wasn't them, yet they still end up getting the blame. And how the hell would we explain to the rest of the world why we nuked Iran in a retaliatory strike when we knew full well it wasn't the Iranians who did it? Especially now that they've supposedly been co-operating with the IAEA and scaled back their enrichment programme to where we want it to be?"

"Makes sense," retorted General Scholl. "I agree with Roni. We need to send someone to talk to the Iranians, warn them of what's happening. But who do we send?"

The last comment had them stymied. For the better part of a minute no one said anything, each looking at the other for an answer that wasn't forthcoming. Until Sharon opened his mouth. "What about Michael Grey?"

CHAPTER 6
POINT OF NO RETURN

Schopfheim, Germany

Michael Grey, Moshe Immelmann and Aaron Cohen were sitting in the drawing-room on the first floor of the villa in Schopfheim. There was no point in being anywhere else, not until they knew where the three transport vehicles were going. The other Mossad agents had taken over the top floor of the villa, there was nothing left for them to do apart from wait for further instructions.

The information on the three transport vehicles had been with Billy McLaughlin for the last four hours. Working as fast as was humanly possible, he had managed to establish where the loads from the villa were destined and what the cargo consisted of. He called Grey, told him he would be sending an email with the data as it was too detailed to relay over the phone, and advised he'd be waiting for further instructions. Minutes later the email arrived on Grey's laptop. It didn't make for good reading.

Fiege had transported a crate to the Port of Rosas in Spain. GKN Freight Services had delivered a crate to Cologne / Bonn airport, destination Cairo in Egypt. Kaufmann Spedition had delivered a crate at Frankfurt airport, destination Athens in Greece. The delivery addresses were known in each case. From one of those addresses the bomb would move to Israel. But which one? What threw the spanner into the proverbial works was the description of the cargo. Each of the three crates was identical in dimension, as was the gross weight of each crate - precisely 324 kilograms. Each contained machine tools, or so the cargo manifests stated. Had the weights been different from one another it would still have been remotely possible to deduce which crate contained the device. Not in this case. Immelmann, Cohen and Grey were busy planning who would go to which of the three destinations and how the teams would be made up, when Immelmann's secure phone rang for the fourth time that day. He listened for a while, said nothing and eventually put the phone down.

"Mike."

"Yeah. What's up?"

"Ever been to Iran?"

"No. Why?"

"Let it never be said that when you work with the Mossad you don't get to see new places. You're going to Tehran. The Global Express's waiting for you in Basel, ready to depart the minute you arrive. You're off to warn the Ayatollahs. Changes our plans slightly. When you're done there, you head for Cairo, I'll do

Athens instead. Aaron, you go to Spain."

"Hold it for a second. You want me to go to Iran?"

"Yes, you. It's all been arranged; they're expecting you."

"You're kidding, right?"

"No, I'm not."

"Shit. I thought you weren't on speaking terms?"

"Officially we aren't. We do, however, have a few channels we can use when we really need to. This is one of those occasions. You'll be collected at Imam Khomeini International Airport by the Iranians. Shouldn't take more than a couple of hours and you'll be out of there again. Let's see," Immelmann checked his watch, "it's 10:00 now, you leave in two hours. Give it around five hours' flight time, with a further two-and-a-half hours' time difference and you'll be there before 20:00. Just in time for supper."

"Okay, so I go to Tehran. What do I tell them?"

"Everything, Mike. The whole lot."

"What if they offer to help us?"

"Use your discretion. Who knows, this may just open a door for future dialogue we haven't yet been able to unlock."

As the Bombardier Global Express carrying Grey took off from Basel, Aaron Cohen, accompanied by two Mossad agents, set off for the Port of Rosas in Spain whilst Moshe Immelmann caught the next possible flight to Athens, where he would hook up with his Athens based colleagues. Which left the small matter of the frozen corpse of Dr Amir Asadi. As soon as darkness set in, it was removed from the villa and placed into a small cold-produce delivery-van. Late that night, a small row-boat slipped quietly from its mooring at the Schluchsee, a large dam in the Black Forest. At the deepest point of the dam, Asadi's body, suitably weighted down, was lowered over the side of the boat and sank 60 metres to the bottom to its final resting place.

Tehran, Iran

Grey looked out of the window of the Global Express at the lights of Tehran in the distance to his left. He had slept for most of the flight, only waking up as the sleek business jet began the descent for Tehran's Imam Khomeini International Airport. The aircraft touched down and taxied to the far end of the apron, some distance away from the main terminal buildings. Only taken into operation in 2004 and located some 30 kilometres away from the city, virtually all international flights landed there instead of at the more central, yet much older, Mehrabad International Airport. The door of the aircraft opened and Grey stepped onto Iranian soil. Waiting for him was a black Mercedes limousine, two gentlemen in dark suits standing next to the parked vehicle. As soon as Grey stepped onto the tarmac one of the men came towards him.

"Mr Grey, please follow me. We will be taking you into Tehran." The man's English was good, the accent decidedly British. *Probably spent time in the UK*, mused Grey, as he got into the back seat of the Mercedes. The man who had addressed him climbed into the front passenger seat, his colleague into the driver's seat and they left the airport. They had hardly left the airport exit when three police motorcycles pulled out in front of them, leading the way, sirens blaring. The small convoy swung left onto Freeway 7, also known as the Tehran Qom Freeway or Persian Gulf Highway, heading directly to Tehran. Grey, with the little he knew about Tehran, lost his bearings entirely when they headed right at the imposing Azadi square, the centrepiece of which was the Azadi Tower, and then, after a few kilometres, left, and into a labyrinth of side streets. They eventually came to a halt outside a modestly appointed residential property. The man who had spoken to Grey at the airport and who, when Grey had tried to strike up a conversation during the trip, had curtly advised Grey he was not permitted to speak to him, got out, opened Grey's door and directed him to the entrance door of the building. There the man knocked twice, the ornate door opened and something was spoken in Persian. Grey entered the house and the wooden door closed behind him. The man who had opened the door gestured to Grey to follow him up a short flight of stairs and into a large, open lounge area. Standing on the far side of the room was a robed cleric. The man again said something in Persian, bowed deeply and left the room. The robed cleric turned.

"Welcome to Iran, Mr Grey." The tone of voice was neither friendly nor hostile. He was wearing a long black robe, the black turban or *keffiyeh* wrapped around his head, his white beard neatly trimmed. It was the elderly cleric's eyes that sent an involuntary shiver down Grey's spine; two dark brown pools, the pitch-black beads of the irises piercing into his very soul. "Please, sit." He pointed at a seat and sat down himself. "Before you tell me why you are here, let me tell you who I am." He adjusted his robes, leaned forward and poured two small cups of tea, pushing one cup across the low, flat table towards Grey. "I am an Ayatollah, a member of the Guardian Council. My name is of no importance to you. The mere fact that I am here, and not a junior functionary, should indicate the curiosity the request from the Zionists for an urgent meeting has sparked off. To say it is most unusual would be an understatement."

"Your Eminence," Grey addressed the Ayatollah in the customary manner, "firstly, I need to thank you for making yourself available to meet me. As you have rightly put it, the request for this meeting is highly unusual, yet crucial under the circumstances. I am also aware that time is a scarce commodity for a man in your position, hence I will get straight to the point. However, let me make it clear from the outset; I am neither a Jew nor an Israeli citizen. I am a South African who holds a British passport. I am currently working with the Israeli Mossad to avert a possible crisis we believe has the potential to tear the Middle East apart."

"Working with the Mossad?" The Ayatollah stoked his beard, his face expressionless. "You are a very brave man coming here and professing to work with the Zionist intelligence apparatus, Mr Grey." Grey noted that the Ayatollah did not mention Israel by name. "You will no doubt be aware of the relationship between my country and the Zionists. Mutual hatred would perhaps best describe it. It would give us the greatest of pleasure were the illegal occupants of Palestine to disappear from the Middle East forever. They, in turn, would like nothing better than to see us reduced to a toothless, feeble and inconsequential state. Not exactly the basis on which to build a cordial relationship, is it? So, Mr Grey, what is it that the Zionists wish to tell us?"

"Your Eminence. Let me reiterate. I am currently working *with* the Mossad. I do not work *for* the Mossad. I am not concerned with whatever differences there may be between Iran and Israel. The reason for me coming here is to brief you on a situation we are faced with that could have dire consequences for the Middle East as a whole." Grey stopped, waiting for a reaction from the Ayatollah.

The Ayatollah remained impassive. "Please, do continue. You have my attention, Mr Grey."

"Unless we are badly mistaken, and I don't think we are, a rogue nuclear device will shortly be detonated somewhere in Israel. Your Eminence, I don't think I need to tell you what the implications would be." Grey sat back, wondering how the Ayatollah would react.

The Ayatollah, even if he was alarmed, showed no sign of it. "Can you prove what you just said?"

"Amir Asadi. Dr Amir Asadi. Does the name mean anything to you?"

"Should it?"

"I was hoping it would. An Iranian. If you do not know the man, it would be in your interests to find out immediately."

The Ayatollah, accustomed to dealing with men who feared him, was not entirely sure what to make of the man sitting opposite him. Not a Jew, yet, by his own admission, working with – not for – the Mossad, and telling him a nuclear device was to be detonated over Zionist-occupied territory. The ramifications, if what Grey had said was true, were only too clear to the Ayatollah. He took a cell phone from his robe and dialled a number, his beady, serpent eyes on Grey as he spoke. A minute later he ended the call.

"Amir Asadi. A nuclear weapons designer and physicist. Disappeared from Iran two years ago. We assume he was captured and killed by the Zionists. He wouldn't be the first. What do you know of Asadi?"

Grey pulled a photograph from his jacket pocket and handed it to the Ayatollah.

"He's dead, Your Eminence." The Ayatollah stared at the photograph of the corpse in the deep freezer. Grey continued, "It's Asadi; the Mossad confirmed it within minutes of seeing the picture. He was murdered about four or five days ago in a small town in southern Germany, and it wasn't the Mossad who did it. We found his body. Over the past two years he built and modified the nuclear device."

"Explain." The Ayatollah sat back and folded his arms.

It took Grey 15 minutes. When he had finished, the Ayatollah stood up, slowly walking across to a window looking out over the street below. "You are quiet correct in your assumptions, Mr Grey. If the device explodes and the international press is fed with sufficient false information, all pointing a finger at - and blaming - Iran, the Zionists will have no choice but to strike at us, even if it was not us who did it. If the current Zionist leaders do not order the strike, they will be removed. Whoever then takes over, and it will more than likely be the military, will launch a reprisal attack against us; popular sentiment will demand it." He pointed out of the window. "Before we know it half of Tehran will disappear in one horrific flash of light." He remained silent for a few seconds. "Would we retaliate in turn? We would, there would be no choice. And, as much as international opinion may differ on the subject... we do have the means to do so. What will happen from there onward becomes very hard to predict, at best, millions will perish." He turned, walked back to his chair and sat down again. "Yes, we would dearly like to rid the Middle East of the Zionists, but not at the expense of our nation. Nor can it ever happen that the world, including our Islamic allies, blames us for unleashing nuclear disaster on the region. A very dangerous and clever plot to say the least. It must be stopped."

"Yes, Your Eminence, it must be stopped at all costs. You will understand how hard a decision it was for the authorities in Israel to send me here to warn you."

"It must have been," mused the Ayatollah. "Yet, considering the circumstances, a very wise decision. Whatever the eventual outcome of the existing antagonism between us, it should not be influenced by the action of an external force, especially a force prepared to use a nuclear device to further whatever aims it may have." The Ayatollah got up. "If you would excuse me, I need to consult my colleagues."

The Ayatollah turned and left the room, leaving Grey alone. Half an hour later he was back.

"Well, Mr Grey, unusual circumstances call for unusual decisions. We have a proposal to make. Until this matter has been resolved, we will put whatever resources we have available to us at your direct personal disposal to prevent this pending disaster. You will appreciate that this does not mean at the disposal of the Mossad. I trust you understand the reasoning?"

"Perfectly, your Eminence," said Grey. "Revealing your foreign networks is something you will want to avoid at all costs, and, if so, then certainly not to the Mossad. Even the Israelis understand that. I will ensure there is no compromise on this; your sources will only be utilised as a last resort, and only if there is no other option."

"I appreciate your professional approach, Mr Grey. It would also be of great importance to me to be kept in the loop on developments. I assume this will be in order?"

"Yes, it will."

"Very good. Here," he handed Grey a slip of paper, "is my personal telephone number. You mentioned you were on the way to Cairo?"

"Yes, I am due to fly there tonight still."

"Then please save this number on your telephone." He gave Grey a second number. "It is the contact number of our key man in Egypt. He controls our entire network in the region. If need be, call him; he has already been instructed to help you in whatever way he can. If you do expose him to the Zionists, he would never be able to work in the Middle East again. But, if there is no other choice, and it helps to prevent a nuclear exchange, then a compromised agent is a very small price to pay."

"Your Eminence. In the event that I do call for your assistance, I will never – ever - reveal the source. I am a military man, a professional in my field. I subscribe to a certain code of ethics. I trust you understand what I am saying?"

"I do, Mr Grey. I was hoping for, and expecting, a response of this nature."

There was nothing more to say. Grey thanked the Ayatollah and headed for the door and the waiting Mercedes. He was about to walk out when the Ayatollah stopped him.

"One last thing. You mentioned you had two of your men in the USA attempting to find out who is behind the purchase of the device."

"I did. Why?"

"I suggest they look closely into the affairs of a certain Brent Delgardo, CEO of a company called Delgardo Technologies Inc."

"Do you think Delgardo may be involved?"

"It's a possibility, Mr Grey. A substantial amount of our uranium enrichment hardware was indirectly acquired though Delgardo Technologies or associated companies. Perhaps Delgardo *wanted* us to build a nuclear device?"

"As it stands right now I would not be entirely surprised, Your Eminence. I will most certainly follow it up. Oh, there is something I did forget to ask you."

"Yes?"

"When I arrived I was not searched for any concealed weapons or possible explosives. Why?"

The Ayatollah smiled. "Because, Mr Grey, I am an excellent judge of character."

Grey left the building and walked across the dark street to the waiting Mercedes. A little over one and a half hours later the Global express took off. The wheels of the aircraft had barely retracted when Grey had Billy McLaughlin on the line. McLaughlin, who had been working non-stop for the past 36 hours, had just shut down his systems and was about to leave his IT empire in South Wimbledon to head home for some well-deserved sleep.

"Mike! Where the hell are you? I thought you were in Iran."

"I was. Finished my meeting with an Ayatollah and went straight back to the airport. We've just taken off. Listen, you need to find out whatever you can about a company called Delgardo Technologies Inc., run by a Brent Delgardo. Can't tell you exactly where it is, but it's somewhere in the USA."

"Give me a minute." McLaughlin had already started up the smallest of the three systems he used and begun typing. "Got it. Delgardo Technologies Inc. Only one name comes up. Based in Spartanburg, South Carolina. Are they involved in this?"

"Possibly. The Ayatollah gave me the name. Listen, I need to hang up and get hold of Jaco van Rensburgh. He's got some work to do. I'll call you once I'm in Cairo."

Spartanburg, South Carolina, USA

Brent Delgardo pulled into the driveway of his home close to the Country Club of Spartanburg. Although not ostentatious, the house was decidedly upmarket, with garages for four cars. He parked his car of choice for the day, a late model Porsche Cayenne Hybrid, and made his way into the main house, kicking off his shoes on the way in. First stop was the answering-machine in the entrance hall. There was only one call, from the pro-shop at the Country Club, advising that his new set of Ping golf clubs was ready for collection. Five minutes later, after changing into his running gear, he left the house and headed for the forest close by. Running along a narrow track he used every day, he vanished into the trees and returned over an hour later, sweaty and spattered with mud. Whereas most executives he knew went to a gym once or twice a week, Delgardo got his kicks out of trail-running; the harder the trail the better. He loved the terrain, no single run the same as the preceding one. After a quick shower he dressed and headed out for the night, this time taking his favourite mode of transport, a 1966 Mk III AC Cobra.

The first stop was Renato's Italian Restaurant. After a leisurely meal of *carpaccio* and seafood *linguini*, washed down with a glass of the excellent house Chianti, he left the premises and made his way to his ultimate destination, a member's only club on the outskirts of the small town of Greer, halfway between Spartanburg and Greenville. It was one of the few places he knew of where privacy of the patrons was rule number one, not compromised under any circumstances. Within 15 minutes he was joined in one of the private suites of the club by four other men, each having arrived by private or chartered jet at Greenville Spartanburg International Airport. Brent Delgardo, 35 years of age, majority shareholder of a company that built components for a variety of Northrop Grumman military products, welcomed the others as they came in. Shortly afterward - he was, after all, the host, as this time the gathering took place in his home town - he called the meeting of The Patriots to order. There were five points on the agenda, the first two by far the most important. The oldest member of the group, 70-year-old Marty Trump, who ran a company renowned for the design and manufacture of, among other items, the guidance systems for a variety of missiles used by the US Air Force, got straight to the point.

"Well, Delgardo, has Morgan been eliminated?"

"Yes. It all went according to plan. Police reports will show conclusively that Morgan died as the result of an explosion caused by a defective seal on the gas stove in his apartment."

"And Schultz?"

"Similar. Although in his case we used an explosive device. At the same time we sent an anonymous tip-off to the FBI that Schultz was about to be taken out by some extremist group he had sold faulty weapons to. If you checked yesterday's papers you'll have seen the reports. No link to us whatsoever."

"Very good." Trump lit a cigar. "That covers point one. Now for point two. The Meinhof Kollaboration. Are they on track?"

"Slightly ahead of schedule." Brent Delgardo walked across the room and dimmed the lights. His laptop computer was connected, via a serial port cable, to a ceiling-mounted projector. On the far side of the room Delgardo had set up a large screen. Moments later the screen lit up, covered by a large map of Europe right through to the Middle East. A number of places on the map had been marked with red circles. Delgardo took a laser pointer and began his briefing.

"Right here," the laser pointer picked out Schopfheim in Germany, "is the town where the device was assembled and modified. The operation was shut down a few days ago after successful assembly of the device. The man recruited to assemble the device has been eliminated. We then sent three crates, identical in size and weight, to three different locations." He pointed out the Port of Rosas in Spain, Athens in Greece and Cairo in Egypt. "At this point only I and the three members of the Meinhof Kollaboration know which of the crates contains the real thing and which of them are bogus."

"Why?" asked Gerald Hopkins, a middle-aged man who had a controlling interest in three companies that designed and manufactured navigation instruments. "Don't you trust us?"

"Trust has nothing to do with it," retorted Delgardo. "Security has. We're not talking about some small-fry project where it doesn't matter if anyone finds out. We're talking about detonating a nuke. If we, as a group, decide the detail needs to made known to all present here, then so be it. I would caution against it. We all know someone is after us, certainly after the Morgan and Schultz incidents. As it stands, I believe we are safe. Which doesn't mean it will stay like that forever."

"I agree," said Blake Wellington. A year younger than Delgardo, the man speaking was the IT whiz of the group, the owner of a highly successful company in Silicon Valley specialising in the production of high-end computer chips for a large number of military hardware sub-contracting firms. "Should one of us get caught, we can't divulge what we don't know. I propose Delgardo keeps the executive detail to himself. By now it's gone so far it'll all be irrelevant in a few days anyway."

"Are we doing the right thing here?" Gary Simms, the last man in the group, owned a company involved in the supply of interior fittings for most naval vessels. The other four men turned as one. "Is there no other way of achieving our objective? Sure, our collective companies will all grow substantially, but does it really require a nuke? We can still stop now. Can't it be done some other way?"

"No." Delgardo could sense the fear in the man who had just spoken. "It's far too late to turn back now. We proceed as planned."

The other points on the agenda did not take long to discuss and the five men left the meeting venue to make their respective ways back to the airport; Delgardo the last to leave. As the Lincoln Continental carrying Gary Simms vanished at the end of the long driveway, Delgardo made a single telephone call. Twenty minutes later, the Lincoln, the driver sticking to the speed limit, was passed by a speeding articulated truck. The driver of the Lincoln, not suspecting anything untoward, continued driving, when suddenly the truck veered into him. He lost control and the vehicle careened off the road, flipped and collided head-on with a large elm tree. The driver and passenger did not stand a chance. By the time emergency rescue services arrived on the scene they could only ascertain the approximate time of death. With no witnesses, the accident would be one of many ascribed to the driver having fallen asleep behind the wheel, having swerved because of a deer crossing the road, or any of a host of other reasons related to driver error.

The leadership group of The Patriots had been reduced to four.

As the corpses were being removed from the accident scene and Delgardo arrived at his home, Jaco van Rensburgh and Gert van Tonder were on the way from Billy Graham International Airport, North Carolina to Spartanburg. Following them by road were the three Mossad agents in the surveillance panel van.

CHAPTER 7
TRANSFER TO TARGET

London, United Kingdom

Billy McLaughlin was attempting the impossible. Three crates had left the villa in Schopfheim, each crate with a different destination. One of the three crates would have to contain the nuclear device. And where the device went, so would, in all likelihood, the three highly elusive members of the Meinhof Kollaboration. Which meant two things – they could have flown to Athens or Cairo or possibly driven to Spain. Flying would mean it could have been from any one of a large number of airports scattered around Europe; those in Germany, France, Switzerland and Austria being the most likely. Driving could have been by rented, stolen or purchased motor vehicle. It was certain that three young people, two men and one woman, would make - or would already have made - their way to the location where the bomb was to be delivered. Or, possibly they hadn't even left yet. Even worse, Grey and his newfound friends were off on a wild goose chase, with the device having been spirited out of the villa by some other means? He needed to find a pattern or something unusual. But what? Billy McLaughlin was not the kind of person to give up on anything; far from it! Situations such as the one confronting him were what he considered mentally stimulating, challenges to be relished. It dawned on him somewhere between 00:00 and 03:00 - Maestro debit cards!

Everyone in Europe, from teenagers to old-age pensioners, use Maestro debit cards. While cash payments in most European countries, including Germany, are still commonplace, nobody operates without a Maestro debit card – nobody! The likelihood of that including the Meinhof Kollaboration, or whoever was linked to the Meinhof Kollaboration, was probably greater than 99.9 percent. Each Maestro card had a unique number and was linked to a unique account, and behind the number was a name and an address of sorts. And precisely there, figured Billy McLaughlin, might be the one mistake the Meinhof Kolaboration had inevitably made. He knew, which the German authorities didn't, that the Meinhof Kollaboration had been located in one spot for the better part of two years. Previously they had moved from one place to the next every two to three months.

In McLaughlin's mind it had the potential to be the one game-changer he, Michael Grey and the Mossad were looking for; something to put the good guys on the front foot and the bad guys on the back foot. He wasn't looking for a name any longer. No, he was looking for a number - the number of a Maestro card that had been used only in various retail outlets and shops in the town of Schopfheim, or the very close vicinity, for two years –

because a card must have been used, even to withdraw money from an ATM - and then suddenly appeared elsewhere. If there was such a card! And if - provided a card fitting the criteria could be found - it would become the identity. Names could change, passports could change, but not bank account numbers. Yes, he thought, that was it! Bank account numbers did not change, no matter who was using the card. There was also no way the Meinhof Kollaboration would operate without a bank account, and no matter which of the three members known to them - Keller, Biedermann or Stegemann - used the card, it would be the same number. So there it was. If there was a card to be found, with activity only in the target area for two years, which then suddenly became active elsewhere, he might just have them! Wide awake, Billy McLaughlin got to work.

It took him the better part of the next 24 hours to develop the software programme to infiltrate the databases of the German target banks he had in mind. The idea was simple; execution a different matter entirely. A custom-designed spyware programme would home in on the systems of every single bank he could find in Schopfheim, then cascade upward to the nationwide databases of these banks. The software would check on millions of transactions, looking for an identical number. The trigger was activity in any retail outlet in the small town in southern Germany, from there it would look for activity of the same card anywhere else. There were bound to be thousands of those, but not many would have been isolated to Schopfheim for two years, and then suddenly appear elsewhere. Depending on how many cards came up fitting the bill, he would narrow it down, and, with a bit of luck, have what he was looking for.

Twenty-three hours later, his spyware programme hit the databases of all the major German banks.

By then, Aaron Cohen, after driving for the better part of a day, had arrived in Port of Rosas in Spain; Moshe Immelmann had disembarked from a scheduled Lufthansa flight in Athens and Michael Grey had arrived in Cairo.

Port of Rosas, Spain

Aaron Cohen, after a marathon drive, arrived in Port of Rosas in the early hours of the morning. Not that the port could be described as a large commercial operation, if anything, the majority of vessels anchored there were multitudes of yachts and pleasure craft. The address to where the crate had been delivered was a small import-export agency not far from the harbour; the size of the warehouse behind the non-descript offices nothing to write home about. It was still early and there was no one about. By the time the offices of the small agency opened, Cohen and his two colleagues had been joined by a Spanish-based Mossad agent, who had been advised in advance as to what he was being tasked to do and had come prepared for all eventualities.

Cohen and the three Mossad agents walked through the doors, making their way across to the reception counter where the young lady who worked there was still busy getting herself ready for the day and the odd client who would possibly visit.

"Good morning," said the Spanish-speaking agent.

"Ah... good morning." The young lady, unaccustomed to the presence of four men so early, was somewhat flustered. "Can I help you?"

"Yes. We would like to speak to your manager."

"May I ask who is calling?"

"Certainly." The Mossad agent opened his wallet, briefly flashed an ID and closed the wallet again. "Mauro Ante. *Servicio de Vigilancia Aduanera.*"

Spanish Customs? *Oh crap*, thought the young lady. In record time the four men were seated in the office of the manager, Pedro Bastidas, who proceeded to make his guests as comfortable as possible; a visit by the Spanish Customs Surveillance Service an event he could quite happily do without. After a few minutes of small talk as they waited for coffee, inevitably about Spanish soccer and the recent poor form of the European soccer giant, FC Barcelona, with Bastidas doing his best to crawl up the collective asses of the men sitting across from him and the receptionist frantically running around organising the beverages, the Spanish-speaking Mossad agent got to the point.

"Mr Bastidas. These gentlemen with me are from HM Revenue and Customs in Britain. There is reason to believe you have a consignment in your warehouse sent from Germany that, of course you cannot know, originated from England. We suspect the consignment may contain narcotics and need to investigate the contents. I, as representative of the *Servicio de Vigilancia*

Aduanera, have been tasked by highest authorities to assist these gentlemen in their investigations."

"Why certainly!" The manager of the logistics company breathed an inward sigh of relief. "Can you give me more details of the cargo?"

"Yes." He took a copy of the cargo manifest from a briefcase. "We are looking for this consignment."

"Ah. Very good. This will help me check." The manager picked up the telephone on his desk, called the warehouse supervisor and gave him the consignment number. Less than a minute later he put the phone down. "I'm sorry, gentlemen. The cargo is no longer here. It was loaded onto a vessel called the *Estrella* yesterday. We believe the boat left port after midnight, about six hours ago."

"Destination?"

"She's headed for Israel."

By the time Bastida's heart rate had dropped back to acceptable levels, Cohen and the three other men were in the harbour, talking to the owner of an Outerlimits 42 Legacy powerboat, the *Calypso*. With more than sufficient range and a top speed in the realms of the ridiculous, certainly in excess of 200 kilometres per hour, they would be able to catch the much slower *Estrella*, a Seaton Expedition 70 yacht, within next to no time. Provided of course they could convince the owner of the boat to hire it to them. He did – at a price! Shortly after 09:00 the powerboat, tanks filled to the brim, left port, the pilot steering the vessel slowly out of the sheltered harbour. Sitting next to him was Aaron Cohen, his three colleagues on the back bench, all of them wearing windbreakers with the *Servicio de Vigilancia Aduanera* logo emblazoned on the back. All were strapped in and all were wearing helmets. In the bottom of the boat, in front of the men on the back seat, lay a duffle bag.

Cohen, who had by then – courtesy of Billy McLaughlin - established that the *Estrella* was owned by one Pedro Alonso, (long suspected of smuggling anything and everything around the Mediterranean, but never being caught with hard evidence), thought it was all a bit exaggerated. Until the boat hit the open waters outside the harbour. The pilot, who had been given the instruction to head in the general direction the *Estrella* had taken at the fastest safe speed possible, opened the throttles. Aaron Cohen, very much used to all sorts of things most people would consider abnormal, as were the three men in the back, very nearly shat himself. The boat surged forward at a rate most sedan motor vehicles would not be capable of. What was fast on tarmac seemed twice as fast on open water. On top of that, the surface, unlike tarmac, was anything but smooth. As the boat accelerated to beyond 120 kilometres per hour, Cohen began to appreciate why he was wearing a helmet and why some powerboat drivers, who competed in these vessels, ended up pissing blood after a long race due to kidney damage. Mind-blowing did not even begin to describe the sensation. It was something like combining a never-ending, extreme roller-coaster ride with downhill snow-skiing on a surface filled with potholes you couldn't avoid. The first ten minutes of the ride were exhilarating, the next ten minutes started becoming painful and, after that, it was sheer, back-breaking agony. The pilot, who didn't seem to have a care in the world, merely commenting on how ideal the conditions were, continued, unrelenting. Cohen, after half an hour, could quite happily have kicked the man in the teeth and strangled him.

After two hours of hard driving the pilot of the *Calypso* shouted across at Cohen, pointing at a radar screen on the dash in front of him. Up at the top right of the screen a small green blip was visible and the powerboat changed course slightly. Fifteen minutes later the blip, the *Estrella*, was visible in front of them, cruising along at a pedestrian eight knots. A further two minutes later the powerboat was alongside the *Estrella*, the Spanish-speaking Mossad agent shouting through a megaphone.

"Estrella! This is the Mauro Ante, *Servicio de Vigilancia Aduanera!* Stop your engines! We are coming alongside and will be boarding your vessel!"

Cohen was watching the pilothouse of the *Estrella*. There were two men on the bridge, talking to each other, arms gesticulating furiously. After what seemed like an eternity one of the men picked up the microphone of the built-in ship loud-hailer.

"Calypso! What do you want? We are in international waters!"

The Mossad agent with the megaphone glanced across at Cohen and grinned, "Leave it to me." Turning back to face the *Estrella* he continued barking through the megaphone, *"Estrella!* Either you stop now and let us board or we will force you! A

Spanish Meteoro Class naval patrol vessel is about half an hour away, coming from the east. If need be, they have orders to sink you! You choose!"

Again Cohen noted the animated discussion going on between the two men on the bridge. This time it didn't take long and the *Estrella* suddenly slowed. The *Calypso* pulled alongside and Cohen and two of the other Mossad agents boarded the *Estrella*, the third agent, who had removed a Heckler & Koch G36E assault rifle from the duffle bag, remaining in the *Calypso* to give cover if required. As Cohen and his men approached the pilothouse, the door opened and one of the men came out to meet them, decidedly unhappy about the unwelcome intruders.

"Spanish Customs, hah? Well how about some fucking ID then?"

Cohen's Spanish-speaking colleague came forward. "You're Pedro Alonso, right?"

"So? What's it got to do with you?"

"Everything, you asshole! We've had you on our radar for some time now and this time round you've fucked up. So," he pulled a 9mm Heckler & Koch USP handgun from his jacket, also standard Spanish Infantry issue and waved it in the man's face, "I suggest you shut up and show us where you stuck the crate you loaded in Port of Rosas."

Pedro Alonso heaved an inward sigh of relief. The crate was stashed away in what had been a dining-room and master bedroom, the interior walls removed to create a relatively large load space. Manhandling the crate into the lower deck had been a bitch of note, and had taken all of ten men. He was sure there was nothing untoward in the sealed crate, the consignment note merely stating it contained high-value machine tools bound for an Israeli engineering firm in Tel Aviv. Why he and his particular mode of transport had been chosen to send a shipment of machine tools to Israel had puzzled him, but he hadn't taken long to accept the consignment, the rate he was being paid was very favourable indeed. It also provided cover for the "real" money-making cargo he had on board on this particular trip – 5000 cartons of contraband cigarettes packed into a hollow space underneath the floor of the lower deck, destined for Cyprus, and two kilograms of cocaine, hidden in a space underneath one of the two John Deere diesel engines, destined for Antalya in Turkey. As long as it was the crate these customs boys were after, then so be it, he would be more than happy to help them.

"The crate?" Alonso was suddenly very co-operative. "Sure! Follow me."

The group of men made their way to the lower deck. "There it is." Alonso pointed at the wooden crate, the strapping intact. "Don't ask me why, but some geezers wanted this to go to Israel and asked us to ship it. Why they didn't use a plane beats me! I mean it's a pile of machine tools. But what do I care, I got paid for it. You wanna have a look inside?"

Ten minutes later the crate was open. "Machine tools?"

"Yeah, why?"

"Because this here's got squat to do with machine tools."

Pedro Alonso stepped forward and looked into the open crate. "What the fuck!" The crate, lined with thick LDPE plastic, was filled half-way to the top with loose building-sand. "What the hell's going on here?"

"You tell me," said the Spanish-speaking Mossad agent, who had started rummaging through the sand, hoping to find something buried. There was nothing. Cohen, who had brought along a hand-held HazMatID Ranger chemical identification device, checked out the contents. It proved one thing only – the contents of the crate were exactly what they appeared to be - sand!

"You're lucky, Alonso. Suppose we can't arrest you for shipping sand, can we? But maybe we should search the rest of your boat, eh?" He looked around, Alonso behind him very nearly shitting his pants. "But, not now." He patted Alonso on the cheek. "Must be your lucky day, *paisan.*"

They made their way back onto the *Calypso*, the *Estrella* and a mightily relieved Pedro Alonso steaming away from them. As the *Estrella* vanished in the distance, the pilot of the *Calypso* started up the engines of the powerboat, opened the throttle and set course for Port of Rosas, travelling a bit slower at Cohen's request. As the pilot tied up the vessel Cohen was already speaking to Michael Grey, who had by then arrived in Cairo.

"Hi Mike. What a complete *balagan.* The crate had already left Spain and was on route to Israel by boat. We chased it, got them to stop and opened the crate. Guess what? The bloody thing was filled with sand."

"Sand?!"

"Yeah, sand. So I guess it's one crate down and two to go. Heard anything from Moshe Immelmann?"

"No, nothing yet. I have to hand it to whoever organised this little lot, using sand to create identical weights. Clever bastard, *né?*"

"Too bloody clever! What do you want me to do now?"

"Can you get to Cairo?"

"Sure. When do you want me there?"

"As soon as you can. I think I might need help down here. I'm starting to have the funny feeling that Moshe's about to find a pile of sand as well."

"Which would leave the crate destined for Cairo. Shit! I'm on my way. I'll call you once I know what travel arrangements I can come up with."

Athens, Greece

Moshe Immelmann had travelled to Athens the day before, arriving at Athens International Airport Eleftherios Venizelos before darkness set in, where he was collected by the resident Mossad Head of Station. From there they made their way to the Holiday Inn Attica Avenue, ideally situated on the A6 Attiki Odos Motorway, avoiding the badly congested inner city of Athens.

Doing anything further at that time of day was not viable, and, after a quick supper washed down with a few drinks, Moshe Immelmann found himself asleep in his room just after 22:00.

The following morning they set off for the small town of Koropi, roughly four kilometres south-west of the airport, where a number of logistics companies had set up shop. Immelmann knew where the crate destined for Greece had ended up, and it didn't take too long to find the premises of the company he was looking for. Unlike the Port of Rosas, however, the Greek logistics company was far larger and more professional, and pulling a stunt like Cohen had in Spain would not have worked. There had to be another way, and, after some discussion and observation, Moshe Immelmann decided a somewhat more unorthodox approach would suit them best. His Greece-based counterpart had, in any event, kept an eye on the place for the past 48 hours and knew it shut down late at night and re-opened the following morning. With not much else left to do besides wait, Immelmann took the opportunity – it was his first visit to Greece – to have a look at the Acropolis and the ruins of the Parthenon, that monumental piece of ancient Greek architecture overlooking Athens.

At 01:00 the following morning the two men were back in Koropi and parked their car a short distance away from the logistics company. Only this time, arranged on the quiet by the Greece based Mossad, they were both wearing the black uniform of the Greek Special Counter-Terrorist Unit – the EKAM. Less than 200 metres away from their parked car was a small electrical sub-station. Immelmann and his partner made their way across to the fenced-in substation and cut a small hole in the fence. Immelmann watched his colleague push his way through the opening and to the transformer that formed the heart of the installation. Within minutes he was back and the two men made their way back to the parked car. As they drove away from the scene there was a muffled *"whump"*. The timed explosive Immelmann's side-kick had attached to the transformer had exploded. The transformer, filled with cooling oil, went up like a roman candle, burning oil crackling and cascading from the destroyed casing. At the same time the lights in half of Koropi went out.

Immelmann and his partner quietly drove off. By then two fire-engines, the police and a disgruntled maintenance technician from the Greek Public Power Corporation – the PPC – were already on the way to the scene of the destruction. They arrived a few minutes after the departure of the Mossad agents, very quickly coming to the conclusion that there had been a catastrophic failure of the transformer. There was no way the transformer could be repaired, it would have to be replaced, an exercise the man from the PPC did not look forward to. Power in the affected parts of Koropi would, at best, be restored within 36 hours; anything earlier would be a miracle.

As the police and the men from the PPC watched the firemen attempt to extinguish the blaze, Moshe Immelmann and his colleague arrived at the premises of the logistics company. The entire area was in total darkness. This time they made their way around the back of the warehouse, separated from the adjacent building by an open plot of land strewn with building rubble and weeds. Knowing there was nobody around at that time of night and that the alarm systems would, in all likelihood, be inoperative due to the power-cut, they scaled the fence surrounding the warehouse, made their way to a side door, picked the lock and entered the dark interior of the building. Should anyone have stopped them, they would have identified themselves as EKAM operators who had noted two suspicious characters moving around on the premises, and were checking what was going on. There had, after all, been the explosion of the sub-station - an incident that could well be construed as terrorist activity – precisely the kind of activity the genuine men of the EKAM dealt with. People didn't argue with men from the Special Counter-Terrorist Unit, it was not generally considered to be a good idea.

It took the two men a little over an hour to find the crate they were looking for amongst hundreds of other boxes, pallets and crates. They had opened the lid and Moshe Immelmann sucked in his breath. It was sand.

Realising that the entire exercise had been a waste of time, they made their way back to the Holiday Inn Attica Avenue. The first thing Moshe Immelmann did was to call Michael Grey in Cairo.

"Mike. Moshe here."

"What's up?"

"Nothing good, I'm afraid. The crate in Greece is bogus."

"Let me guess. It was filled with sand?"

"Yeah, it was. How the hell did you know?" The surprise in Immelmann's voice was evident.

"'Cause the one in Spain was also full of sand," muttered Grey. "Aaron called me late yesterday to let me know."

"Shit." Immelmann walked across to the bar fridge in his room and grabbed a bottle of Delphi Pilsner. "If Spain's a no-go and Greece as well, then it leaves you and Cairo." He opened the bottle and took a swig of the cold beverage. He would have preferred a couple of ouzos, but those weren't available so early in the morning.

"Suppose it does." Grey got up, pulled back the blinds in his hotel room and looked out at the sun popping up over the horizon. In the distance loomed the Pyramids of Gizah, barely visible through the haze of pollution so prevalent in the sprawling, chaotic megalopolis of some 16 million people. "Only thing is, my crate hasn't arrived yet. Billy managed to find out that it'll only be here later today, coming in on an Egypt Air flight out of Cologne / Bonn if everything's on schedule. I'm heading out to the airport in a few hours from now to check out where the cargo collection area is. Maybe I can pick up something as they unload, although I doubt it."

"Bit bloody brazen, isn't it?" said Immelmann. "Egypt Air flight? You'd have thought they'd use some obscure one-man-show type airline to cart a nuke around. No, they use Egypt fucking Air. So, what's your plan once it's there?"

"I'm working on it. Assuming the bomb's in the Cairo crate,

the one option is to pick it up and leave it at that. End of story. But, where does that leave us? Nowhere. What we need are the people behind this. If we don't get rid of them, then who's to say they won't try again?"

"I hear you. Don't know if I agree entirely, but you've got a point. Promise me one thing though, will you?"

"What's that?"

"Whatever you do, don't let them detonate the nuke!"

London, United Kingdom

Billy McLaughlin's idea to track the movements of Maestro debit cards was proving to be a nightmare of monstrous proportions. He could access the data, but there was so much of it, that it became a problem to sort it into any meaningful order. For the past ten hours he had been working on a programme to do it for him, which meant sorting transactions per card over a two year period, at least, for every bank he had tapped into, and then seeing whether or not a card used in only one place over a long period of time had suddenly been used at a different geographical location. He ran his pilot programme for the first time shortly after midday and found the first errors in his software. An hour later he tried again, ironed out another series of flaws, and then ran it for a third time in the early evening. This time it worked; the programme pulling up transaction data from a whole series of banks, looking for purchases made in Schopfheim over a two year period, and, if something was found, checking if it had been used elsewhere. With the programme running, he went for a bite to eat, slept for three hours and then went to check on what his programme had found so far.

He wasn't disappointed. Only two Maestro debit card numbers had registered usage in Schopfheim over the period McLaughlin had defined – just to make sure, he had set it up in such a way that the search start-point was two months after they knew for sure that the Meinhof Kollaboration had moved to Schopfheim, and ended two months before the device left the villa. Both cards were Maestro debit cards linked to the largest public banking group in Germany, the Sparkasse. One of the cards was linked to an account held at a Sparkasse branch in Hamburg, the other to an account held at a Sparkasse branch in Schopfheim itself. The likelihood of the Schopfheim card being the one he was looking for was remote, but he checked a bit deeper just to make sure. It belonged to a Mrs Trüter, a pensioner living in an old age home in the town. One call to the old age home sufficed. There was indeed a Mrs Trüter living there, who had moved in well over eight years earlier and was now over eighty-nine years old. One last check showed that the card had only ever been used in Schopfheim – Mrs Trüter clearly did not travel anywhere, certainly hadn't over the past six years, nor had she been anywhere over the past three months. Mrs Trüter, Billy McLaughlin surmised, could be excluded from any wrongdoing.

The second card was a different matter entirely. It was registered to one Annemarie Schubert, the physical address a flat in Hamburg, a post box number given as a postal address and a cellular phone number as a contact number. It took McLaughlin ten minutes to find out exactly where the flat was, and a further five minutes to establish that the flat in question was rented by a Turk called Omar Umut, an immigrant who had lived there for the past four years with his family. It also didn't take long to establish that the phone number was not actively used, the monthly bill paid by stop order from the Schubert account. *Who, Annemarie Schubert, are you?* mused McLaughlin. Later still, it was close to midnight, McLaughlin had found enough for the entire elaborate plot hatched by the Meinhof Kollaboration and whoever else was behind them, to start unravelling.

Cairo, Egypt

Michael Grey had barely left the hotel, the Cairo Heliopolis Radisson Blu, a stone's throw away from the airport, when his telephone rang for the second time that day. When Billy McLaughlin called it was usually important.

"Billy. What's up?"

"I think I've got them, Mike. Will take a bit of explaining. You got a few minutes?"

" The Meinhof Kollaboration? How?"

"Bank accounts; bog standard German debit cards no one operates without. I checked out the German banks on debit card transactions over the past two years. Christ, what a mission, but it worked. I managed to isolate two cards that had been active only in Schopfheim over the past two years. Figured if the Meinhof Kollaboration holed themselves up down there for the period and went nowhere else, which we assume happened, then there'd have to be traces of sales transactions linked to a debit card, they'd never have paid for everything in cash, and, even if they did, they'd have to have drawn the money from an ATM. No one I know of carries around cash to last for two years. To cut a long story short, two cards actually did pop up. One belongs to an old lady who lives in an old age home down there, and the other to guess who?"

"Fuck. I don't know. Jens Keller?"

"No. One Annemarie Schubert, account held at a Sparkasse branch in Hamburg."

"Annemarie Schubert? You've got to be shitting me!" Grey was flabbergasted. "You sure it's not Anne Biedermann?"

"No, not 100 percent sure, but the probability is very high we're talking about one and the same person here."

"Surely Biedermann wasn't stupid enough to use a first name so close to her own?"

"It's only stupid if you get the connection right. You know how many women are called Annemarie and how many Schuberts there are in Germany? Both names are common. It could be anyone. Here's the clincher. Around two years ago a sum of US $5 million was transferred into the account. Guess from where?"

"Not the elusive American account?"

"Precisely. Now we have a link to the Americans, an Annemarie Schubert, who is, in all likelihood, Anne Biedermann, and an account I can track movement on. It's all starting to tie up! It gets even more interesting. Over the past couple of days the account activity shifted. First activity in Frankfurt, then on to Magdeburg and now Berlin. Also, the card was active in Berlin at the same time Senator Golding was assassinated. It's them, Mike! It's the Meinhof Kollaboration! And now I can track the movements of the card user as close to real time as dammit!"

"Anyone ever told you you're a genius?"

"Once or twice. What do you want me to do now?"

"Keep an eye on that debit card. If the thing is used, I need to know immediately. Can you do that?"

"Sure, problem is there can be a bit of a time lapse between actual transaction and the data records reflecting in the Sparkasse data centre."

"I get you. Still, it's better than anything we've had so far. With Keller and his cronies on the move I suspect they'll make their way here over the next day or so."

"I wouldn't bet against it," replied McLaughlin. "Anything else?"

"I think you better inform Abel Sharon; he needs to know as soon as possible. I spoke to him earlier today. To say he's stressed would be putting it mildly. He needs to give his Prime Minister some positive feedback and this may just do the trick. One last thing. Get hold of Jaco van Rensburgh in the US. He needs to know as well."

"I'm on it. Good luck!" McLaughlin ended the call as Grey drove slowly past the main terminal of Cairo International Airport.

Finding the cargo section of the airport was not difficult, getting a close look at the aircraft being loaded and unloaded however downright impossible. Neither was there a vantage point high enough anywhere in the vicinity, certainly not one he could make use of without trespassing or creating unnecessary suspicion. The Egypt Air flight was scheduled to land after dark at 21:25. With nothing else left to do, and assuming the cargo would be collected by someone hitherto unknown at the Egypt air cargo terminal, probably the following day, he reluctantly made his way back to the hotel. He had hardly entered his room when his telephone rang for the third time. It was Aaron Cohen, advising him of his imminent arrival in Cairo. Grey, who had been somewhat frustrated by the lack of meaningful activity on his part, began to feel decidedly more comfortable. He had grown to like Aaron Cohen and the other Israelis he'd been working with, and having Cohen in Cairo made life so much easier. Deciding two hours of sleep would do him a world of good, he closed the curtains, lay down on top of the bed and closed his eyes.

Tel Aviv, Israel

As Grey fell asleep, Abel Sharon finished preparing his notes for the briefing session he had convened, attended by Prime Minister Roni Ezra, General Chaim Scholl and Samuel Goldberg. Ezra and Scholl he respected, but Goldberg? To Sharon, Goldberg was worse than a pimple on his ass – painful, irritating, uncomfortable, and of no use whatsoever. This time around, if he got too clever, he'd simply tell him to shut up until he knew what he was talking about. How the hell Goldberg had ended up being in charge of the Ministry of Public Security baffled Sharon; at best the man would have been suited to running the administrative department of an accounting firm. He packed his briefing files and made his way to the Prime Minister's office. Scholl and Goldberg were already waiting. Without the need for any pleasantries Sharon went straight into briefing mode.

"Afternoon, Prime Minister, gentlemen. Here," he handed each of the men a three-page typed document, "it sums up what I'm about to tell you." He continued as the men started reading. "I'll start with Grey. He's been to Iran and was met by an Ayatollah from the Guardian Council. He says the meeting went well, the Iranians hate us as much as we hate them, but they don't want someone meddling in our differences, certainly not when it involves a nuke. They realise the implications and what it would mean if the thing did go off over Israeli territory. This Ayatollah's gone as far as offering Grey the help of their intelligence apparatus. Grey has been given the direct contact number of the man who runs the Middle East region for the Iranians and has been advised to use him if needed."

"What?!!" General Scholl stopped reading and dropped the

document in front of him. "Are you telling me Grey's got access to the man who runs the Iranian agents in the area? Damn, it's unbelievable! He needs to tell us who it is! We'd be able to dismantle their entire network!"

"Sorry, Chaim, not gonna happen. One of the conditions the Ayatollah had was that Grey should only use him as a last resort. The Iranians know full well that, if the man is used, then he's also burnt. They'd have to move him back to Tehran. Grey was quiet blunt about it; if we demand he exposes who it is, he'll walk away. So, while it's a pity, it's an absolute no-go!"

"Abel's right, Chaim," said Ezra. "If Grey did tell us, and with the little I know of him he won't, and we did destroy the Iranian network, then the only door we have open with the Iranians will close forever. Doesn't matter what our differences are, we'll always need a conduit to get messages across when we have to."

"Damn! You realise it would've been the intelligence coup of the century?"

"What else is new?" demanded Goldberg, who had by then also finished reading, the tone of his voice decidedly antagonistic.

Sharon, noting the sarcasm, continued. "Three crates left Germany, all identical, to three different destinations, Spain, Greece and Egypt. Aaron Cohen and Moshe Immelmann handled Spain and Greece respectively. The contents of those crates are confirmed as bogus, all they contained was sand. The third crate is due in Cairo later today, so we assume the device is going to come in via Egypt. Grey's in Cairo. Aaron Cohen left Frankfurt this morning, in fact he'll probably have joined up with Grey already..."

"So why don't we just stop this thing right now? If the device is on the way and we know when it'll arrive, then why don't we intercept it and that's the end of it? Or don't *you* have the right resources in place?" demanded Goldberg, glaring at Sharon.

"Because, you fool," Sharon lost his temper, "if we do that we'll have the device and nothing else!" He banged his fist on the table, Prime Minister in the room or not. "At what fucking point do you think the people behind this will try it again, hah? At what point? If you're so fucking clever and you have the right resources, then why don't you just go and handle this shit yourself?"

"Calm down, Abel, will you?!" Prime Minister Ezra decided it was time to pull rank. "And you, Samuel, if you can't be constructive, I'll ask you to excuse yourself. Your comment about the right resources was way below the belt! Abel, carry on."

Sharon took a deep breath. "My apologies, Prime Minister. As I said, Grey's in Cairo and the device appears to be on the way. He thinks, and I agree, that the three MK terrorists are on the way as well, or will be there shortly. We know the device has to be collected, since there was no forwarding address. Cohen, Grey and our other men down there will monitor the Egypt Air Cargo Terminal around the clock. The minute someone arrives to collect they'll be onto them."

"And then?" queried Prime Minister Ezra.

"That's up to us to decide. Grey suggests we let them move

the device and follow. When the timing's right we apprehend the entire lot."

"Fine. I go along with Grey's plan. It'd better work. Anything else?"

"No, that's it. I suggest we reconvene tomorrow, at say, 09:00? Any objections?"

As the four men went their separate ways, Michael Grey, who had by then been joined by Aaron Cohen, received a call from Billy McLaughlin. He had just observed that the ominous Maestro card had been used. The purchase was for three airline tickets from Emirates. It hadn't taken McLaughlin long to get into the Emirates database. Whoever the Maestro card belonged to had just bought three tickets from Warsaw to Cairo, via Dubai. The Meinhof Kollaboration were on their way.

Spartanburg, USA

Jaco van Rensburgh, together with Gert van Tonder, and the three Mossad agents, arrived in Spartanburg within a day of each other. They checked into the low-cost College Inn, roughly five kilometres away from the residence of Brent Delgardo. By mid-afternoon the unmarked panel van was parked less than 200 metres away from Delgardo's home. Had they been in Spartanburg a day earlier, they would have been privy to what would prove a vital telephone conversation. But, they were late and they missed it.

Delgardo, who, with the blessings of the other leaders of The Patriots, had taken charge of the tactical execution of the project, arrived back home and put into motion the last phase of what The Patriots had termed Operation Grail. One call, and from then on, the success of Operation Grail was entirely out of the hands of The Patriots. Delgardo had known all along, as had the other members of The Patriot leadership, that the Meinhof Kollaboration were merely a vehicle. Yet they were a vehicle with the ability to turn into an unguided missile, if not controlled properly. So far, all had gone well, but there was no way the end phase of Operation Grail could be left entirely in the hands of those whom The Patriots considered to be useful, yet misguided fools. There was simply not enough trust in Keller, Biedermann and Stegemann. The decision had thus been taken some time back to ensure that the final phase of the project would go ahead as planned, irrespective of what the Meinhof Kollaboration did or did not do.

As a result, and unbeknown to Grey or the Mossad, a group of ten men had departed from three different locations on the planet, all en route to Cairo, 48 hours before the device was due for delivery in Egypt. Three of the men left Moscow, all ex-Soviet Spetznaz operators. Four others, all ex-members of the Bulgarian 68th Special Forces Brigade left Sophia. The last three, two ex-Navy SEALs and an ex-US Ranger, retired Colonel Max Preston, the man who would take overall charge of the mission, left the United States from Atlanta, Georgia. Professional and highly disciplined by virtue of years of training, they had left their respective armed forces and become guns for hire, men who didn't care who they worked for or what the cause was, as long as they got paid. None of the three members of the Meinhof Kollaboration knew about them, and unless something happened that wasn't deemed part of the script, they never would. Not until they reached their final destination, that is! It would, however, make Michael Grey's life a lot more difficult over the next 48 hours.

Neither had it escaped Brent Delgardo that he needed to look after himself. The events over the past days had proven conclusively that someone out there knew a little too much about what was happening. At some point during the morning he made the decision to vanish until Operation Grail had reached its logical conclusion. He made two telephone calls and by 17:00 the Porsche Cayenne with Delgardo behind the wheel was on the way out of Spartanburg, heading towards Asherville, then Johnson City, and on to his destination, a holiday home he owned at Watauga Lake, nestled in the Blue Ridge Mountains in North Carolina.

The home, small as it was, reflected Delgardo's lifestyle. Not far from the small town of Butler, it overlooked the lake; the shoreline less than 100 metres away from the main house. At the end of a small jetty was a private boathouse, the mooring place for what Delgardo considered to be one of his favourite toys, a customised Bayliner 335 Cruiser, far too big and ostentatious for a lake the size of Watauga. He walked through the front door just before 23:00 and went straight to bed.

What he did not know was that his two telephone calls earlier that day had been picked up by the Mossad agents in the unmarked panel van. Only this time, he had made the calls from a different cell phone, the one he used on a day-to-day basis. It made very little, if any, difference to van Rensburgh and van Tonder; they had come to find Delgardo and take a long and hard look into his affairs. Delgardo's decision to relocate to his holiday home was a bonus; it had changed the terrain in which van Rensburgh and van Tonder would have to operate, terrain far better suited to the unique skills of the two South Africans. As the lights went off in Delgardo's holiday home, van Rensburgh and van Tonder moved in. The likelihood of the place being kitted out with security measures such as beams was remote; there were simply too many raccoons, deer and other wild creatures roaming in the area for beams to be of any use, the alarm would have been set off far too often. By the time 03:00 the following morning arrived, van Rensburgh and van Tonder had scouted out the surrounding area and established that the location of the Delgardo home, secluded and private as it was, provided anyone with an ulterior motive for being there with more than enough cover.

At sunrise Delgardo left the dwelling and headed out for his morning run with no idea he was being watched from a distance. An hour later he returned, unlocked the front door and walked into the open plan lounge / dining-room area. The smell of freshly brewed filter coffee wafted through the air and his thoughts immediately turned to his housekeeper, who he assumed must have gotten up early enough to ensure breakfast was ready by the time he got back. However, the housekeeper, a 56-year-old divorcee without children, was neatly tied up, gagged and locked in the bathroom of the small one-bedroom outbuilding she called home. When Delgardo turned to close the door he found himself confronted by Gert van Tonder. Delgardo, not expecting anything untoward, certainly not within ten hours of arriving at Lake Watauga, froze. Gert van Tonder used Delgardo's momentary paralysis to full effect. His right fist snapped forward, connecting with the nerve-endings in the lower part of Delgardo's chin. Delgardo's lights went out and he dropped like a sack of potatoes. When he came around a few minutes later he was lying on the sofa in the lounge, his hands and feet tied. Looking down at him were two men. Still dazed, he tried to focus on the two faces.

"Who are you?" he mumbled.

Van Rensburgh, who commanded the mission, folded his arms. "None of your business, Delgardo."

Behind him, Gert van Tonder was busy dialling a number on his cell phone. Seconds later the unmistakable sound of a ringing telephone came from Delgardo's bedroom. Van Tonder, his own cell phone still active, left the lounge area and returned moments later. In his hand were two cell phones, one of which he handed to van Rensburgh.

"Here, it was this one."

Van Rensburgh took the telephone and sat down on a dining-room chair he had moved to where Delgardo was lying on the couch. "Well, my friend," he bent forward slightly, "looks like you've got some explaining to do."

"What do you want?" The minute the telephone in his bedroom had started ringing he knew that the very people he'd been on the run from had found him. How they had figured out where to find him so quickly escaped him. He noted the foreign accent of the man speaking to him, but wasn't able to place it. Strange as it was, he felt no fear, rather rage at his own stupidity. He should have switched the telephone he used for Patriot business off and hidden it, but then there had never been a reason to do so before, so why now? But how had they gotten hold of that one particular number? Not that it mattered any longer.

"You know exactly what we want, Delgardo," said van Rensburgh quietly. "For starters, you can tell us what Keller, Biedermann and Stegemann are up to with the nuke you bought for them." He turned and spoke to van Tonder, this time in Afrikaans, and handed him Delgardo's telephone. Van Tonder nodded and left the house.

By then it had dawned on Delgardo that the two men were South Africans who knew far more than he thought possible, and that his comfortable life was in the process of coming to an abrupt halt.

"What nuke? And who the hell are Keller and Bieder... who did you say?"

Van Rensburgh sighed. "Listen, Delgardo, by the time we've finished with you you'll have told us everything you know anyway.

Thing is, I don't have a hell of a lot of time, which means I need you to talk quickly. You will, you know."

Van Tonder had, in the meantime, handed Delgardo's telephone to the Mossad agents in the surveillance van. Not only were the three Mossad agents in the van experts in the monitoring of any electronic signals, one of them was an expert in cellular telephone technology. There wasn't a phone on the planet he did not know of, and he promptly commenced taking the Sony device apart, extracting whatever data the phone and the SIM card held. Five minutes later van Tonder was back with van Rensburgh. Delgardo's life was about to become infinitely more miserable.

"Got anything?"asked van Rensburgh.

"I'd say," replied van Tonder. "You're not going to believe this but Delgardo didn't only store the numbers, he stored the names as well."

"He what?"

"Stored the names. The guys in the van have already sent them through to McLaughlin."

Van Rensburgh stared at Delgardo, incredulous. "Surely you aren't that fucking stupid?"

Given the names and numbers, Billy McLaughlin identified exactly who the people listed on Delgardo's telephone were in next to no time. Abel Sharon was immediately informed. He promptly called for an emergency meeting with the Israeli Prime

Minister. The meeting lasted less than fifteen minutes, after which Abel Cohen went to his office and made two telephone calls. The first call went to Michael Grey, who, after listening for a few minutes, had to concede that what Sharon told him was about to happen was, as much as it was undesirable, an unavoidable consequence. Stating clearly that he did not want his men involved, Grey advised Sharon that he would be recalling his men from the USA. Sharon understood completely and ended the call. He then called Victor Stahl, Mossad Head of Station in the USA. Stahl, who had been in the loop all along and had seconded the three Mossad agents, together with the surveillance van to van Rensburgh and van Tonder, listened to Abel Sharon's instruction and acknowledged the order.

At the same time Michael Grey called Jaco van Rensburgh. That same evening the two men boarded a direct flight to London at Charlotte's Douglas International Airport in South Carolina, from where they would fly on to Cairo.

As the two men left the United States, the Mossad-operated surveillance van was heading for Atlanta, Georgia. Only this time there were not three, but four men in the vehicle, one of them the bound and gagged Brent Delgardo. The housekeeper at Delgardo's holiday home had been released by what appeared to be two FBI agents, who informed her that Delgardo had noted the intrusion, fled the scene and then contacted the police. They told her that the suspects had terrorist connections and had been apprehended, Delgardo was safe, and that she was not to mention a word of the incident to anyone as it was a matter of national security. They also advised her as to what the penalties would be if she did talk to anyone, which was enough to ensure that she would never open her mouth. By the time the pseudo FBI agents had left, (they were actually two of the Mossad operators from the surveillance vehicle) the housekeeper, although still shaken, had largely recovered from her ordeal. It would not be too long before two real FBI agents would be speaking to her.

Cairo, Egypt

Michael Grey and Aaron Cohen watched as the passengers from the scheduled Emirates flight from Dubai made their way out of international arrivals. The task of identifying the individuals they were looking for would have been well nigh impossible at any of the larger European airports, but this was Egypt, and the incoming Emirates flight was not the run of the mill tourist charter flight. The majority of the passengers were of Middle Eastern origin, although there were still a surprising number of European passengers who came through in dribs and drabs, mixed in among their darker-skinned fellow travellers. Most of the European passengers appeared to be tourists. It was Cohen who spotted the first of their targets. He tapped Grey on the shoulder.

"There! That's Stegemann, isn't it?"

Grey, who together with Cohen, had spent the past two hours going over the identikits of the three members of the Meinhof Kollaboration, studied the man who was carrying a large backpack hefted over his shoulders, walking past them less than five metres away. He nodded in affirmation. "Yeah, that's him all right. Tail him. I'll follow when the other two have come through. Go!"

He watched as Stegemann, who stopped every few metres to consult what looked like a pocket guide to Egypt and look about, continued on his way. Stegemann was clearly scanning his surroundings. *Not bad*, mused Grey, *he's definitely got some idea of fieldcraft.* Cohen's fieldcraft was, however, a lot better than Stegemann's, and he slotted in behind his quarry, blending in so well that Stegemann would have had to be a highly-trained spook to realise he was being followed. Working on the premise that Keller, Stegemann and Biedermann would group up somewhere outside the airport, Cohen was tasked with following the first person positively identified out of the airport and Grey the last, even if they recognised only one of the three it would still be good enough. It would have been good to have van Rensburgh and van Tonder around as extra manpower, but they were still en route from the USA. The next supposed member of the Meinhof Kollaboration to walk into the arrivals hall was a female who looked like Anne Biedermann, followed five minutes later by someone remotely resembling Jens Keller. Grey tucked in behind the man he thought to be Keller and followed him outside. He did not have to go far, the person he was following joined up with the two other suspected members of the Meinhof Kollaboration at the drop and go area. To Grey's left, some ten metres away, Aaron Cohen casually observed what was happening. Five minutes later, time enough for Keller and Stegemann to smoke a cigarette, Keller hailed a taxi and the three climbed in. The taxi had hardly pulled away from the curb when Grey and Cohen climbed into the next taxi available and told the driver to follow. They didn't travel far; the taxi they were following stopping outside the Novotel Heliopolis hotel within the precincts of the airport complex. Keller, Stegemann and Biedermann entered the hotel foyer and walked across to the reception, followed by Cohen, who kept his distance. Noting the three taking card-keys for three rooms and then taking the elevator to the second floor, Cohen returned to Grey who was waiting in the taxi.

"They've checked in," he said to Grey. "No idea what their next move's going to be, but I suggest you get the car. In the meantime I'll check us in as well. The minute they move, we follow."

As Cohen made his way back into the hotel, Grey told the driver of the taxi to take him to the car park where they had left their hired Audi A3. Ever since Abel Sharon had told him what was happening in the United States and he had called back van Rensburgh and van Tonder, the entire mission they were on had lost its edge. It had suddenly all become rather routine and dull, taking down the Meinhof Kollaboration a mere formality, something they would do as soon as Keller, Stegemann and Biedermann went to collect the device and had it in their possession. Earlier that morning, Grey and Cohen had been joined by three additional teams of Mossad agents – each team consisting of two men - who had spread themselves out, covering the routes in and out of the airport. So far their three adversaries had made it all too easy. The taxi stopped, Grey got out and made his way to the parked Audi. By the time he arrived back at the Novotel, two of the Mossad teams had arrived as well. The third team remained in position well away from the hotel, out there as cover, in the event that the Meinhof Kollaboration suddenly got inventive and gave Grey, Cohen and the others the slip, which was highly unlikely, considering that there were now six watchers in place. The Meinhof Kollaboration would be going nowhere without their knowledge. Cohen had already advised Israel of the developments. It was all just too bloody routine.

Tel Aviv, Israel

Which was pretty much what Abel Sharon was thinking in Israel. They now knew who the American connection to the Meinhof Kollaboration was; that Keller, Stegemann and Biedermann had indeed arrived in Cairo and all signs pointed at a quick and painless resolution of the problem they had been grappling with for the past days. There was a collective sigh of relief when Sharon finished his briefing.

"So that's it?" Prime Minister Roni Ezra closed the briefing folder in front of him. "All we need to do now is take them out when they collect the device?"

"Yes," grunted Sharon. "We've got more than enough men in place. The way it stands we're eight against three. I've arranged to collect van Rensburgh and his partner as soon as they land in London. They'll be in Cairo in the next ten or so hours as well, by which time it may already be game-over. If it happens that the Meinhof Kollaboration don't move before they arrive, it'll be ten against three. By this time tomorrow I reckon it'll all be done and dusted."

"And the American side of things?" asked General Scholl.

"Give it a few days and we'll have it sorted out as well. I've got a team of interrogators on the way to Atlanta; once they're there they'll pick the rest of Delgardo's head clean."

"Can't our men over there sort it out? Wouldn't it be quicker?" asked Goldberg, this time a lot less confrontational.

"They're not equipped to handle this kind of thing. They're all damned good field officers, but are not trained in high level interrogation. Delgardo's told them quite a bit already; there wasn't much point in denying anything, not after what was pulled off his telephone. But he won't have told them everything. Also, he's got two telephones, one for all his day-to-day calls and then the other one. Right now it's the day-to-day phone we're interested in, but it'll take us a month of Sundays to sift through what's relevant and what isn't. That's why I want some specialised men there; they'll know exactly how to go about it."

The meeting ended and the men went their separate ways. Abel Sharon, although more than happy with developments, couldn't get rid of the quiet, uneasy feeling gnawing ever so slightly in the pit of his stomach. Something was telling him it was all going to go pear-shaped. Why, he didn't know; but he didn't head up the Israeli Mossad for nothing, and, when his gut started telling him something was not entirely right, his gut was usually bang on the money. Back in Cairo Michael Grey was having similar thoughts. Something was about to go wrong. But what?

CHAPTER 8
DEADLY TWIST

Cairo / Ismailia, Egypt

Whatever is was that the Meinhof Kollaboration were up to, they were taking their time about it. By mid-morning the following day, Keller, Stegemann and Biedermann had still not left their hotel rooms. Grey and the watchers knew exactly which rooms they were holed up in. They hadn't moved, spending most of their time in Keller's room, supper, breakfast and a host of beverages sent up via room service. They eventually came to life shortly after the breakfast session in the hotel had ended. First Keller appeared at the reception desk. Grey watched from a distance as Keller appeared to settle the bill. Not much later Biedermann and Stegemann made their appearance, Stegemann carrying not only his own, but also Keller's backpack, the only luggage items they had arrived with. Grey, in constant eye contact with one of the Mossad agents waiting near the front door, nodded his head ever so slightly. The agent acknowledged the signal, left his post and made his way out of the main entrance.

As the three members of the Meinhof Kollaboration walked out of the hotel, Aaron Cohen and Michael Grey fell in behind them, keeping their distance.

Outside the hotel entrance, Keller and his cohorts stopped. Keller glanced at his watch and lit a cigarette. He had hardly taken the first drag when an old sand-coloured Bedford TK truck, with drop-sides and a canvas canopy, drove into the hotel parking lot and came to a halt. The driver got out, looked about and saw two men and a woman walk towards him. Grey, Cohen and the two Mossad teams at the hotel were ready to move, the third Mossad team still on station and waiting in close proximity to the two exits of the airport complex. Grey watched as Keller handed the driver of the Bedford a wad of cash. The man counted the money, shook Keller's hand and hailed the next taxi he could see. As the taxi disappeared around the corner, Keller, Stegemann and Biedermann climbed into the Bedford and drove out of the hotel parking lot.

Not far behind followed Grey and Cohen in the Audi A3 and the two Mossad teams, each team driving a Land Rover Discovery. The EgyptAir cargo terminal was not too far away, and shortly after leaving the hotel the Bedford turned into the entrance of the cargo terminal. The three vehicles making up Grey's contingent found places to park nearby and waited. Within half an hour the Bedford truck drove out of the collection area and headed off in the direction of Cairo International Road, the modern dual carriageway leading to and from the airport complex. Once more, the Audi and the two Land Rovers slotted in behind the

Bedford, keeping sufficient distance between them so as not to arouse any suspicion. By then the third Mossad team, also in a Land Rover Discovery, had been alerted. At the first major interchange the Bedford truck swung right, and then right again, onto the Ismailia Highway heading out of Cairo towards the Suez Canal. The Land Rover driven by Team 3 had tucked in a few cars behind the Audi and the other two Land Rovers. So far the entire exercise had been a walk in the park, the Bedford making its way slowly through the traffic. *Too easy,* mused Grey, *too easy.*

An hour and a half later they had cleared most of the heavy traffic and were nearing Ismailia. Up ahead, on his left, Grey could make out a number of centre pivot irrigation systems of a large commercial farm. To his right was open desert, the sandy, barren land stretching to the horizon and beyond. And still the Bedford was driving along at a sedate 70 kph. How the hell Keller, Biedermann and Stegemann had failed to notice they were being followed was beyond Grey, nor did he care. It was time to make their move. He glanced across at Cohen who was driving the Audi.

"Let's do this, Aaron."

Cohen grinned, took the two-way radio that connected him to the three Mossad teams and gave a single instruction in Hebrew. As Grey watched, one of the Land Rovers peeled out and shot past them. The Bedford truck was still 200 metres away from the fast-approaching Land Rover when Grey noticed a shadow moving rapidly along the ground some 10 metres away from the Audi to his left. He cranked down the window, the relatively warm air outside rushing into the air-conditioned interior of the vehicle. The window open, he heard the unmistakeable, repetitive "whup whup whup" of a helicopter.

Before he had time to react the helicopter came into view in front of them, a sand-coloured Huey Cobra, the side doors of the low-flying chopper wide open. Sitting in the open doorway of the chopper, clearly visible, was a white male dressed in khaki combat fatigues, holding what looked to Grey very much like a Russian made RPG7 rocket-launcher, the bulbous nose-cone of the missile pointing down towards the Land Rover in front of them. Cohen, who had by then also seen the chopper, was screaming a warning into the two-way radio.

It was all a little too late. Grey watched in horror as an orange spurt of flame belched from the shoulder-held launcher and the missile hurtled down towards the Land Rover. The Land Rover didn't stand a chance; the missile went straight through the side door and blew the vehicle and the occupants to smithereens. What Grey hadn't noticed was the presence of a further chopper behind them. By the time he did, the second Land Rover had been hit as well, the blazing wreck catapulting off the road. As he watched, utterly dumbstruck, one of the occupants was flung from the vehicle, burning, coming to rest in the middle of the road. He watched in horror as the man tried to get up. Grey could hear his demented shrieks. There was nothing he could do. The Mossad agent collapsed, consumed by the flames. When the third Land Rover, the last of the makeshift convoy, erupted in a ball of flame and the helicopter in front of them swung around, Grey knew he had to get out of the vehicle if he wanted to remain alive. If anyone had asked him later how he had done it he wouldn't have had the answer, yet somehow he managed to unbuckle his seat-belt, open the door and fling himself out of the vehicle in what must have been less than two seconds. The last image Grey had of Cohen was a wide-open mouth, trying to scream a scream that never came, his hands furiously twisting the wheel of the Audi, staring in disbelief at the smoke-trailing missile heading straight for him. As Grey hit the tarmac the missile penetrated the windscreen, exploding as it hit Cohen in the face. Of Cohen and the Audi there was nothing left; only two of the wheels torn off in the explosion wobbling off into the sandy wasteland.

Covered in grazes, bruised and bleeding from a cut on the back of his head, his shirt and trousers ripped open, Grey found himself lying on the warm tarmac, the wrecks of the four vehicles around him billowing black smoke into the air. Pretending to be dead, he lay on the tarmac listening to the sound of the two helicopters hovering above them like two oversized dragonflies. They were clearly searching for survivors. Finding no obvious signs of life, they flew off in a southerly direction and vanished into the desert. Grey staggered to his feet and surveyed the carnage around him. He didn't bother to look if anyone was still alive, he had seen enough similar damage in his life to realise that the only thing needed was a fleet of mortuary vans. Behind the wreckage the traffic was beginning to pile up. One of the dumbstruck locals, a young man on a 125cc Honda motorcycle, who had, up until then, been minding his own business and was on the way to Ismailia, drove bravely around the burning vehicles through a black cloud of smoke, checking to see if there was anything or anyone he could save. By the time he noticed the beaten up figure of Grey standing in the middle of the road it was too late. Grey desperately needed transport and the young man had exactly what was needed.

"Sorry," muttered Grey, as he punched the young man straight off the motorcycle. Knocked senseless, he lay still in the middle of the road, the motorcycle falling over a few metres further on. Grey hobbled across to the prone figure, pulled off the *galabeya* the young man was wearing - the loose-fitting Egyptian robe worn by many men – and slipped it over his head. Next he removed the crash helmet and crammed it onto his own head, the shell too big, but in this case, a loose fit was certainly better than a tight fit or no fit at all. Seconds later he was on the motorcycle, had driven over the median of the dual carriageway and was headed back in the direction of Cairo, past the growing number of gawking onlookers who were gathering at the scene. In the distance Grey could already hear sirens and he pressed on, putting as much distance between the accident scene and himself as possible. He had to get out of there. Whatever he'd had in the car with him was gone, including his cell phone and wallet. The only good thing was that he'd booked into the Radisson Blu hotel for a full week, his remaining clothes and some extra cash in the hotel room safe would still be there.

The pandemonium behind them had not escaped the three

occupants of the Bedford.

"Scheisse!!" screamed Anne Biedermann, as the first Land Rover exploded behind them and the helicopters came into view. Karl Stegemann, who was driving, saw the same through the rear view mirror. He didn't need a second invitation and nearly rammed the accelerator through the floor-board. The truck lumbered forward like an elephant. Jens Keller, who had been attempting to sleep, suddenly awoke.

"What's happening?" he demanded, looking about him in a confused daze.

"No idea!" cursed Stegemann. "Looks like we've been followed and…"

"Followed?!! What…"

"Look behind us, will you?!" yelled Anne Biedermann. "There were a couple of cars following us! Someone in two helicopters just went and blew them up!"

"What the fuck?!"

"Blew the fucking cars up! Three or four of them!"

"How the hell…?"

"I don't bloody know! Those helicopters came out of nowhere and next thing they start shooting the cars off the road!" Biedermann was losing the plot ever so slightly.

"Where the hell are they now?" demanded Keller.

"Gone," replied Stegemann, beads of sweat on his brow, "last

I saw they were heading off into the desert."

Keller, who had been sitting in the middle of the cab, leant across Biedermann and stuck his head out of the window, looking in the direction from which they had come. Racing past them on the other side of the road were three police vehicles followed by an ambulance. In the distance, four columns of black, oily smoke marked the spot of the attack. He watched for a minute, and sat back in the cab.

"Marvellous! Absolutely fucking marvellous!!! Someone's been following us! Then someone else, fuck knows who, goes and shoots them off the road!! Who the fuck was it?! And who the hell was in those cars?!" He banged his fist on the dashboard of the truck. "Can someone explain to me how we didn't notice we were being followed?!" There was a brief moment of silence. "I'll tell you why! Because whoever it was knew what the hell they were doing! What they obviously didn't know was that someone else was onto them as well. And, nor did we!"

"But who the hell knew about us?" demanded Biedermann. "Who?!!"

"How would I know? Do I look like Jesus Christ?" Keller sat back, pensive. "Let's think about this. A couple of cars follow us. From where, we don't know. Why, we don't know. Nor do we know who they were. Nor did we bloody notice them, did we? Right now I assume nobody survived. So who the hell was in the helicopters? They didn't blow us up. Why them and not us?"

For the next few minutes nobody said anything. "You

know what?" Stegemann scratched his nose. "I think they were protecting us. Can't be anything else, can it?"

"Yeah, right," said Biedermann. "And who the hell would want to protect us? From what?"

"From getting caught with a nuclear device on the back of the truck?" ventured Stegemann, a hint of sarcasm in his voice.

"But why? How would they know?"

"Don't know and don't care. Can't think of anything else." In the distance the town of Ismailia came into view and Stegemann slowed down a fraction, sticking to the speed limit once more. "Looks like we have someone out there who knows what we're on about and seems to want to make sure we succeed. Or maybe not?"

"You know what? It might be the answer," muttered Keller. "The last time I spoke to Delgardo he said we didn't have to worry about anything; that we'd be safe. Maybe he sent out a squad of people to make sure we'd do what he'd planned. That's what I think happened. Whoever Delgardo sent must have seen us being followed and taken them out. Well organised, you've got to hand it to them! Flying around in helicopters definitely means they aren't small-fry amateurs. Still, we can't be sure. If those guys in the helicopters are what we think they are, then clearly Delgardo doesn't trust us. If he did, he'd have told us there was a protection screen. Can't blame him; we don't trust him either, never have." Keller remained quiet for a moment, thinking. "Thing is, we don't know what their real mission is, do we? Let's assume for a second that we're next on the list. Right now all they know is that we're in a Bedford truck. So, slight change of plans on our side, when we get to Ismailia we find different transport. We have to get rid of this truck as soon as possible and use something else."

" And then?" asked Biedermann.

"We continue," replied Keller.

"I suppose there's no point in contacting our American friends and letting them know about it?"

"No, not after what's just happened," retorted Keller. "Also, the minute we landed in Cairo all contact with Delgardo ceased. That's the way it was arranged. We're on our own."

A further 100 kilometres to the south the two low-flying Huey Cobra helicopters landed in a cloud of dust and sand close to two military-style transport vehicles. As the blades slowly stopped rotating, Colonel Max Preston climbed out of the front seat and made his way to a small tent that had been pitched next to the trucks, his 2IC, ex-SEAL Lieutenant Simon Groves, close behind him. Preston dropped his wiry frame into a camp chair, reached into a cooler-box and pulled out two ice-cold bottles of beer. He tossed one at Groves, who popped the cap with his teeth.

"Bit of a turkey-shoot, wasn't it?" said Groves, grinning from ear to ear.

"Yup." Preston took a long swig of his beer and put the bottle on a small, fold-up table. "I reckon we got everyone; didn't see any survivors."

"Yeah, couldn't see any myself."

"But," frowned Preston," we can't be too sure, can we? I would've liked to have landed and checked. Still; good mission all round."

"So what's next?" asked Groves, watching the rest of his men cleaning out the choppers.

"We move closer to Rafah. That's where they're heading, aren't they? All we've got to do for our last US $2 million is make sure they get there in one piece. That's it, and then we're out of this dump."

"Wonder what they're up to?" mused Groves.

"No idea. Whatever it is, it's bound to be no good, not for Israel. Otherwise why pay us two million up front and two million when it's all over. For all I care they're a bunch of lunatics who want to get into Israel and blow up the Knesset. Whatever. I don't give a shit!"

"Wanna tell your contact what happened?"

"No point." Preston finished his beer and reached into the cooler-box for another bottle, swatting a fly from his face at the same time. "My contact is off the air. He told me once we were here we wouldn't hear from him again, nor would he respond if I called. For the next few days we're on our own."

"I can live with that."

"And so can I. Means we can do what we want and don't have to listen to someone else's crap."

"No chance anyone noticed us flying the choppers down here?"

"No," grumbled Preston, "none at all. We flew in far too low. Last time anyone saw them was yesterday and those flights were all nicely declared and legal."

"Can't use them again, can we?"

"No, we can't."

"So what the hell do we do with them?" asked Groves.

"We leave them right here and continue in the trucks," said Preston, as he got up and stretched. "Tell the men to dump their camo fatigues into the choppers and get dressed up in their archaeologist kit. We head out in 30 minutes from now."

"What about the guys we hired the choppers from? Won't they be all over us like a sore rash?"

Preston grinned. "First they'd have to find us or the choppers. Both scenarios are highly unlikely. We chartered them for a full week, didn't we? Then we removed the transponders on these things that tell them where we're going, remember? Nah, they'll never find us! They'll think we're still where we were this morning. Will they eventually find the choppers? Maybe. But us? Never. By the time they've figured out what happened we'll be long gone." Half an hour later the two trucks left the Huey Cobras behind them, heading off into the desert in the general direction of Rafah.

At around the same time Michael Grey had reached the

Radisson Blu hotel, dumped the motorcycle, *galabeya* and helmet and made his way as quickly as he could through the hotel reception area and up to his room. On the way a number of people stopped and stared at him, clothes in tatters and caked with dried blood. Minutes later he was in his room. For the first time in three hours he noticed his system winding down. Grey knew exactly what would come next. He had just lost his entire team, seven men dead, one of them Aaron Cohen, a man he had come to view as a friend, rather than an involuntary "business" associate. Wiping away the thoughts flooding his mind, he picked up the handset of the telephone on his bedside table and dialled the number of Billy McLaughlin. Twenty seconds later the call was answered.

"McLaughlin speaking."

"Billy. It's Michael."

"Mike! You sound like shit! What's up?"

"Can't talk, Billy. I'm in trouble. Listen, my cell phone's gone and I don't know if this line's safe. I need a secure phone, like now. Can you do something for me?"

McLaughlin grimaced. Never before had Grey lost a cellular telephone, certainly not an encrypted one. Something had gone horribly wrong. He didn't know what, but he knew exactly what to do; he'd always assumed that one day a call like this would come. He'd made it his job ever since the day they first solved the Zaire kidnap assignment, that he'd never, never, leave Grey in the lurch when the time came. McLaughlin had known all along that he was the supposed safe element, never in the line of fire, the go-to guy when Grey really needed it. So far he had operated more in the background than anything else, happy to provide the ELINT Grey needed to carry out his work on the ground. Right now his closest friend and business partner was in obvious trouble and he needed help.

"Where are you?"

"The Cairo Heliopolis Radisson Blu, near the airport. Room 315."

"Okay, got it. Don't move from where you are. I'm sending you what you need. It'll take roughly seven hours to get there. When you get it, call me." McLaughlin hung up and made the next call. An hour later a hand-to-hand courier left London on a private jet.

By the time the cellular phone arrived in Cairo, Grey had been through the entire gamut of emotions, the intense emotional pain that came with the loss of his comrades, the feelings of guilt – wondering what he could have done to prevent it – and the despair. Nor had he been able to make contact with van Rensburgh and van Tonder, who he knew had arrived over four hours ago, and were probably thinking the worst. Grey's entire strategy had gone up in flames. So had that of the Israelis. There was only one good thing; the decision Grey and McLaughlin had taken years back to instantly update each other's telephones the minute a new number or contact was entered had now paid handsome dividends. Grey, his new phone fully-charged and loaded with all the data he needed, went active. The first call he made was to Jaco van Rensburgh who answered at the very first ring.

"Mike! What the fuck!! Where the hell are you? We've been sitting here at the airport with our fingers up our asses waiting for you! What happened?"

"Too much to tell you over the phone. Listen, I need you two to catch a taxi and get across to the Cairo Heliopolis Radisson Blu. It's not far from where you are. Once you get there call me, I'll come down to collect you." Without saying anything else he ended the call.

Van Rensburgh, sensing the tension in Grey's voice, could feel his stomach knotting up. Van Tonder, a foot shorter than van Rensburgh, looked at him curiously.

"And?"

"Sounds like we've landed ourselves in Shitsville, my friend," replied van Rensburgh as he waved down the next closest taxi he could see. "If you ask me, I think our little picnic has just come to an end."

As van Rensburgh and van Tonder loaded their gear into the trunk of the taxi, Grey was busy on his next call, this one to Billy McLaughlin, who also picked up immediately.

"Mike! Thank God! I was waiting for your call! What the hell's going on?"

"We're in trouble, Billy, deep trouble. And I don't know exactly what to do about it, not yet anyway."

"What happened?"

"Well, it was all going to plan. We were following Keller and his cohorts with the bomb. About an hour or so out of Cairo we were about to make our move..."

"Sorry Mike. Who's we?"

"Cohen, myself and six other Mossad agents. In total, four vehicles. Cohen and I were together in one of them. Like I said, we were about to stop Keller and co., who were driving in front of us in some old clapped-out Bedford, bomb nicely stashed away in the back of the truck, when suddenly two choppers appeared out of nowhere. Sixty seconds later they'd blown us off the road."

"Holy crap! And the others? Aaron Cohen? Where are they?"

There was a moment of silence. "Dead, Billy," replied Grey quietly, his voice quivering. "They didn't make it." He paused once more. "I'm the only one who got out alive and that was pure luck."

"My God!" Billy McLaughlin felt like throwing up. He could hardly imagine what Grey must have gone through. The two had always known that Grey's activities were fraught with danger and there had been times when it had been close. But this? McLaughlin shuddered involuntarily. "Are you okay? Do you need medical help?"

"No, only a few cuts and bruises, nothing major."

"What about the bomb?" asked McLaughlin, dreading to hear

the answer he knew had to come.

"Gone. Together with the Meinhof Kollaboration. And I'm fucked if I know exactly where they're taking it!"

"Oh shit..."

"You got that right."

"Does Abel Sharon know about this?"

"No," said Grey, "not yet. I couldn't talk to him, not using the telephone in the hotel and then definitely not for dialling a number in Israel. Egyptian intelligence would have been all over me in about two seconds flat if I'd tried. We might all think they're just another bunch of inept Arabs, but they're not stupid, far from it. That's the next call I need to make."

"What do you want me to do? How can I help?" asked McLaughlin.

"Don't quite know yet. But I need you to be next to your telephone for the next few hours because we're going to need you. Jaco van Rensburgh and Gert van Tonder are on the way here; at least then I'll have a small team back in place. They should be here any minute. I need to call Sharon now. I'll call back in an hour or so when we know what our next move will be."

"I'll be waiting." For a short moment there was silence. "And Mike, it wasn't your fault! I know what you're capable of. You'll find the bomb."

Grey ended the call. Less than 30 seconds later his phone rang once more. Van Rensburgh and van Tonder had arrived and were waiting in the lobby. A few minutes after that they were in Grey's room, listening as Grey talked to Abel Sharon.

"Michael! Thanks for calling. I was getting a bit nervous here. How did it go? Got the bomb and the Meinhof Kollaboration?"

Grey, dreading what he had to tell Sharon, spat it out. "No, Abel. We haven't. They got away from us. Your men, including Aaron Cohen, are all dead. I'm the only one left alive. I've just been joined by Jaco van Rensburgh and Gert van Tonder. The bomb's gone, Abel!"

"What!!!? How the hell did that happen?" Sharon felt cold beads of sweat forming on his forehead.

"Someone, and I don't know who, shot us off the road. Two choppers; if I saw correctly they were older model Huey Cobras. Took less than a minute. I'm the only one who got out alive; still don't know how. All I know is the bomb's gone, probably heading east towards the Israeli border. Your men are dead. With my two men, who arrived a few minutes ago, we're down to a team of three as it stands."

"Jesus wept! Aaron and the others dead? What now?"

"No idea, Abel. I don't know. And I'm sorry, I really am. This shouldn't have happened! Someone out there knew what we were up to. Who? I need to ask you something; it's been on my mind ever since we were taken out. Is there any chance there's a leak on your side?"

"A leak? Bloody hell, I certainly hope not!"

"I may be completely wrong, but think about it, Abel. Up until now the only people who knew what was going on were Billy, myself and your people. Jaco van Rensburgh and Gert van Tonder knew only parts of it, and that was on a needs basis. I'll vouch for them, also for Billy. Who'd you meet with? Who else knows the full detail on your side?"

"Only four of us. General Chaim Scholl, IDF Chief of Staff, Samuel Goldberg, Head of Ministry of Public Security, our Prime Minister, Roni Ezra and myself. Why?"

"Any chance it could be one of them? Listen, Abel, I don't want to cast any undue doubts here, but someone knew exactly what our movements were, they knew we were here and what we were doing. How else do you explain them wiping us all out at once? Had they taken out myself and Cohen it would have been one thing, but the others as well?"

"Do you know what you're suggesting here?"

"Hell yes, I do! A couple of dead men, some of whom had wives and kids, would be asking pretty much the same thing! We got screwed over, Abel! By whom?"

"Mike, I'm not about to point a finger at any one of those men, certainly not Roni Ezra. Me personally you can count out as well. That leaves Chaim Scholl and Samuel Goldberg. No, Mike, it isn't them either. Scholl's straight as an arrow and Goldberg? Yeah, I think he's a complete and utter prick, but he's so conservative he makes the average practising Jew look like a heathen. No, there's no leak from this side. Right now, as much as I regret the loss of life – and I mean it – we've got an entirely different problem. The bomb..."

"I know, Abel. I'd like to discuss it with my men and come up with a plan of sorts."

"I can't send more men from my side, you know that?" asked Sharon.

"I do. And if you do have a leak, I don't think I'd want them here," said Grey. "I suggest you think carefully about what I said. Whatever meetings you have from now on, make damn sure it's with people you can trust. My personal suggestion? Get your borders blocked off – airspace, border crossings, the works. If you ask me they'll try to get the device in via the tunnels in the Gaza Strip. I know you wiped most of them out, but it may be time you arranged another ground offensive in the Strip just to make sure there aren't any left, 'cause I'm willing to bet there'll be new ones."

"Get real, Grey. We can shut down all our borders in the next 10 minutes, but a ground offensive in the Gaza Strip? Not likely, even we can't get our shit together that quick. No, there's got to be something else."

Grey, who had been thinking it through as he was speaking, his confidence restored by the mere presence in the room of two men he would go to hell and back with, figured out there and then what to do next. "I have the offer from the Ayatollah. I think the time's come to make use of it. I suggest you meet with Roni Ezra and let him know what's happening. And, if you do have a mole, try and flush him out."

"You want me to tell Ezra what's going down and that we're no longer actively involved on your end?"

"Yeah, exactly. Well, maybe not directly. Simple fact is right now you're not in a position to help, whether you like it or not." Grey glanced across at van Rensburgh and van Tonder, and it dawned on him what he needed to do next. "Shut down your borders, Abel. I'll find the device before anything happens, I promise..."

"You're damned sure of yourself, Mike. So what do I tell Ezra?"

"Tell him he doesn't have a choice. Unless you guys want to go it alone, which isn't going to work and you know it. Right now, as much as I didn't want to find myself in this mess, I'm probably the only choice you have. "

"Doesn't sound like I don't have too many options, does it?"

"No. You don't."

"Anything else?"

"One last thing. I called van Rensburgh and van Tonder back from the US because I didn't want to be associated with any Israeli wet activities. I take it you still have Delgardo alive?"

"Yeah, we do. Why?"

"Find out from him if he sent in a back-up squad. Then find out as well if he has any Israeli connections who feed him information. It'll clear up very quickly whether you have a leak or not."

"The thought had already crossed my mind. Good luck, my friend. From here on in we may go different routes but with the same objective. In as much as I can't help you going forwards, I can certainly try to protect you wherever I can. And please, keep me informed, will you?

"Will do, Abel."

"Stop this thing, Mike...for the love of God, stop it!"

Tel Aviv, Israel

Abel Sharon sat back and mulled over what Grey had told him. Once again Israel had lost men who had been tasked with keeping the country and its citizens safe. It was at times like this that Sharon wondered if there were someone out there who could do a better job than him. The loss of the seven men disturbed him deeply, since he had come to know them personally over the past years. Now he would have to inform their next-of-kin and loved ones that they would not be returning home. First though, he would have to tell Roni Ezra what had happened and do so without the presence of Chaim Scholl and Samuel Goldberg. Somehow he needed to find out if there was a leak, and the only way of doing that was to entice the mole, if there was one, to do something premeditated and flush him out. If there was a mole! He couldn't help thinking – if it turned out to be true – that it could only be Samuel Goldberg. He picked up the phone, dialled the number of the Prime Minister's office and told Ezra's private secretary that he needed to see Ezra immediately.

"Sorry, Mr Sharon," she replied, "the Prime Minister went into a meeting with a representative of the Swedish government five minutes ago. He won't be available for the next hour."

"Hmm." Sharon wondered if he should scream at the lady. "Tell you what. You interrupt the meeting and tell the Prime Minister I need to see him, like now."

"But I can't..."

"You can. And if you don't, I can assure you your cushy job will be a thing of the past by tomorrow morning. So I suggest you get going. I'll be there in ten minutes." He slammed down the receiver and cursed, "Bloody civilian know-it-all bitch!"

Cairo, Egypt

As Sharon made his way to the Prime Minister's office, Michael Grey was busy on his next call. Van Rensburgh and van Tonder were fully in the picture as to what had happened. The bomb was gone and they were down to three men. Somewhere out there were the three members of the Meinhof Kollaboration and somewhere else were a bunch of highly organised men, who somehow knew what Grey and his men were up to. That posed a huge problem. Eight against three had been highly favourable odds. Three against three was still acceptable. But not three against three, plus what Grey estimated must be anything up to fifteen other men; men who knew how to fly choppers, had access to weapons such as anti-tank rockets and knew how to use them. Those odds were unacceptable and had to be evened out. But how? Flying more men in from South Africa was no longer possible, time didn't allow it. The local help Israel could provide had been eliminated with no hope of infiltrating more men in from Israel, at least not into Egypt. It had left Grey with one last option. He let his telephone ring for close to a minute and was about to give up when a quiet voice answered.

"Yes?" came the response in Arabic.

"Sorry," replied Grey, "I do not speak Arabic. Do you speak English?"

"Yes, I do. How can I help?"

"Am I talking to the baker shop? I am told you bake the best bread in Cairo. I would like to order four loaves," replied Grey, repeating the code sentence given to him by the Ayatollah.

"Ahh! Yes Sir, you have the correct number. In fact we have a few loaves left that we could deliver immediately. Would that be suitable?" came the sing-song voice.

"Yes it would, thank you."

"And what would the address be?" asked the voice.

"The Cairo Heliopolis Radisson Blu at the airport. Do you know of it?"

"Yes, we will deliver in 30 minutes. Our delivery man will meet you in the lobby. How will he recognise you?"

"I will be wearing a short-sleeved shirt and my left arm is bandaged. A small accident."

"I am sorry to hear that. We will be delivering shortly." With that the call ended.

Fifteen minutes later Grey was in the lobby, waiting. Van Rensburgh and van Tonder had, in the meantime, checked in as well and were holed up in van Rensburgh's room. From where he was sitting Grey had an unobstructed view of the entrance. Minutes before the half hour was up, an elderly man, immaculately dressed in a suit, entered the hotel. He stopped and looked around, and spotted Grey with his bandaged arm, smiled and walked across to where Grey was sitting.

"Mr Grey," he said, holding out his hand in greeting, "a pleasure to meet you."

Grey stood up and shook the offered hand of the man facing him. *So, this is the man who runs Iranian intelligence operations in the region,* he mused, *and he knows my name!* Grey guessed that he was probably around 60 years of age, his neatly cut, jet-black hair interspersed with streaks of grey, a thin pencil moustache traversing the upper lip.

"Thank you, Mr...?"

"Call me Mr Aman." He looked about and pointed at three free lounge chairs around a low coffee table at a more secluded spot at the far end of the lobby. "Perhaps we should continue our discussions over there?"

"Certainly," answered Grey. As they made their way across the lobby Grey signalled to a waiter and asked for two cups of coffee. Well out of earshot of anyone the two men made themselves comfortable, the coffee arriving moments later.

"Well, Mr Grey, I am glad to see you are still alive. I thought you too had perished on the road to Ismailia."

Grey nearly spurted coffee out through his nose. "You know? How the hell..."

Aman, or whoever he was, smiled. "We monitored your movements, of course. I must say you and your men were rather efficient, nicely spaced out so as not to make it too obvious to the three occupants of the Bedford truck that they were being followed. What we were not aware of was the presence of the men in the two helicopters who blew you and your men apart. Nor, obviously, were you. Our man who was following you was roughly eight cars behind you when it happened. By the time he got to the wreckage it was all over; there were no survivors, only dead bodies. By then the first police had arrived on the scene so it was impossible for him to check further. At that point we thought you too had perished. I cannot tell you how pleasant a surprise it was when you called earlier, we were certainly highly concerned."

"Are you telling me you had us covered from the minute I got to Cairo?"

"I am. The Ayatollah you met? I don't think you realise just how powerful he is in Iran. He called me when you were still in Tehran and explained that you might contact me. He also told me what it was about and that we should monitor your movements at all times. Let's just say we were tasked to provide some necessary protection for you and to interfere only when necessary. Well, it wasn't necessary, you had it all very neatly tied up, until yesterday afternoon, that is."

"Fine, Mr Aman, I hear you and appreciate it. If that's the case then you'll probably know where the Meinhof Kollaboration are now and where the bomb is."

"Unfortunately, Mr Grey, and here it does get a little more complicated." The gentle smile on Aman's face had vanished. "The simple truth is, we don't. We had arranged for you to be followed in such a way that every 10 or so kilometres a different vehicle would be on your tail. Our man following you when the incident happened was due to be replaced by the next vehicle once you got to Ismailia. He immediately contacted us to advise us of what had happened. Naturally we put our men in Ismailia on high alert, but unfortunately it was a little too late; there was no further sign of the Bedford truck."

"What? How the hell is that possible?"

"Oh, it is easy. Whoever was in the truck, and we assume it must have been this Keller who came up with the idea, obviously realised that they were being followed and decided to get rid of the truck and find a new one. At least so it seems. You see, we found the Bedford about four hours ago, in a side street on the outskirts of Ismailia. It was empty. There was nobody about to ask how it got there, so we assume they found a different truck, probably bought it at some ridiculous price the owner wouldn't be able to refuse, transferred the cargo and continued on their way. There's no way we can ask the entire population of Ismailia if someone sold a truck, even we wouldn't be able to find out so quickly."

"So you're telling me they're gone?"

"Yes, I am."

"What about the men in the choppers? Any idea who they were?"

"Yes and no. We made some discreet inquiries. There are, after all, not many places that own or hire out choppers such as those which were used. They belonged to a Cairo-based organisation and were rented for a period of six days by a man who called himself John Anderson. He said that he needed the choppers to get to an archaeological dig somewhere out in the desert. Apparently there were two qualified pilots in the group, hence they didn't need pilots from the hiring company. I don't need to tell you that there is no John Anderson and that the archaeology story is just that – a story."

"Any idea how many men there were?" asked Grey.

"According to the helicopter hire company there were ten men. Oh, I need to mention that the choppers have also vanished. The transponders were removed so the hire company could not track them any longer. Well, not quite. As far as the hiring company was concerned they were stationary at a place around 50 kilometres to the east of Ismailia. We checked and found the transponders. Pretty neat, I must say, they'd been removed and hooked up to a separate power source to keep them active. Whoever the ten men are, Mr Grey, they are no fools! And, as you have found out, they are extremely dangerous."

"Let's assume Keller and his two colleagues are headed for Rafah and the Israeli border. Surely you have connections in Hamas who'd be able to keep a look out for them and stop this from happening?"

"Hamas? Ever since the last Israeli incursion into the Gaza Strip the organisation is more splintered than it has ever been. There's severe in-fighting between the various factions and we know of five major ones. We assume one of those factions is, and please excuse the pun, collaborating with the Meinhof Kollaboration. But, I digress. As the Ayatollah mentioned to you, in as much as we Iranians do not like the presence of Israel in the Middle East, we certainly would not want to get rid of the Zionists by means of starting a nuclear war. Also, in recent times - and this is strictly off the record - it has crossed our minds that perhaps a more lasting solution needs to found. But, back to Hamas, as far as the *Al-Qassam* Brigades are concerned we do control one of the larger, more moderate factions. They have been activated and are on the lookout."

"I suppose it's time then to get to Rafah and into the Strip?"

"It is, Mr Grey. We have arranged transport as you need to be quick. We know of the other two gentlemen who joined you earlier today. The three of you can leave in the next 30 minutes; there is a plane waiting to take you to Rafah. That is, if you wish to continue your mission, of course."

"Yes, we do. This thing must be prevented, no matter what. Will you be coming as well?"

"No, I won't. You will be met in Rafah by a man called Adofo. He will assist you from there onward. He also understands that he is under your command. As I understand, you are an accomplished military practitioner, not so? So are your two men. The men under my direct command are not trained in semi-combat operational matters, they are trained field operatives, people who by and large work alone. Hence they will not be of use to you, not for this exercise. The *Al-Qassam* Brigade we control will be."

"What about weapons?"

"No problem, of those you will have more than sufficient. Now go, Mr Grey. Time is against you. And us."

Grey got up. "How do we get to the airport? To which aircraft?"

"See the gentleman standing near the entrance?" Aman pointed at a man standing outside, smoking a cigarette. "He will take you."

"I suppose all that's left is to thank you." Grey turned and started walking away when Aman stopped him.

"One last thing, Mr Grey. You promised not to let the Mossad know who I am or what you are going to be exposed to. I trust that still stands?"

"Mr Aman," replied Grey quietly, "do you know what the last comment of the Ayatollah was when I asked him why he trusted me?"

"No, perhaps you would enlighten me?"

"He said he was a good judge of character," Grey paused. "He is, you know."

The two men parted company. Within the hour a King Air 90, carrying Grey, van Rensburgh and van Tonder, left Cairo International and swung east, heading out over the wastes of the Sinai Peninsula and towards Rafah.

Tel Aviv, Israel

As the aircraft took off, the meeting between Roni Ezra and Abel Sharon was drawing to a close. It had not been pleasant, not by the wildest stretch of imagination. Israeli meetings, even at the highest political level, are conducted in a far less formal manner than would be the case in Europe, the USA or many eastern countries. In the case of the meeting between Ezra and Sharon, who had known each other for years, both being products of the same school in Israel and both having served their compulsory military service in the 188th Armoured Brigade, any form of formality went straight out of the window. After an initial three minute period of extreme agitation and shouting at each other, the two men got down to figuring out what their next move would be. The fact that neither Scholl nor Goldberg were present didn't please Ezra, but he understood why. In addition, as much as he vented in those first minutes after finding out what had happened, he knew there was absolutely no blame to be apportioned to Sharon - he simply had to vent at someone and Sharon was the only person around. On top of the missing nuke, which by then must surely have been well on way to the Israeli border, Ezra was concerned about the possibility of a mole among the four men. He too knew it wasn't Sharon or himself, and he counted out Chaim Scholl as well, the man was simply far too patriotic and thought the Americans were, in general, a bunch of *schmucks;* necessary, yes, but *schmucks* all the same. But Goldberg? Ezra knew he had to inform both men of what had happened; after all they controlled the resources that now needed to be activated. Both men were summoned urgently and arrived ten minutes later. This time the shouting match lasted the better part of five minutes before it simmered down to reasonable levels, with Samuel Goldberg predictably making most of the noise. Once again, much of what was said by Goldberg was directed at Sharon and his perceived inefficiency, yet this time Sharon sat back in silence and absorbed whatever came at him – he didn't really have much of a leg to stand on and he knew it. He had, after all, whether his fault or not, been in charge of the operation that had now gone bad.

What did come out of the meeting was that General Scholl would immediately increase the Israeli Defence Force - the IDF - manpower seconded to border patrol duties three-fold, as well as arranging aerial surveillance of the entire area at the southern end of the Gaza Strip around the clock. If anything or anyone in the area decided to do anything stupid, the likelihood was that it would be picked up. Goldberg, on the other hand, would put his own internal security organs on high alert. The reason they would give to the various unit commanders and other heads of operational departments would be that there was credible information of yet another pending mass incursion of Hamas terrorists into Israel, in this case, one supported by a German terrorist organisation. Of the device nothing would be mentioned. An hour later the instruction had gone out to the IDF and the Israeli Police Services, who reacted in the usual manner and immediately stepped up their activities – they were, after all, used to the ongoing threats emanating from across the borders of Israel.

A good while after the meeting had concluded there was a knock on Abel Sharon's office door. Sharon, who was busy planning which of his agents he would move to where to be able to give Grey as much assistance as possible without sending men into Egypt (knowing it was impossible anyway considering the time element) looked up.

"Come in," he called out.

The door opened quietly and Roni Ezra entered. This was somewhat unusual; normally Sharon would have been called to Ezra's office. Unusual too was the fact that Ezra hadn't announced he was coming to see Sharon.

"Roni!" Sharon got up. "What brings you here?"

Ezra pulled up a chair and sat down. "Needed to talk to you, Abel." He ran his hand through his thinning hair. "Listen, I'm sorry for having a go at you earlier on, I know you did everything you could – and more. We were so close. Damn!"

"Yeah, we were," said Sharon as he sat down again, "and apologies accepted, but you didn't need to apologise. I know my job gets the better of me from time to time; personally, I've got no idea how you handle yours. I'd have gone mad a long time ago. So, out with it. You obviously want something."

Ezra smiled wrily. "Your honest opinion, Abel and I won't hold you to it. What's going to happen?"

Sharon frowned. "You really want to know what I think? Not what I know or can verify?"

"Your opinion, Abel, your real opinion. What's going to happen?"

Sharon stood up, removed his reading glasses and placed them on the desk in front of him. "If you ask me there're three things happening all at once. Grey's hooked up with the Iranians and won't tell us a lot more than that. It concerns me; I hope he knows what he's doing. Then there's the Meinhof Kollaboration. We don't know exactly where they are, but we have to assume they're going to try to move the device into Israel via the Gaza Strip. This means that they must have some connection to one of the Hamas groupings; the probability is high they'll try to move the device in via a tunnel, but which tunnel? It'll be one we have no idea about, probably very deep and very long. On top of that there's this group of men from the chopper who threw the spanner into the works in the first place. What I can't come to grips with is who the hell they are and what their real intent is."

"Okay, I get you. Back to my real question. What the hell's actually going to happen?

"I think there's going to be a small-scale war somewhere in the southern part of the Gaza Strip, on one side Grey and his men, together with whatever Hamas faction the Iranians control, on the other side the Meinhof Kollaboration and the Hamas faction they're aligned to. Then throw in the protection element the Meinhof Kollaboration appear to have behind them, although I still don't know what exact role they'd play. If Grey wins, we win. If Grey loses, the bomb will find its way into Israel; if that happens it's over to us and our own devices."

"What about contact with Grey? Still possible?"

"Yes, it is." Sharon shrugged. "He'll keep us posted so we'll know what's happening. I just wish we could give him more help."

"You a hundred percent sure we can't send men in to assist?" asked Ezra.

"I am. The men we could use down there are dead. Infiltrating more will take too much time, and the risk of them being caught out is far too high. It takes months of preparation to plant one of our field officers, never mind seven or eight men all at once."

"Last question. Goldberg? Do you really believe he's a mole?"

Sharon frowned. In so much as he disliked Goldberg, he couldn't get himself to believe that the man was leaking information. Of all things abhorred by Israeli's, betrayal of the State by an Israeli national was something so incomprehensible that it simply didn't happen. Yet when it did, and there had been cases, the Israeli reaction was usually swift and uncompromising, as Mordechai Vanunu, a former Israeli nuclear technician, had found out. He had leaked details of the Israeli nuclear programme to the British press in 1986, after which he had been lured to Rome, abducted by the Mossad and returned to Israel to face trial, ultimately spending 18 years in prison.

"No Roni, I don't think he is. But the man has a bit of a bent ego on him, no idea why. If you ask me he might go and blurb something somewhere where it falls into the wrong hands, but I don't think he'd intentionally pass on information."

"Thanks Abel," said Ezra and got up to leave. "I didn't think so either. Still, we can never be absolutely sure. Here's what I need you to do. Keep in contact with Grey, anything you hear from him pass on to me immediately, no matter what time of day. As for Goldberg, I want you to put one of your men on him. I want to know who he talks to, when he farts and whatever else he does. If he does leak, we'll catch him. If he doesn't, well, we'll owe him an apology."

CHAPTER 9
TUNNEL WAR

Gaza Strip

The Gaza Strip. An area approximately 50 kilometres long and between 6 to 12 kilometres wide, it is bordered on the north and east by Israel, to the west by the Mediterranean Sea and at the southern end, where it is the widest, by Egypt. Close to two million Palestinian people live in the Strip. Since its inception in 1949, the Gaza Strip has been in a state of perpetual turmoil, a hotbed of anti-Israeli activism and Islamic fundamentalism. Free movement into and out of the Gaza Strip, ruled de facto since 2007 by Hamas, is non-existent. As a result, and much to the chagrin of the Egyptians and in particular, the Israelis, the inhabitants of the Gaza Strip, that is to say those with the necessary resources, and who happen to be primarily Hamas-funded, have resorted to building tunnels underneath the borders. The tunnels were designed to smuggle consumer goods into the Strip as well as - in the case of tunnels leading into Israel – to infiltrate Hamas fighters and terrorists into Israel. Looking for the tunnels, difficult to locate in the first instance, and destroying them, is an ongoing activity conducted by both the Israelis as well as the Egyptians. Yet, as the tunnels found are destroyed, new ones are built just as quickly. The Israeli Defence Force is on record as saying that they alone had found and destroyed at least 30 such tunnels leading into Israel by mid-2014, with the estimated cost of building an average tunnel around US $3 million.

Of interest also is the relationship between the Hamas political leadership and its military wing, the *Izz al-Din al-Qassam* Brigades. In so much as the Brigades form a part of Hamas, they are also able to act independently. Hence, what Hamas says and what the Brigades do, are not always one and the same thing, a state of affairs that could well be exploited by those with devious intentions and who know how the system works.

The Patriots, who had spent time and a substantial sum of money on finding out, knew exactly how the system worked. The minute the purchase of the South African-built nuclear device had been concluded, they employed the services of a well-placed middle-man and made contact with one of the *Al-Qassam* Brigades, whom they immediately commenced supplying with a number of rather high-tech combat weapons; weapons smuggled in through one of the tunnels the Brigade operated between Egypt and the Gaza Strip. In addition, they provided the Brigade with previously unheard of funding. There was, however, one condition, accepted by the Brigade without question. As a result, and, unbeknown to both the Israeli and the Egyptian authorities, the construction of a further two tunnels commenced; one from

Egypt into the Strip and one from the Strip into Israel. The big difference between those two tunnels and the existing ones was, to say the least, startling; so too was the price tag.

The tunnel to be constructed first was the one between Egypt and the Gaza Strip. The starting point was inside a medium-sized cement block manufacturing company that had been set up specifically to disguise what was really happening. Cement block factories need sand, lots of it, and how better to get rid of the sand and rock extracted during the tunnel-boring process than using it to make cement blocks. It also provided sufficient reason to erect closed-in buildings for manufacturing purposes. Within a month of the factory commencing production, the parts of a completely dismantled tunnel-boring machine had been delivered to the factory. By then a shaft had already been sunk. One month later, the boring machine assembled in an underground cavernous vault excavated for the purpose, the tunnel-boring operation commenced. With a diameter of just over 1.5 metres, concrete-lined and reinforced, running 60 metres below the surface - well below the level of all the other tunnels - and over 2 kilometres in length, it was a feat of engineering to be proud of. The tunnel terminated in the basement of a building used by the Brigade in Rafah. When completed, after a marathon effort of only six months, the tunnel-boring machine was dismantled and moved once more, this time to the town of Khirbat Ikhza'a, close to the border with Israel, not far from the Kibbutz Nir Oz in the south east of Israel.

Again, the tunnel-boring process started. The second tunnel

was just on four kilometres long and had taken eight months to complete, surfacing in a small patch of arid, unoccupied land surrounding the ancient synagogue of Ma'on. The tunnel-borers punched through the surface in the early hours of the morning and immediately ten men followed, rapidly installing a lid with an earth-covering roughly one metre thick. It was all over within 30 minutes; the last man to leave was one of the Brigade members who had the responsibility of camouflaging the exit. He would be back in the Gaza Strip two hours after the others, entering via one of the other, far more rudimentary tunnels used by Hamas. The men who had been employed to build the tunnels, contractors from Russia who had been paid exorbitant salaries, in advance, for their services, left the completed tunnel in body-bags, executed on their last day on the way back to the tunnel entrance. Nobody else knew of the tunnels, except The Patriots and a few select members of the *Al-Qassam* Brigade. For the next months the two tunnels lay idle, waiting to be used.

The Commander of the *Al-Qassam* Brigade, Ahmad Shabaan, who had overseen the tunnel construction, was beginning to feel somewhat frustrated at the lack of any further progress – he had, after all, been advised that the planned activities would contribute largely to the complete annihilation of Israel. He eventually received the message he was waiting for. His benefactor, and he still had no idea who it really was, merely advised him to expect three persons, two males and one female, who would arrive at the cement block factory within 48 hours and that he should be ready for them and their cargo – an explosive device. What he wasn't told was exactly what type of explosive device it was. He immediately ordered 15 of his men to be sent through the tunnel to the cement block factory on the Egyptian side of Rafah.

At the same time three other groupings were also on their way to the Egyptian side of Rafah – Michael Grey and his small team of men in the KingAir 90, twenty-five members of a different *Al-Qassam* Brigade who would link up with Grey and his men (and who had the backing of Iran), as well as Colonel Max Preston and his men. On top of that the IDF massively stepped up patrol and surveillance activities in the area. Even if the Meinhof Kollaboration and Ahmad Shabaan had been aware of the developments, it would have made very little difference; the point of no return had long since come and gone.

Atlanta, USA

The interrogation of Brent Delgardo had proven to be an exercise with mixed results. The two men who had flown in from Israel to handle the process had been ruthlessly efficient. There were ways of extracting information, and, in Delgardo's case, it was neither physical nor chemical methods that did it, rather the threat of exposing his activities to the US government. Delgardo, a hard-core Republican supporter and well-versed with what would happen if he ended up in one of the state penitentiaries, decided that cooperating with the Israelis would be better than being an involuntary guest of the US government. Also, the Israelis, lying through their teeth, had promised they would not harm him so long as he told them everything. Delgardo talked. The entire interrogation session lasted the better part of a full day, Delgardo hooked up to a polygraph for the duration. At the end of it, with Delgardo neatly tied up and isolated in one of the bedrooms of the safe house, the Mossad operators sat down to take stock over a few cold beers.

"So he wasn't lying," stated the man who had been responsible for the polygraph testing and who had been studying the printouts generated by the machine. "Everything he said was the truth, the needles didn't even flicker. Or he's the best liar I've ever come across."

"No, he told us all he knew," said the lead interrogator. "What I can't figure out is why he came clean so quickly, no effort to resist whatsoever. Never seen that before."

"Nor have I," commented the second member of the interrogation team. "Personally, I think Delgardo assumes if he tells us everything he might get off lightly, we told him from the outset that if he came clean we wouldn't harm him, didn't we? The richer they are, the more they have to lose, and he definitely doesn't want to lose everything. Bit late, mind you."

Victor Stahl, Mossad Head of Station in the USA, who had been watching the entire proceedings, nodded in agreement. "Okay, it's a wrap then. We now know exactly who The Patriots are, where they live, the companies they own and how they went about this. We also have a name – Operation Grail. Delgardo handled the final execution bit of Grail. What concerns me is the group he sent in to keep an eye on the Meinhof Kollaboration. If those ten guys are as good as he described them to be, then Grey's going to have more than just a bit of a problem. Problem is they can't be re-called, Delgardo made sure there was a point of no return, which was the moment the device landed in Cairo."

"But what the hell for? I've never heard of anyone launching an operation without a re-call option in place," said the lead interrogator.

"Does happen with some deep-cover operations, especially the black ops type," replied Stahl. "The reason's rather simple. With operations of that nature, and Grail's a real beauty, there's always the possibility of last minute doubt creeping in, especially if more than one man is involved in the decision-making process. To remove the risk of making decisions based on sudden remorse or doubt, or to avoid being linked to a possible negative outcome, communication lines are completely shut down, starting with the destruction and disposal of all cellular communication devices, which is exactly what Delgardo's instructions were. The Meinhof Kollaboration and the ten other men in Egypt know that, even if they tried to make contact, it wouldn't work. Conversely, it wouldn't work either – we've tried. The telephone numbers Delgardo used to contact what he calls the protection unit and the Meinhof Kollaboration go straight to voicemail."

"So unless Grey manages to stop them this thing's going to happen?"

"That's about the size of it. Nothing we can do from our side to help him, not anymore. Had we been 48 hours earlier we'd have stood a chance."

"What about The Patriots?" asked Stahl's 2IC, who had accompanied him on the trip to Atlanta. "What do we do about them?"

Stahl shrugged. "We've received pretty clear instructions as far as they go. What they planned is beyond evil. If we let them live and have them arrested, especially with the money and influence they've got, they'll be back on the streets within five years, max! Provided of course that there's enough hard and fast evidence to lock them away in the first place. You know the American legal system as well as I do, Delgardo and his merry men will employ an army of legal experts and lawyers, pay them a fortune and create a legal quagmire that'll make the OJ Simpson trial look like child's play. Not only that, they'll drag the trials out for years without any guarantee of a result. And we mustn't forget that, if this ever went to trial, we'd be implicated as well, which is an absolute no no." He paused. "No, they cannot go on trial. The only choice we have is to remove them ourselves. If we don't, and even if Grey succeeds, they'll try again. What we shouldn't forget is by doing what they did The Patriots declared war on Israel. That mere fact changes the rules, gentlemen. One of the original group of five of the Patriot leadership is already gone, thanks to Delgardo. Over the next few days the four remaining leaders will all have rather unfortunate accidents, the first one happening tonight."

"Who's first?"

"Delgardo."

Five minutes later, Victor Stahl, this time alone in a different room in the safe house, was on the line to Abel Cohen. The first question Sharon posed after listening to Stahl concerned the possibility of contact between Samuel Goldberg and The Patriots.

"What about Goldberg, Victor. Did Delgardo say anything about possible contact with him?"

"No, Abel, as far as we could establish there was and is no contact. We asked him the question on five separate occasions, each time phrased differently. The gist of the answers was always the same; Delgardo has no idea who Goldberg is and definitely hasn't had any contact. He went as far as saying that they'd tried to get close to a number of highly-placed people in Israel for a long time but had never been successful. In Delgardo's own words, the man they'd tasked to establish the contact was actually told to go and fuck off in one particular instance, whereas in other cases he was told pretty much the same in a more polite manner."

"You're telling me there's no leak on our side?"

"That's affirmative, Abel. At least none that we know of."

Sharon breathed a sigh of relief. Yet still there was something about Goldberg that bothered him, but it would have to wait.

"Then how did the men who shot Grey and our people off the road know so intimately what was happening?"

"Easy. They were sent by Delgardo to look after the Meinhof

Kollaboration. Thing is, The Patriots didn't entirely trust Keller and co., so they came up with this back-up plan. The men sent by Delgardo, and there are ten of them, are there to shield Keller. Also, if Keller deviates in any way from the plan, they are there to make sure he gets pulled back into line."

"Any idea who they are?"

"A bunch of retired special-ops characters. Seven from Russia and Bulgaria, the other three from here. The leader of the group is an ex-US Ranger, one Colonel Max Preston, retired."

"Jesus! That's some serious muscle! And they knew all along exactly what the movements of the Meinhof Kollaboration were?"

"Yes, they did. Delgardo didn't know that they'd already been actively involved and we didn't tell him either. But yes, they know the full plan as well as the time-frames."

"Time-frames? You mean Delgardo told you exactly when this was going to happen?"

"He did. In three days from now. The device is due to be set off in the early morning hours."

"Where?"

"In a place called Tirosh."

"Christ, even I don't know of every last little place in Israel! Where the fuck's Tirosh?"

"I hope you're sitting down, Abel. The place is basically right on the southern side of Sdot Micha."

"What!! Sdot Micha!!??" Sharon exploded. "That's where we've stationed our Jericho 1 and 2 ballistic missiles! God Almighty! If that thing goes off there it'll be the start of World War Three!"

"Don't I know it, Abel! At least we know where the device is headed and Sdot Misha is far better than Tel Aviv or Haifa. We can cordon it off tighter than a duck's ass."

"Did Delgardo say how they were going to bring it in?" Sharon could feel his heart pounding in his chest. This wasn't good for his health, not one little bit.

"That too. Via two tunnels specifically built for the purpose. One into the Gaza Strip, from Egyptian side, the other from the Strip into Israel."

"Did he say where these tunnels are?"

"No," replied Stahl. "All he knows is that they were built by Russian contractors under the watchful eye of one of the *Al-Qassam* Brigades he had contact with. Problem is, all contact with the Brigade has been stopped as of yesterday, part of the operational planning. He used to talk to a Commander Ahmad Shabaan. This Shabaan and his Brigade is also responsible for infiltrating the Meinhof Kollaboration into Israel. Only thing is, Delgardo doesn't know where the tunnels are located. Oh, the contractors were exterminated upon completion of the tunnels, so it's no use even trying to find out exactly who they were."

"Unbelievable, Victor, un-bloody-believable!"

"I thought so as well, Abel. At least we know what's happening and can act."

"Damn right we can! And we will. If those bastards even attempt to bring that thing into our country they'll have to get past the entire IDF first, that much I promise you! What about Delgardo and the other assholes in this Patriot organisation? You're going to remove them?"

"We'll have to. Starting tonight."

"Do me a favour, will you? Make it slow and let them suffer. With what they're busy doing to us, it's the least they deserve." Abel Sharon hung up, left his office and made his way to the office of Roni Ezra. This time he didn't bother announcing his arrival; he simply marched straight past Ezra's startled secretary - who tried to say something but was stopped by Sharon's withering, thunderous glare - and barged into Ezra's office without bothering to knock.

At the same time the panel van with the three Mossad operators and sedated Brent Delgardo left Atlanta, heading back in the direction of Watauga Lake in the Blue Ridge Mountains. By the time they arrived at the lakeside home, Delgardo, who had been woken and then pumped full of drugs, was as high as a kite. He didn't have a clue what he was doing, but suddenly the Mossad operators were his best friends, or so he told the shocked housekeeper when he arrived. And yes, he had invited them to take a slow cruise on the lake in his Bayliner. At night? Delgardo clearly had no idea what he was doing or whether he was Arthur or Martha. Suspicious to the extreme, the housekeeper watched as the men made their way to the boathouse, waited until the Bayliner moved slowly onto the dark lake and vanished around a headland and then called the police. They arrived an hour later and sat in the dark, waiting for the Bayliner to return. When two hours later there was still no sign of the boat, they decided it was all a little too odd and called for help. Half an hour later a police vessel headed out onto the lake. They found nothing; the Bayliner had vanished. It was eventually found two days later by police divers, resting at the bottom of the dam wall at the far side of the lake, the bow completely caved in. In the cabin, up under the ceiling, floated the bloated corpse of Brent Delgardo. Of the three men who had been with him there was no trace. What the police did find when they retrieved the boat was a number of syringes and three sealed sachets of heroin. Clearly Delgardo had been high on drugs and had somehow managed to ram the Bayliner into the dam wall.

When the FBI finally arrived on the scene three days later and questioned Delgardo's housekeeper, she confirmed that she had never before seen Delgardo in the state he had been in on the night of the incident, that there had been three other men who had already made their way to the boathouse, hence she couldn't describe them, and that Delgardo had behaved strangely from time to time. She also mentioned the previous incident and that the FBI had already spoken to her at the time. It didn't take long for the real FBI to establish that something very strange had happened; there had definitely been no FBI personnel in the area for more than seven months. With no leads, no descriptions of the three suspect men and nothing else to go on, the case was eventually closed, with Delgardo's cause of death being recorded as a drug overdose.

Rafah, Egypt - Gaza Strip Border

The KingAir 90 carrying Michael Grey, Jaco van Rensburgh and Gert van Tonder landed at an old Israeli air-base some 50 kilometres from the Egyptian border with the Gaza Strip in the early morning. Mr Aman, Grey's Iranian contact, obviously had more influence than Grey had thought possible, the permission to land at the MFO airbase - controlled since the Israeli withdrawal from the Sinai by the Egyptians - not being easy to obtain. Waiting for them was a dark-skinned young man who introduced himself as Adofo. Not much later they were heading out through the sparsely populated arid countryside towards the Egyptian side of Rafah.

Rafah, Egypt – The Meinhof Kollaboration

At the same time Jens Keller, Anne Biedermann and Karl Stegemann drove their truck into the outskirts of Rafah. Not far from the single border crossing - they could see the complex of buildings at the crossing in the distance ahead of them - they turned left, and a further two kilometres later arrived at the cement block factory. Anne Biedermann, who had been giving Jens Keller directions, tossed the detailed map of the area behind her seat and climbed out of the truck, joined moments later by

Stegemann and Keller. There was nobody visible; the entire factory yard was a dustbowl. Biedermann scuffed the dirt with her canvas military-style boots, the slight breeze blowing eddies of dust into the air. The trip had taken well over a day and they would have arrived on time late the previous night had it not been for the need to change vehicles in Ismailia. After more than 24 hours in the same clothes, driving in a truck that sadly lacked any form of air-conditioning or other creature comforts, Keller, Biedermann and Stegemann, their shirts sweat-stained and covered in dust, were beginning to feel the effects of the journey. A shower would have been nice, but would have to wait. There was work to do.

"Hello? Anybody here?" Anne Biedermann could feel the fatigue starting to set in. She turned to face Keller. "*Wunderbar! Here we are and nobody's home.*"

"Relax, Anne," replied Keller. "They'll be here. We're a couple of hours late, remember?"

He had hardly finished his sentence when a shout came from across the yard. "Don't move! Get your hands up! Drop whatever weapons you have on the floor!"

Okay, someone's been expecting us after all, thought Keller as he lifted his hands slowly above his head, Biedermann and Stegemann following suit. "No weapons!" Keller shouted back, wondering who was going to emerge from the shadows.

"Are you Keller?" came the response.

"Yes."

Seconds later 15 figures emerged from the behind a few scattered heaps of sand, the main building and from behind two trucks parked on the far side of the yard. They were all dressed in black fatigues and black balaclavas, only their eyes and mouths visible. Wrapped around their heads were green headbands displaying Arabic writing. Each carried an AK-47 rifle, the weapons trained at the three individuals standing in the middle of the yard. They stopped less than ten metres away, encircling them.

"Damn," whispered Stegemann, "it's them. Hamas." One of the black-clad figures, who Keller figured was the leader of the group, came closer and stopped a metre away from him.

"Who's Keller?" asked the man, his rifle at the ready.

"Me," replied Keller. "I've come to see Farouk. Is that you?"

"Yes, I'm Farouk," came the response. "You have the cargo with you?"

"In the back of the truck." Immediately Farouk barked a command in Arabic and two men detached themselves from the circle, slung the AK-47s across their backs and made for the truck, climbing into the back. A short while later Keller heard them prising open the lid of the wooden crate. They emerged once more, one of the men running across to Farouk and whispering something in his ear. Farouk nodded and the men resumed their position in the circle. Suddenly his hand came up and he pulled the balaclava from his head, revealing a young face with tousled black hair, the other Hamas fighters lowering their weapons.

"*As-salamu alaykum,* Mr Keller! Welcome!" He stepped forward and greeted Keller in the customary Arabic fashion, three light cheek to cheek kisses, repeating the same with Stegemann and Biedermann. "Come," he said, "let's get under cover. My men will unload the cargo." As they moved across to the enclosed factory building he looked up at the sky, searching.

"Problem?" asked Keller, who was walking next to Farouk.

"No, not yet, but the longer we stay out here the greater the chance of being spotted by the drones the Zionists use in this area."

Moments later they were sitting around a rickety table, Farouk offering cold bottles of water to the three Meinhof Kollaboration terrorists.

"We were expecting you last night," he smiled as he spoke, "what happened?"

Biedermann and Stegemann sat back letting Keller do the talking. "We had to change trucks. Someone was following us." Keller went on to explain what had happened outside Ismailia the previous day.

"That is bad, Mr Keller." Farouk's smile had vanished, his expression suddenly cold and ruthless. "Are you sure you weren't followed here?"

"Positive. We drove for hours through the desert and there was nothing behind us. We also kept our lights off for most of the way and stopped every 20 or so kilometres to see if there was anything."

"And you saw nothing?"

"We noted 20 cars and 14 trucks pass us as we were stopped, and they drove past without any hesitation. No, we were not followed.

Farouk's smile gradually returned. "Good, very good. But we cannot be careful enough. Speed is now of the essence; we need to move; today! Commander Ahmad Shabaan is waiting for you in Gaza." He turned to one of the Hamas fighters and gave a further command, again in Arabic. "Let me show you the tunnel. I hope none of you suffer from claustrophobia."

They got up and walked into the cement block manufacturing part of the factory building. It was still too early, the 'official' work for the day had not yet commenced and there was nobody about. At the far end of the open-plan building was what looked like a small brick office block, albeit without any windows and only a single, locked, steel door. Farouk walked across the open expanse of floor, followed by Keller, Biedermann and Stegemann. Behind them five of Farouk's men pushed a trolley, on top of which, cradled between two blocks of wood, was the nuclear device. Farouk unlocked the door, stepped into the dark interior and switched on a light, beckoning the others to follow him. The interior of the room was startling. To the right it was empty, the floors swept clean. On the left stood a large steel gantry, under which, suspended by four thick steel cables, was a steel platform approximately one metre wide and two metres long. Each of the four steel cables was connected to individual electric winches mounted to the gantry. Below the suspended steel platform the vertical shaft leading to the main tunnel dropped 60 metres into pitch black darkness.

"Well then, my friends," said Farouk as he stepped onto the steel platform, "are you ready?"

Cautiously, Keller, Biedermann and Stegemann stepped onto the steel platform which was swaying ever so slightly, wondering whether or not the contraption would bear their weight, never mind the weight of the device. Moments later Farouk pressed a red button mounted within reach on the concrete wall next to the gantry. The motors of the winches hummed softly and the platform dropped away into the dark shaft. To Keller and his colleagues it seemed like an eternity, none of the three saying anything on the way down. When the platform eventually came to a halt, Farouk took a torch from his pocket, illuminated the darkness and stepped off the platform. To his left was yet another light switch and he pressed it. The bottom of the shaft was suddenly bathed in brilliant white light. Keller involuntarily sucked in his breath.

On one side of the platform, the lights fading away in the distance, was the tubular entrance to the tunnel. On the other side loomed a large cavernous vault. It was empty, excavated for the sole purpose of assembling the tunnel boring machine. The tunnel was not quite big enough to stand in; it required him to crouch slightly if he didn't want to keep on banging his head on the rough concrete ceiling. Bolted into the smooth concrete floor, two parallel steel tracks disappeared into the distance. Right in front of the platform stood a modified coco-pan, the entire top removed and replaced with a flat deck, not much more than 30 centimetres above floor level. Keller was more than suitably impressed, as were Biedermann and Stegemann. If the tunnel out of the Gaza Strip was the same, then this was going to be a walk in the park.

Rafah, Egypt – Colonel Max Preston

Colonel Max Preston and his men eventually arrived in Rafah some ten hours later than planned. The idea had been to get there well before the Meinhof Kollaboration, which, had the latest maps of the area he'd acquired at great expense been accurate, would have been more than possible. However, the maps weren't - what they failed to show was a great trench that had been cut through the desert for a pipeline. There was no way the two trucks they were driving could get through, and, after driving for two hours to find a crossing point, without success, they decided to fill in the trench and build their own crossing. That exercise had taken a further four hours, plus an hour to manoeuvre the vehicles - completely stripped of everything they could to reduce weight - across the soft, man-made crossing. They too knew exactly where the cement block factory was and made their way there as quickly as they could. What Preston did not know either was that Delgardo had failed to mention to the *Al Qassam* Brigade, now attached to the Meinhof Kollaboration, of the presence of Preston and his men and what their purpose was. That omission was to cause untold complications in the life of Colonel Max Preston in the hours ahead.

Rafah, Egypt – Michael Grey

It was by sheer coincidence that Michael Grey and his team, accompanied by Adofo, the Iranian, arrived in Rafah minutes before the Meinhof Kollaboration. Their particular destination however was a small house, one of 30 or so clustered around an intersection close to the border with Israel. They all looked the same; the only difference between the house Grey and his team arrived at and the others being a large basement, accessible via a staircase hidden behind a large wooden cupboard in the small living-room of the home. To get to the staircase one had to open the cupboard doors, step into the interior and swing open the backing panel. The permanent residents of the house were an old couple, both well into their 80s; ardent supporters of Hamas and all things anti-Israel. Their only son, who had joined Hamas and one of the *Al-Qassam* Brigades, had been killed by Israeli gunfire during the IDF ground operations in the Gaza Strip in July 2014. When the commander of the Brigade their son had been attached to met them at their home to express his condolences, they offered their dwelling to him should his Brigade ever need it. And so it happened.

Three months later the basement had been dug and this

particular *Al-Qassam* Brigade had a safe house on the Egyptian side of the Gaza Strip border. It was also the Brigade the Iranians had chosen to support. Unbeknown to the fighters in the Brigade and to Hamas, their Commander was actually an Iranian deep-cover operator, infiltrated years earlier into the Gaza Strip. In as much as Hamas thought it had some form of control over the Brigade in question, it was the Iranians who had full control. Nor did it escape the Hamas leadership that this particular Brigade was by far the most professional and successful of all the *Al-Qassam* Brigades. The Commander of the Brigade, using the first name of one of the all-time heroes of the Palestinians, was simply known as Commander Yasser.

Commander Yasser, at the age of 35, had seen more mayhem and violence in his rather short life than most men. Initially trained in Iran, he had taken over command of his Brigade seven years earlier, and had personally been in charge of infiltrating more than eighty-seven terrorists into Israel through two tunnels his Brigade had built and operated. One had since been destroyed by the Israelis in a raid. The other had survived, albeit with severe damage. In as much as Yasser hated the Zionists and what they stood for, he had a grudging respect for the IDF. Had any of the countries surrounding the Zionist state - Jordan, Syria, Lebanon or Egypt - been able to produce an armed force even remotely as capable as the IDF, the Zionists would have been thrown into the sea long ago. But they hadn't, and, until they did, the largely futile battles with the Zionists would continue. Yet nuking the Zionists? He had been quietly told about what was intended to happen by his superiors in Iran, that a Michael Grey and some of his men would be making contact and that it was his task to ensure that the plan failed. Yasser shuddered, knowing full well what the consequences of such an action would be, the death of a larger part of his home nation as well as the death, if not complete annihilation, of the Palestinians, never mind the Zionists. This Michael Grey, whoever he was, would need his help.

Three rapid knocks on the wooden door of the cupboard at the top of the staircase bought him back to reality. He stood up as the back panel of the cupboard slid open and four men descended the stairs, three of them European. They grouped up in front of him and one man stepped forward, holding out his hand. Yasser studied him intently. Somewhere between 40 and 50, he mused, definitely a fighting man. There was steel in the man's eyes, something he hadn't seen in anyone's eyes for years. He took the offered hand, noting the physical strength of the man as it squeezed shut over his. Here was a man you didn't want as an enemy.

"Mr Grey. Welcome. I am Commander Yasser."

Grey too studied the man in front of him and knew immediately that this was not simply another misguided fanatic leading an equally misguided bunch of fanatical, brave, yet incredibly emotional and stupid men. No, Yasser was of a different mould.

"Thanks, Commander." He gestured behind him. "I'd like to introduce you to my men, Jaco van Rensburgh and Gert van Tonder."

"Three men, Mr Grey? A bit ambitious considering what you have in mind, not so?"

"I take it from your remark that you've been briefed?"

"Yes," replied, "I have."

"Then you must have been told what happened 36 hours ago?"

"No, I was only told you would be arriving here and about the nuclear device. What happened?"

A few minutes later Grey had given him the full story and Yasser frowned. "So, what was up until 36 hours ago a rather routine mission went completely wrong in the space of minutes and cost seven Zionist agents their lives?"

"It did," retorted Grey. "And I blame myself for what happened. Don't get me wrong, Commander, as I told your superiors in Iran, I'm neither a Jew nor an Israeli, and my opinion on who's right or wrong in this part of the world is of no significance. But I do have a severe aversion to the use of nuclear devices, even more so considering the possible consequences. Thing is, I don't have a real plan up my sleeve. What I do know is that the device needs to be smuggled into Israel, and the likelihood of the Gaza Strip being used as a transit point is, in my opinion, a given. I assume you have eyes and ears on the ground that could assist?"

"Yes, I do. What do you propose?"

"Spread your people out as wide as possible in Rafah and the surrounding area. The minute they come across anything even remotely suspicious, they get hold of us and we move ..."

He was interrupted by shouting, all of it Arabic, coming from the ground floor of the building, where six of Yasser's men were standing guard. Yasser held up his hand, stopping Grey in mid sentence, listening. Seconds later he was bolting up the stairway, shouting at Grey as he went.

"Grey! The trunk on the far side of the room; there're weapons in there! Arm yourselves! Then get up here - we've got shit going down!"

Grey, van Rensburgh and van Tonder didn't hesitate. Moments later they too ran up the staircase, each with an AK-47, a couple of full magazines and a few grenades stuffed into their pockets. Four of the Brigade fighters were positioned around the ground floor, one of them jerking his thumb at the top floor of the dwelling when he saw Grey. Ten seconds later Grey and his men had joined Yasser on the top floor.

"What's happening?" demanded Grey, leopard-crawling across the floor towards Yasser, who was crouching at the window.

"There's shooting going on about 200 metres away from here." Yasser pointed towards a few buildings not far from them. "Somewhere behind there." Grey could hear the staccato sound of rifles being fired.

Grey crawled closer to get a better look. "Israelis?"

"No." Yasser listened intently. "They use mainly M-16s, they sound different. This is AK-47 fire. It doesn't make sense! Who the hell's fighting who?"

Grey crawled to side of the window, sat up with his back against the wall and looked across at Yasser. "You know what? I think we might just have located the Meinhof Kollaboration."

"You said there're three of them? What I'm hearing sounds like a lot more shooters than that."

"Don't ask me to explain, 'cause I can't, but I reckon the shooting's between whoever's with the Meinhof Kollaboration and the guys who blew us off the road. We need to get there. Like yesterday!"

"Then let's move out." Yasser scrambled away from the window, shouting commands in Arabic. Crouching low, Grey, van Rensburgh and van Tonder left the building, following the scuttling fighters of Yasser's Brigade. Ahead of them the sound of gunfire was getting louder. As he ran after Yasser, van Rensburgh and van Tonder close behind him, it occurred to Grey that the Israelis would very soon decide to have a real close look at what was happening. The Israelis however were two steps ahead of him. Alerted by an informer, who had contacted his controller, the news of the activity had immediately been passed on to the IDF. The rapid response was consistent with the usual way of IDF operations. Within seconds of being informed, the controller of an Eitan drone flying high above the southern Gaza Strip re-routed the unmanned aerial vehicle, and a further two minutes later the Israelis had an exact view of what was happening.

Rafah, Egypt – The Cement Block Factory

Colonel Max Preston, on the other hand, was wondering what on earth he had gotten himself and his men into. He was being paid to protect the Meinhof Kollaboration without interfering – unless there was a deviation from the plan - and he was doing just that. He and his nine men, split into two teams of five, the one team led by Lieutenant Simon Groves, the other by him, had slowly approached the factory. Groves had cautiously driven in through the main gate as Preston made his way to the far side of the factory perimeter. Preston's mission directive had always been to make sure the Meinhof Kollaboration got to Rafah unhindered and only once there to expose himself to Keller. After that he was to assist directly, providing cover for the Meinhof Kollaboration as they moved through the Gaza Strip until they entered Israel, at which point he and his men would disengage and head for home. Part of the deal should have been that the *Al-Qassam* Brigade knew of their presence.

But they didn't know, did they? As far as failure to communicate went, that failure ranked as epic. Delgardo, out to avoid any possibility of a protracted argument with Ahmad Shabaan, who would in all likelihood have refused the help of Preston and his men, had planned to tell him about Preston and the role he played at the last minute. But his capture by van Rensburgh and van Tonder had made that impossible. As a result the Brigade detachment led by Farouk had no idea who Preston and his men were, nor what they wanted.

As Lieutenant Simon Groves and the other four men in his team climbed out of the truck, not expecting any hostilities, they were being watched by nine of Farouk's fighters, who were concealed around the factory yard. Noting the men climb out of the truck, the gear they were wearing, the arms displayed and the fact that they were definitely not Arab in origin, one of the fighters came to the logical conclusion that a group of Israeli commandos had stumbled across them. He didn't hesitate. Shouting *"Allahu Akbar"* at the top of his voice, he opened fire, spraying bullets at the perceived enemy. The other eight fighters, all of whom had come to the same conclusion, immediately joined in. Groves and his men didn't stand a chance, being literally ripped apart by the deadly fire. Preston, who had pulled up in his truck on the far side of the perimeter, gaped in stunned shock. Seconds later he and his men were out of their own truck, scrambling for whatever cover they could find. They too carried AK-47s and, moments later, commenced returning fire. Ten seconds later three of the nine Brigade fighters had gone down and the remaining six regrouped, slowly retreating to the factory building as they traded shots. Preston, with half his men dead, needed to find better cover, and he his remaining men began moving forward. It took the better part of five minutes to get into a safe position, his highly-trained men knowing exactly what to do. In the meantime, the last of the six remaining Brigade fighters was sprinting for the factory entrance, the other five already inside, firing at their adversaries through windows they had smashed the glass out of. Two metres from the open door the running figure was cut down by yet another burst from Preston's AK-47, the sickening meaty "thwack" sound of bullets punching into the man's back, legs and arms audible above the din, the last round penetrating and exploding the skull, spraying brains and gore onto the walls near the factory door.

By then Commander Yasser, Michael Grey and the men with them had closed in on the scene, just in time to see Preston and his men move towards the factory entrance. Taking cover, Grey, next to Yasser, and the others scattered around them, they watched as one of the men crumpled in a heap as a bullet hit him in the chest. Ten bodies lay scattered around the factory yard, five of them in close proximity to the truck Groves had arrived in. It was then that Grey got a clear view of one of the running men.

"Yasser! It's him!"

"Who's him?!"

"The man who just ran across the yard? He's the guy who shot the rocket at us from the chopper!"

Yasser squirmed forward, closer to Grey. "You see who they're fighting against? The bodies dressed in black with the balaclavas? It's an *Al-Qassam* Brigade!"

"Shit. What now?"

"We take them out. The Brigade fighters as well if we have to. Not much else we can do." He slid back down the slope of the dirt mound. "You ready to move?"

"Give me a second." Grey crawled to his left to where he had a direct view of van Rensburgh and van Tonder. Using hand signals from their days in the South African Defence Force, he motioned at his two colleagues. Yasser watched as the affirmative signal came back, impressed.

"Not the first time you're doing this kind of thing, is it? One day you need to tell me who the hell you are."

"Maybe." Grey grinned. "Yasser. I need that man alive. Can you get that across to your men?"

"Yes." Grey watched as he signalled one of his own men, four fingers up, followed by a cutting motion across the throat, then pointing at Preston and raising his thumb. Grey observed as the same signal went down the line of men and they moved forward, Yasser to his right and van Rensburgh, together with van Tonder, immediately to his left.

Up ahead of them Colonel Max Preston was seething with rage. Five of his men were dead and now he was facing the single biggest cock-up he had ever found himself in. Why the hell they'd been attacked escaped him completely; it shouldn't have happened! There wasn't much point in continuing the counter-attack; he knew they were outnumbered. Their mission was well and truly botched. The only thing left was to get the hell out of there and head for home before more damage was incurred. Anyway, they'd been paid in advance, and unnecessarily risking the lives of his remaining men, as well as his own, was something he no longer considered as worth it. The gun-fire from the factory had begun to diminish and he gave the signal to his men to start pulling back. He didn't realise that retreating would expose him and his men to far greater danger than an advance into the factory building would ever have.

As Preston gave the order to retreat to what he presumed would be safety, Yasser, Grey and their armed force had moved forward and were now in firing range. Effectively caught from behind, Preston and his remaining men were sitting ducks. When the expired Lieutenant Simon Groves had mentioned to Preston - after landing the choppers in the desert – that blowing the Israelis off the road outside Ismailia had been a bit of a turkey-shoot, what happened next was more like a lame turkey-shoot. Outnumbered three to one, they didn't stand a chance. Preston watched as, in the space of two seconds, his remaining men were mowed down. Preston, who'd been convinced that nobody had survived the ambush outside Ismailia, stared in horror as he recognised the man who'd been so clearly visible in the passenger seat of the Audi. It couldn't be! His mind went into a state of paralysis; he didn't feel the bullet that shattered his right knee. He fell sideways, watching in complete disbelief as another European closed in and swung the butt of his rifle at him. Then it went dark.

Rafah, Egypt – Tunnel 1

At the bottom of the shaft leading into the tunnel, Keller, Biedermann, Stegemann and Farouk heard the sound of muffled gunfire the moment it started. Not sure what was going on above them, Keller, fearing the worst, jumped onto the platform of the lift and hit the start button for the winches. Before Farouk and the others had time to react, he was already two metres up the shaft.

"What the hell?!" Farouk watched as the platform moved up into the dark shaft. "Keller! What are you doing?"

From above came the muffled, receding response. "The bomb! I have to get the bomb!"

When Keller arrived at the surface, he found the five Brigade fighters positioned behind the support pillars that held up the factory roof, weapons facing the factory entrance on the far side of the large hall. Keller shouted at them in English hoping they'd understand. One of them did.

"The bomb!" screamed Keller. "Push it onto the platform! Now!"

The Brigade fighter, with the little English he understood and spoke, shouted at his colleagues. Two of them sprinted across to the trolley. Together with Keller they pushed it onto the platform, then returned to their defensive positions. Keller, not knowing whether to leave them there or not, shouted and gesticulated with his arm at the platform, pointing downwards, wanting the men to join him.

"Come!" he yelled. "Quickly! There is no time!" Outside in the factory yard the intensity of the shooting had increased, one or two bullets whizzing into the factory hall through shattered windows.

"No!" came the shout in broken English. "You go! Now! We stay! We fight! Is okay! We go back different way!"

Keller didn't require a second invitation to leave and pressed the button. Once more the winch motors hummed and the platform with Keller and the nuclear device dropped away into the darkness. He arrived at the bottom, stepped off the platform and faced Farouk.

"Listen, Farouk. We've got to get the bomb across. Now!"

Farouk jumped onto the platform and looked back up the shaft. "My men! Why did you leave them?"

"Because they didn't want to come, that's why! Farouk," Keller stepped back onto the platform as well, "I have no fucking idea what's happening up there, but I can tell there's a hell of a lot of shooting outside. Someone's attacking us, God only knows who. I told your men to come down with me but they refused, said they'd stay to fight and go back via a different route."

"But who's attacking us? The Israelis? It can't be!"

"Doesn't matter, Farouk." Keller felt the adrenaline surge through his system. He patted the cold steel shell of the device. "Let's get this thing onto the rail trolley."

They manhandled the heavy device onto the low flatbed rail trolley, nearly dropping it in the process. Pushed by Keller, Stegemann and Biedermann, the wheels rumbled ever so slightly as the trolley moved off into the sporadically lit up tunnel. They had moved less than 20 metres when the insanely loud crack of a single shot resonated, the noise amplified by the close confines of the tunnel. Behind them, still at the start of the tunnel, Farouk was busy hefting his AK-47 across his shoulders.

"What the hell was that for?" Keller, who had had dived for cover as the shot went off, slowly got up.

Farouk grinned as he passed the three, pushing his way past the trolley to the front of the column. "Shot out the power button to the winches. Those circuits are spaghetti now. The platform's stuck ten metres up the shaft. If anyone decides to follow they'll have to abseil down the shaft, never mind getting past the platform. If they do get down, we'll let them into the tunnel."

"What?" asked Stegemann. "Are you mad?"

"No." This time Farouk's voice was cold as ice. "See here?" He pointed at an oblong block mounted next to the first light, the lights spaced at intervals of 50 metres down the entire length of the tunnel. "C4 explosive. All connected. Once we get to the other side we'll blow the tunnel up. If anyone does get down the shaft and past the platform, they'll be in the tunnel when we blow it up. Happy?" Without waiting for a response he turned and started walking down the tunnel, crouching slightly. "Let's go. We're running out of time."

Rafah, Egypt – The Cement Block Factory

The remaining ten fighters of Farouk's detachment of Commander Ahmad Shabaan's Brigade stared at each other in sheer bewilderment. They were about to move out after the retreating attackers when, out of nowhere, a sustained barrage of gunfire erupted. Someone out there was firing at the same group of men they had been fighting for the past ten minutes. They grouped up, one of the fighters, the most senior of them, taking over the leadership. It didn't take him long to convince his nine comrades that the best course of action - now that their foes were being wiped out by someone else, only God knew who - would be to get back into the Gaza Strip. Perhaps the men they'd been fighting hadn't been Israelis after all and now real Israeli commandos had become involved? It was all a little too confusing and too fraught with danger. The decision was made, and, one by one, the ten remaining fighters left via the far side of the building, well away from where the fighting was taking place. Within minutes they were all gone, making their way to a different tunnel some three kilometres away. At the same time Yasser, Grey and their men left the scene of the fighting in the opposite direction, heading back to the safe house.

Michael Grey, with Yasser and van Tonder standing next to him, watched as van Rensburgh dumped the blindfolded, bound and still unconscious Preston onto the floor of the basement.

"What do we do with him?" Yasser lit a cigarette and inhaled deeply. "Get rid of him? We definitely can't take him with us."

Grey sat on his haunches studying the man who had nearly killed him. "No, I have a better idea. Yasser, you've got to trust me on this one." He reached for the encrypted cell phone in his top pocket. "I'm going to call the Israelis. We're handing him over."

Yasser froze. Next thing he reached for his side-arm, yanked it out of the holster and levelled it at Grey's head. A split second later van Rensburgh and van Tonder had their rifles up and aimed at Yasser's head; the other six Brigade fighters in the room aiming their rifles at van Rensburgh and van Tonder. "Give me the phone. Now! If that thing is switched on, you're dead!"

To Grey it was almost like a surreal comedy show, everyone aiming their weapons at someone else. As tense as it was, Grey could not help himself. He dropped onto the floor, sat against the wall and burst out laughing. Yasser, totally confused by Grey's reaction, glanced at van Rensburgh and van Tonder, who in turn stared at Grey, wondering if he'd gone mad.

"Jesus, Yasser," Grey was still laughing, "you wanna shoot me? You know what, go ahead! This is such a fucking circus I would leave this world a happy man just to get away from it all." He got up slowly. "Do me a favour and stick the bloody gun away, will you? We come here, get involved in a fire-fight at your side and now you think I'm gonna screw you and your men over? Get real, man, the phone isn't switched on. You really think I'm that stupid? Here." He handed the phone to Yasser. "See for yourself."

Yasser slowly lowered his side-arm and took the phone. It was off. "And who says the minute you switch it on the Zionists won't be able to pinpoint the exact position of the phone? Maybe wipe all of us out with a quick air strike?"

"Because the damned thing's encrypted, the GPS location finder is deactivated, and the Israelis need us alive, not bloody dead! Do you really think I'd let the Israelis or anyone else track our movements after what I promised your Ayatollah?"

"How the hell would I know?

"Give me some credit, will you? I promised I wouldn't expose anything to the Israelis unless there was no other viable alternative. That's not the case here, is it? Now, do you mind if I make the call? We haven't got much time to waste."

Yasser paused for a brief moment, thinking. "Okay." He handed the phone back to Grey. "Go ahead. One condition. I listen to what you tell them."

Grey shrugged. "I can live with that."

"Then make the call. I hope for the sake of you and your friends that I can trust you, Grey."

"Don't worry, Yasser," said Grey, looking Yasser straight in the eyes. "Tell me, you're a professional, aren't you?"

"Yes," Yasser frowned, "I like to think I am. Why?"

"So am I, Commander Yasser. In my world professionals keep their word. I don't know about yours."

Hatzerim Airbase, Israel

Abel Sharon arrived at the Hatzerim Airbase not far from Beersheba in the early morning hours, flown there by a military helicopter. Upon his arrival he took over the office of the senior military intelligence officer. Now he was sitting at the desk watching live coverage from the Eitan drone. Although he couldn't identify faces, he knew that somewhere down there Grey and his men were involved in some serious fighting. By the time the Egyptian police and the military arrived on the scene it was all over except for the bodies lying about in the cement block factory yard. He continued watching - the camera of the high-flying drone capturing the scene in startling clarity - as a number of Egyptian policemen, together with a few soldiers (he counted in total 11 men) - entered the factory building and disappeared from view. Suddenly, and without warning, he saw a few of the corrugated iron roof sheets blow upward and off the roof, followed by a cloud of dust rising rapidly into the air through the destroyed roof section. Six of the Egyptians stumbled back out of the factory, one of them collapsing a few metres away from the entrance. Of the others who had entered the building there was no sign. Farouk, with the Meinhof Kollaboration and the bomb safely on the other side of the tunnel, had activated the destruct mechanism. As Sharon, the Eitan drone capturing perfect images but no sound, watched the silent carnage in morbid fascination, his telephone rang. It took him a split second to realise who was calling.

"Mike! Where are you?! You okay?"

"Fine, Abel. Listen, I can't talk for long. Looks like the bomb, together with Keller and friends has made its way into the Gaza Strip. Went in via a cement block factory in Rafah, on the

Egyptian side. Must have had a tunnel starting there. I'll see if I can get there to check it out."

"Don't bother," came Sharon's response. "I've been watching your factory for the past minutes. There're dead bodies all over the place and someone just went and blew something up; a pretty big explosion as well. I guess whoever it was destroyed the tunnel. Place is crawling with Egyptian military and police so I suggest you stay away. What else?"

"The men who shot us off the road in Ismailia and killed your men? We got them. We've got their leader with us; he's unconscious with a gunshot wound. The rest are dead. I want you to come and get him."

"Fuck! You for real?"

"As real as it gets. We'll drop him off a few hundred metres away from the eastern end of the Israel-Gaza Strip border. You won't miss him; he'll be sitting in the middle of the road. Send a chopper, quick in and out and you've got the man. He'll be there all tied up within the next 20 minutes."

Sharon glanced across at the intelligence officer standing next to him, cupped his hand over the handset of the phone and gave a brief order. As the officer rushed out of the room, Sharon continued his conversation with Grey. "Okay, choppers on the way, I'll have the drone flown across to keep an eye on the place. Can't tell you how happy I am to be able to get my hands on that murderous bastard!" The scenery on the large screen in front of him began to change rapidly as the drone started moving position. "What about the bomb?"

"Leave it to me and my newfound friends," replied Grey. "What I suggest you do from your side is stick another couple of drones up there and monitor the entire Gaza Strip border 24/7. The bomb's gone in by tunnel; it'll leave by tunnel. I reckon the entrance to whatever tunnel they'll use next is nicely hidden away so it'll be difficult to find. The exit's a different matter. It'll have to come up somewhere in open territory, there's no other way. Also, it'll have to be within five kilometres of Israeli territory. Just wish I knew the final destination."

"For once we're ahead of you," muttered Sharon. "We got Delgardo to talk. The target area, of all places, is out at Sdot Micha."

"Sdot Micha? Where's that? And what's so important about it?"

"Oh, nothing much, except that Sdot Micha is where we've based all our ICBMs."

"God Almighty!"

"You can say that again. Then again, we've got the place sealed off so tightly there's no way they'll get close, never mind getting in. So maybe we let them come and take them out when they get close enough."

"Are you telling me you want me to hold back?" asked Grey.

"Hell no! But assume you fail. What then? Even if we sent troops into the Strip now, it's far too late. So, over the past 24 hours we've shifted the entire 7th and 188th Brigades to Sdot Micha and the surrounding area. Every road, dirt track and whatever else in a ten kilometre radius around Sdot Micha is blocked off. Then we've moved in a further two infantry brigades and declared a 24-hour around-the-clock curfew for all civilians. If anyone moves within the circle who happens to be non-military, police or secret service, they'll be considered hostile. Anything and anyone approaching the circle from outside will be stopped and interrogated."

"Damn. The place must be crawling. One thing you might want to consider."

"What's that?"

"Get Billy McLaughlin into Israel. I get the feeling that Keller will blow the thing either way. If he sees he can't get it close enough he'll probably set it off anyway. If he does, my guess is it that it'll still give the three enough time to get away. Somehow I don't think suicide is part of their plan. I reckon that arming the device will involve some sort of timer software, in which case I'd like Billy to be around in case you find it and need to disarm it, assuming Keller and Co. have managed to gap it and are no longer around. Not that I'm saying your men can't do it, it's just that Billy is extremely good at what he does."

"Consider it done; we'll have him here as quickly as we can. And you?"

"I carry on from this side. We'll catch the bastards, Abel. I promise."

"Oh, one last thing."

"Yes?"

"We don't have a leak. Delgardo confirmed it."

Portsmouth, Virginia, USA

Marty Trump walked into his luxury condo within spitting distance of Little Creek Cove, tossed his hold-all onto the floor at the bottom of the staircase leading up to the master bedroom and made his way to the kitchen. The last few days had been stressful, more so than usual. Not only had he encountered an unexpected problem in the negotiation process for a large Navy contract, the entire exercise he and his colleagues of The Patriots had embarked on was beginning to gnaw at his conscience. Then, to top it all, the one man he had been closest to in the group, Gary Simms, had inexplicably died in a car wreck. According to the police it had been due to driver error. Driver error? With a highly trained, professional chauffeur at the wheel?

Trump trembled slightly, opened the door to the fridge and took out a bottle of chilled white wine. He was beginning to regret the day he had gotten involved with The Patriots. What had seemed like such a good idea at the time was now turning into something which he felt he no longer had control over. And then there was Brent Delgardo. He'd never really liked the man, who was proving to be a real megalomaniac. And now he too had vanished into thin air. He sighed as he uncorked the bottle, absentmindedly watching as the pale liquid poured into his wine glass.

Trump closed the fridge, took the open bottle and the glass and made his way to the lounge. He switched on the large, flat-screen television and selected the Bloomberg Channel. As the commentator carried on his discourse about recent hikes in interest rates by the Federal Reserve, he sat down, kicked off his shoes and took his first long sip of wine, then another, emptying the glass. He was about to reach for the bottle for a refill when he felt something he had never experienced before. Somehow, it was as though his heart had skipped a beat. He frowned. There! It was happening again! And again! By the time he realised there was something very wrong it was far too late. His last conscious act was to let go of the empty glass he was holding when his heart gave its last beat. He slipped into unconsciousness and the life hereafter in one smooth slide.

Five minutes later the front door opened silently, and a middle-aged man stepped into the condo. He walked past the prone body of Trump, lying back in the chair, and removed a small electronic listening device from behind a picture frame that had been planted there earlier that day. It had been necessary; after all, he hadn't wanted to enter the condo while Trump was still alive. He took the opened wine bottle and replaced it with an identical bottle, making sure the level of liquid was the same. Last, but not least, he took the wine glass and replaced it with a different, clean glass. Before he left, he poured enough wine into the glass out of the replacement bottle to be able to swirl the liquid to wet the inside walls. A minute later he left the condo, pulled off his latex gloves and walked away. Marty Trump was as dead as a doornail;

the body only found two days later. The autopsy report would reveal that he had died of a massive heart attack. What was not discovered were during the autopsy were traces of the chemical that had been injected into the original wine bottle through the top of the cork with a long-needled syringe. Those had long since dissipated. The leadership of The Patriots was down to two men.

Sdot Micha, Israel

Lieutenant Ben Sachs stretched, surveyed the scene around him and zipped his army issue winter coat to the top. It was late evening, the sun was going down and the cold was beginning to become noticeable. Other than that it had been an uneventful day, one of many such days he had endured in the past year. Behind him, grouped together and covered by camouflage netting, were the four Merkava Mark IV main battle tanks of his small troop. His own tank, the command vehicle, was no different to the others except for the assortment of antennae protruding from the top of the flat turret. Scattered around him, some sleeping, others playing cards, and others – the more religious of them – busy with their evening prayers, were his fellow tank-men of the Israeli Defence Force.

Fighting in tanks, driving and living with these steel monsters, might have been the dream of many young boys, but he knew all too well that it was anything but fun. Exhilarating yes; fun? Definitely not, not unless one considered a hot, cramped, oily and noisy environment a fun place to be. He would never forget the day when, while active in the Gaza Strip, an anti-tank rocket fired by an *Al-Qassam* Brigade fighter had somehow managed to penetrate the armour of the tank of one of his comrades and the vehicle had caught fire. All the crew bar one, the commander, had managed to bail out of the stricken vehicle. The commander had not been so lucky, his lower legs burnt so badly that they had to amputate the charred stumps. He had nearly died of the shock. Sachs sometimes woke up at night, the demented screams of the commander resonating in his head. He'd finally been airlifted out to a military hospital, but the experience was enough to stay with Sachs till the end of his days. Sure, maybe a lot of young girls looked at tank drivers with some sort of misplaced awe and admiration, but he knew better. The life of a tank crew was hard, uncomfortable, mostly boring, and supremely dangerous when in combat.

And now they had been moved to Sdot Misha; not only his small troop, no, their entire Brigade, as well as one additional complete Brigade. Plus infantry. There was more fire-power encircling Sdot Misha than anywhere else in Israel, so much so that even a field mouse would have had difficulty getting in and out of the place without the right papers. Ben Sachs knew exactly what was based at Sdot Misha, as did most Israelis, and the presence of so much armour in the place could only mean one thing – there had to be a very credible threat. He called his three tank commanders who ambled across and told them to remain extra vigilant.

Hours later, close to midnight, he received orders to move his troop of tanks to a place called Kibbutz Nir Oz, to be precise, a small historically ancient synagogue close by. It didn't surprise him – there were, after all, so many tanks surrounding Sdot Misha than even the most cautious and prudent of military planners would have had to agree it was complete overkill, and that some of the available resources could be better deployed elsewhere. Less than half an hour later four flat-bed trucks arrived to load the tanks for the transfer. A further four hours later the Merkava tanks rolled off the flat-bed trucks and took up their new positions in the middle of some shrub land, a few hundred metres away from the synagogue. Concealed once more, the tank crews commenced doing what they had become so good at doing. Watching and waiting.

Khirbat Ikhza'a, Gaza Strip

Grey, van Rensburgh, van Tonder and ten men of Yasser's *Al-Qassam* Brigade moved quietly down the dark side streets of Khirbat Ikhza'a. Grey could feel the exhaustion creeping up on him. At some point he knew he'd have to sleep for a few hours, as would his compatriots. First they'd been involved in the fighting and subsequent capture of Max Preston - successfully extracted from the Egyptian side of the border to the Gaza Strip by seven Israeli commandos, who had flown in and out by chopper before the Egyptians had had time to react. Then the entry into Gaza via a tunnel Grey would not have sent his worst enemy into, a dark, dank affair with minimal lighting, definitely not designed for someone of Grey's height. It was neatly summed up by van Rensburgh with his usual aplomb – "If God had decided to make me a mole I'd have avoided this fucking place like the plague!". Then the trip through Gaza from Rafah to Khirbat Ikhza'a. Yasser had by then been in touch with his Iranian controller and explained the situation. That had sparked off all sorts of activity, including the hasty arranging of transport for Grey and his men in an enclosed truck; travelling in Gaza as a non-Arab was something to be avoided at all costs. The Iranians had also managed to confirm who commanded the *Al-Qassam* Brigade associated with the Meinhof Kollaboration. It was not good news.

"It's Ahmad Shabaan," stated Yasser, as though he was talking about the local carpenter, "a really dangerous bastard."

"Oh?" asked Grey. "Why's that? I thought you all worked together?"

"Yes and no. You need to understand how this thing works. You ever heard of plausible deniability?"

"Yes, why?"

"Well," continued Yasser, "it's like this. The Hamas leadership doesn't really control the *Al-Qassam* Brigades. Sure, it may appear that way, since we are, after all, the Hamas military wing. But each Brigade commander can essentially do what he likes, which is why enforcing a ceasefire when the Israelis hit us is so difficult. You see, we don't have to listen and some of us don't. Shabaan's one of those who thinks the Hamas leadership is too soft, and it's usually him and his men who cock it all up."

"Why doesn't Hamas tell them to tow the line?" demanded Grey.

"They don't want to. Makes them look good, you see. Like – "we told them but we can't force them". So Hamas ends up looking morally good no matter what happens. Clever, and a load of crap at the same time."

"I get you. So what about Shabaan? You know where he is?"

"Sure do. Except, like I said, he doesn't listen. Thinks he's some kind of a military genius."

"And?"

"I've been told by Iran to stop Shabaan. We know where he is. Also, and I haven't told you this until now because I wasn't permitted to, we knew about the two tunnels a while ago. Our roots are, after all, pretty deep here."

"You knew all along?!" Grey exploded. "And you're only telling me now? Why the hell not earlier? You know how much time we've wasted?!!"

"Relax, Grey! We haven't wasted any time. There's been a purpose behind our movements ever since we came into the Gaza Strip through our tunnel. Listen, Shabaan's not far ahead of us. I simply couldn't tell you, you needed to prove you could be trusted first."

"Fucking marvellous! There's a rogue nuke out there, I nearly get myself killed, and now I need to prove I can be trusted! Anything else?"

"Calm down, will you? You'd have done the same if you were in my position! We're not playing a game here! People die if we're not careful, and you know it!"

"You're right, Yasser," conceded Grey, "I'm sorry. I would have done the same. This isn't easy on me, especially after what happened outside Ismailia. I should have stopped all of this when we had the chance in Cairo. I waited, Yasser, and it cost seven men their lives. Now it may cost a couple of million their lives as well. It's really starting to stress me out..."

"I'm not surprised," said Yasser. "I've lost more than enough men, and every time it happens I blame myself. But that's our profession, Grey. We're soldiers, remember? We deal with conflict. People will die in the process, sometimes men we command. Neither you or I will change that. We either accept it, or we get out. But we can't get out, can we?"

For a while the two men sat there, silent. Yasser's words had been blunt, but it was the brutal truth, wasn't it? People died because of what the likes of Grey and Yasser did. Sometimes the good guys, sometimes the bad guys, and sometimes the innocent. Sure, they could get out and watch from the sidelines. But that wouldn't change anything, would it? No, thought Grey, Yasser was right. They were soldiers by profession, they commanded men, and death was a regrettable part of the job description.

"I suppose it takes a soldier to understand a soldier, Yasser," said Grey. "Back to reality. You think you know where this Shabaan and the Meinhof Kollaboration are heading?"

"Yes. It'll have to be the next tunnel. We've got a pretty good idea where it starts, that's if our informer wasn't lying. What we don't know is where the second tunnel surfaces. But it doesn't really matter. That bomb cannot explode, either here in Gaza or in Israel. The consequences are too severe. Yet it poses a problem I am not sure how best to handle."

"Let me guess," retorted Grey. "One *Al-Qassam* Brigade fighting another. Not exactly the kind of thing Hamas would want, is it?"

"Well concluded, Grey. It would cause more of a problem than you may be aware of; certainly, it will create a major rift in an organisation that is a touch disjointed as it is. And, as you will be aware, it is not something Iran views as conducive to the greater cause."

It was van Rensburgh who came up with a solution to the predicament. He was sitting on the floor in the room of the house they had temporarily occupied, cleaning his AK-47.

"Why don't you blackball the bastard?"

Grey and Yasser looked at each other, then at van Rensburgh. "What?"

"I've been listening to what you've been saying. If this Shabaan character's the right royal twat you say he is, why not blackball the bastard?"

Yasser leaned forward, "Explain."

"Well, you've got the means to communicate with the Hamas

leadership, right?"

"Obviously."

"Then tell them Shabaan's been cooperating with an outside force, a force hell-bent on making Hamas look like they've lost control and that you've got proof."

"And how," asked Yasser, "would you go about this?"

"Easy. Tell Hamas the Israelis are about to air-drop a present they'll be very interested in. Then Mike lets the Israelis know where the drop needs to take place and bingo! Preston ends up in the hands of Hamas for a quiet chat. Knowing Preston, he'll talk, simply to save himself. At which point Hamas will know that Shabaan's been taking things a bit far. If Hamas doesn't give you the go-ahead to remove Shabaan's Brigade after that, I don't know what will."

"But what if Preston doesn't know about the bomb?"

"I think he does. If by any chance not, we can always make sure by getting the Israelis to stick a note in his pocket explaining what this is all about. You think Hamas would want to be associated with a nuclear device detonating in Israel? Even they're not that mad! There'll be so much shit raining down on them they won't know which way to turn. If you ask me, it'll mean their demise. They'll want this thing stopped even more desperately than Iran and Israel combined."

Yasser stared at van Rensburgh, then turned to face Grey. "You know what? He's got a point. You think the Israelis will do it?"

"It's worth a try." Grey watched van Rensburgh get up off the floor, stretch and scratch his armpit. "Anyone ever told you that you're quite a devious bastard?"

"Yeah," piped up van Tonder, who'd been sitting next to van Rensburgh, "his ex-wife did."

An hour later a Lockheed C130 military transport aircraft took off from Hatzerim Airbase, climbed as fast it could to a height of 5000 metres, then headed out towards Gaza City. Four minutes away from the border between Israel and the Gaza Strip, the loadmaster opened the back cargo-door of the lumbering aircraft. Colonel Max Preston, strapped to a mountain rescue stretcher, the stretcher, in turn, strapped to a padded pallet, didn't say anything – he was too sedated. As the aircraft crossed the border, the narrow strip of open terrain visible far below them, the loadmaster received the instruction from the pilot he had been waiting for and released the drag chutes from the back of the aircraft.

"Don't know what you did," he shouted as the pallet with Preston strapped to it slid out of the back of the aircraft, "but have a nice day! And welcome to the Gaza Strip!"

Far below, four Hamas operatives, field binoculars trained on the aircraft high above them, watched as the pallet left the aircraft. Twenty seconds later the main parachute opened, swinging gently in the wind. An hour later, with Preston revived and in the hands of Hamas, Yasser got the call he had been expecting. It was a simple, two-worded message.

"Destroy them!"

CHAPTER 10
ENDGAME

Khirbat Ikhza'a, Gaza Strip

The inhabitants of Khirbat Ikhza'a had long since settled down for the night by the time Yasser, Grey, van Rensburgh, van Tonder and the 20 men accompanying them neared the location of the entry point to the second tunnel. The village was not as congested as Grey had expected. Surrounded in the main by small farm plots and a scattering of greenhouses, the total population of Khirbat Ikhza'a couldn't have been much more than somewhere between 2000 and 3000 people. Yasser, who was leading them, stopped the group and called Grey to one side.

"There," he whispered, pointing at a greenhouse complex less than half a kilometre ahead. "That's where the tunnel starts, from what we know, it's in the third greenhouse from the right."

"Clever bastards," muttered Grey. "I suppose that's how they hid the earth they dug out of the tunnel, stashed it away in all the other greenhouses, right?"

"Yeah." He signalled to his 2IC, van Rensburgh and van Tonder to come closer. They scuttled across and the five men huddled down. "Okay," he said quietly, "here's what we do. Grey, you and your men head off to the right. From here on in you're on your own. You've got a 15-minute head start." He checked his watch, the luminous dial glowing in the dark. "At precisely 22:50 my men and I will move in. Shabaan and his men will think it's an Israeli attack. That'll help us, the norm for *Al-Qassam* Brigades is to pull back when the Israelis attack, as their weapons and firepower are simply too superior, plus they usually have artillery support which is impossible for us to deal with. They definitely won't know it's another *Al-Qassam* Bridage they're up against. That'll give you the time to move in from the side facing the Israel border, that's the one direction Shabaan and his men won't flee in. Just do yourselves a favour. Keep your heads down, will you?"

"You got that right." He watched as van Rensburgh and van Tonder gave their weapons a final check. "Ready?" The two men nodded. "Go!" He watched as they ran across the road and vanished into the darkness. Before Grey followed his two friends, he turned one last time. "Yasser. We might have different ideas on a whole number of things, but it's been a real pleasure working with you. Thanks."

"Likewise, Grey. Now get going."

Jens Keller was sitting on a plastic garden chair, watching as four of Shabaan's men lowered the device into the shaft that dropped down towards the tunnel entrance. He still couldn't comprehend exactly how the hell they'd been found. Not that he was concerned about a bunch of dead people, it didn't bother him in the least. What did bother him was that whoever was after him was a clearly a tenacious and dangerous bastard. Sure, after the fiasco in Rafah nothing more had happened, they had gotten through the tunnel and moved the device on the back of a pick-up truck to their current location. But he knew that more was going to come, it couldn't be any other way. Even worse was that the likelihood of the Israelis knowing about it were odds even the most cautious of betting men would have put money on. They were bound to be on the lookout for them. But they wouldn't know where the target was, nor where the tunnel would surface, would they? Anne Biedermann, who had taken to mouthing a continuous stream of profanities in German for most of the day, swearing to kill the motherfucker who was after them, was catching a few minutes of sleep. Karl Stegemann, on the other hand, hadn't said much, rather keeping to himself, checking and re-checking his 9mm Parabellum. Shortly now they'd be on the move again, down the longest and deepest tunnel ever dug between the Gaza Strip and Israel. Once they entered Israel they'd be on their own, the last thing Shabaan's men would help with was the loading of the device into the back of a Ford Transit van that would hopefully be waiting for them on the other side. Then, twelve hours later, once they were well away from the scene, the device would detonate at Sdot Micha. Boom! At least that was the plan.

On the floor next to him was a bottle of illegal, potent, home-brewed Vodka someone had managed to organise. He reached down for the bottle, took a long swig and swallowed. He was about to close his eyes for half an hour – he hadn't slept for well over 24 hours - when Yasser's men moved in.

Commander Ahmad Shabaan's detachment consisted of 30 men, including himself. Together with Keller, Biedermann and Stegemann, they totalled 33, 10 more than Yasser and his men. But it made very little difference. Yasser's men were conveniently kitted out with night-vision goggles and could see everything in the darkness. Shabaan's men were not, and that swung the odds decidedly in Yasser's favour.

Less than 100 metres away to the right of the furthest greenhouse, Grey, van Rensburg and van Tonder, also wearing night-vision goggles, watched the attack unfold. Shabaan, knowing that the possibility of a further attack was pretty high, had positioned his men in a circle around the greenhouse. Four of his thirty fighters had been given the task of getting the nuclear device down the shaft to the tunnel entrance.

Yasser had planned the advance to perfection. The first of Shabaan's men to go were three perimeter guards who were quietly approached from behind whereupon their throats were slit. From then on, it became a fire-fight. Yasser had clearly been exposed to some serious military training; the way his men moved forward was not something a semi-amateur grouping of freedom-fighters would have been capable of. The fire and movement of Yasser's men was of a standard even the Israelis would have been proud of – Grey was definitely impressed.

The first salvo of rounds was fired in the space of two seconds; single shots, not the expected automatic fire that sounded so highly effective, yet more often than not did little else than chew up bullets, most of which missed the target anyway. Grey could see some of the muzzle-flashes and watched as three of Shabaan's men went down. Outside of his field of view another series of shots were fired in rapid succession and six more fighters of Sabaan's Brigade commenced their premature journey to the promised paradise and the waiting virgins.

Shabaan, the second he heard the first shots, sprang out of the chair he had been resting in, snatched up his AK-47 rifle and bolted for the greenhouse entrance, shouting a series of commands in Arabic. At the same time Keller, Biedermann and Stegemann, startled and suddenly wide awake, ran towards the shaft. The platform of the hoist, similar to the one in the cement factory and on the way back up after dropping off the device far below, was still a metre away from the top of the shaft. Keller didn't wait. He jumped, followed by the other two. The four men on the platform had also heard the muted shots and Shabaan's shouted commands. They froze, waiting for someone to do or say something. Keller, noting the paralysis of the four men, took charge. Seconds later the platform dropped away into the darkness of the shaft once more.

Shabaan, busy trying to find out who was shooting at them, watched in horror as one by one his Brigade fighters fell. The fools! They were firing on automatic, blindly, the protracted muzzle-flashes giving away their positions. Each long burst was followed by a single muzzle-flash from the darkness, and that was it; man down. On top of that his men on the far side of the protective circle he had set up, hearing the commotion, left their positions and made for the scene of the fighting, unfortunately for them with far more bravado than brains. Not only were they too firing blindly, they were also screaming the name of Allah as they approached. Only half of them got close, the others were cut down from the side by the fast-closing Grey, van Rensburgh and van Tonder, who had decided to join the fray. In less than a minute Shabaan's men had been reduced to less than half their original number.

By then it became clear to Shabaan's remaining men that they were fighting a losing battle. Not only could they not see their enemies, they figured out that what was facing them had to be a highly trained military force. Zionist Commandos! As if by unspoken command they began to flee the scene of the fighting. Dying in the process of killing Zionists they could see and ending up a martyr was one thing, but dying for no reason by trying to fight a battle they believed they could not win - against an enemy they could not see - was an entirely different matter! What really caused panic to set in was when Shabaan's screaming of commands was suddenly cut off in mid-sentence. One of the fighters closest to Shabaan saw him hit by four bullets, three in the chest and one in the head, close enough to hear the impact of the rounds. As Shabaan staggered and pitched forward, the fighter shouted at the others to run. The remaining fighters of Shabaan's *Al-Qassam* Brigade didn't need a second invitation. They dropped their weapons and ran, as fast and as far away as possible. By then Grey, van Rensburgh and van Tonder had closed in and were making their way into the greenhouse after slashing open the thin, fabric wall at the back of the structure.

Yasser shouted a curt command and his men ceased all fire. One of the shots that had killed Shabaan had been his own. He walked across to where the corpse was lying in the dust and pushed it over with his foot. It was Shabaan all right, the three bullet entry-points in his chest oozing blood, the left eye and socket destroyed by the bullet that had hit him in the head, the back of his head a mangled mess of blood and bone. Followed by two of his men he made his way into the greenhouse and across to the dark hole of the shaft. Of Grey and his men there was no sign.

Seventy metres below the border to Israel, the four remaining members of Shabaan's detachment were pushing the flat trolley with the device strapped to it along the steel tracks on the floor of the dimly-lit tunnel as fast as they could. The trolley and the device together weighed in excess of 500 kilograms, making for heavy going. Keller, Biedermann and Stegemann, 50 metres ahead of the men pushing the trolley, were making their way as fast as they could to the other side of the tunnel. Keller knew that they would soon hit an upward slope, signalling the imminent end of the tunnel. He had also been told that at the top of the tunnel was an electric winch, fastened to the concrete wall below the heavy door that concealed the exit. It had been placed there for a purpose, even ten men, for whom there was no space in the tunnel anyway, would have battled to push the trolley up the slope. Four men would find it impossible.

As the trolley rumbled along in the distance behind them they reached the start of the slope. Soon after they were at the top, the last ten metres of the tunnel levelling out ahead of them. Keller found the winch, set the clutch mechanism to neutral and pulled at a large hook fastened to the end of the steel cable. The drum turned easily. He passed the hook on to Stegemann, who promptly made his way back down the slope. Keller and Biedermann watched as the drum rotated, the layer of cable traversing left to right and back again. Half-way through the last layer of cable the drum suddenly stopped. Stegemann had arrived at the bottom of the slope.

Keller breathed deeply. They had now been on the go for well over two days and the strain was beginning to show. Biedermann was sweating profusely, after two days the odour of unwashed body was becoming noticeable. Not the most feminine woman at the best of times, right there and then she could be best described as an ugly, smelly, dishevelled mess.

"So?" mouthed Biedermann. "What next?"

"We bring the device up here, that's what," replied Keller.

"I know that!" snapped Biedermann. "I mean what do we do once it's up here? This whole mission's been a fuck-up since the word go."

Keller looked at her, his eyes blazing. "Shut the fuck up, Anne! This mess wasn't any of our fault, was it? So stop fucking bleating, will you?" There was a tug on the steel cable. Keller switched the clutch mechanism of the winch to wind-up mode, pressed the starter button and the electric winch started up, quietly reeling in the tensioned steel cable. "Here's what's going to happen. When the bomb's up here I'm going to arm it. There's no way we're going to get this thing to Sdot Misha, not in a million years. By now the Israelis will know what's happening. They might even know where it'll happen. So, surprise, surprise! We'll blow it up right here."

"What about the man in the van waiting for us up there?" She pointed at the exit lid above them.

"It'll be our getaway vehicle. Works out very nicely."

"But what about the people in the Gaza Strip? They'll be killed as well!"

"So? You think I care? As long as the thing blows up and takes a shitload of Jews with it, I'm happy. If a couple of thousand Palestinians end up dead as well, so be it. Call it collateral damage."

"Yes, but..."

Keller cut her off. He'd had enough. "Listen to me! We're fighting a goddamned war against imperialists, capitalist pigs and the Jews! We're about to strike at the Jewish pigs harder than anyone else ever has! We're making history here, dammit!!" He stopped, watching as Biedermann went into a sulk. "Anyway, while you were sleeping I discussed it with Karl and he fully agrees."

"What?!" shot back Biedermann. "You discuss something like this with Karl and only tell me now? You bastard, you traitor..."

Keller snapped. He took a step forward and slapped Biedermann across the face, splitting her bottom lip. Biedermann reeled back, dumbfounded.

"Bitch!" hissed Keller. "Remember one thing. I'm the leader of this outfit and, until that changes, you'll do whatever the fuck I say. Got it?"

He had hardly finished speaking when the trolley appeared at the end of the slope. Keller let the winch pull the trolley up onto the short level part of the tunnel below the exit then stopped the motor. Stegemann, who had come up on the back of the trolley, came across and joined them, followed minutes later by two of Shabaan's remaining men. The other two remained at the bottom of the slope, providing cover just in case someone had managed to get into the tunnel and follow them. Keller stepped across to the trolley and stroked the cold, steel cylinder. Strapped to the top was a small box. He removed it, prised open the lid and removed the one item without which nothing would happen. The laptop. Fitted with a battery that would last at least ten hours, he powered up the machine, Biedermann and Stegemann watching in morbid fascination. He talked as he went about his business.

"Here goes. First, we need to attach the USB cable to the device. Karl, if you would?" Stegemann plugged the one end of the cable into the small port at the top of what looked like a release valve for a pressure vessel. "Before we connect the cable to the laptop, we set the timer." He punched a couple of commands into the laptop and a large clock display appeared on the screen. "Now for the time of detonation." Moments later the display changed from a series of zeros to 60:00:00 depicting minutes, seconds and milliseconds. "One hour to boom time. All I have to do now is plug the cable into the laptop, press enter and the clock counts down."

"Jesus!" whispered Stegemann. "It really is simple, isn't it?"

"It is." Keller stepped back. "And no-one will be able to stop it once it's started."

"How so?" queried Biedermann, acting as though nothing had happened. "What happens if someone disconnects the laptop from the device?"

"Instant explosion. Amir Asadi set it up that way. Same thing happens if someone tries to switch off the computer. The only thing that can be done is to re-set the timer, that's the only fail-safe there is, but never to more than an hour. After ten hours the battery will run flat, at which point it will once again be game over. Boom!"

"And replacing the battery or using a different power source?"

"No-go," smiled Keller. "Remove, or even remotely tamper with the battery, and once again it will be boom. Nor can you plug in a power source; Asadi removed the connector."

"So once you set the timer in motion, the best anyone could do is to keep re-setting it to one hour, but only for ten hours maximum until the battery runs dead?"

"*Ja.* Once we connect the laptop to the bomb and I hit enter, the Jews will be well and truly fucked. But before we do that, let's see that our escape route is open."

He had hardly finished speaking when the sound of shots resonated up from the lower part of the tunnel. The two *Al-Qassam* fighters, who had remained at the bottom of the slope, had seen movement in the gloom of the tunnel and opened fire. Grey, van Rensburgh and van Tonder had, however, seen them a few seconds earlier. It took three carefully placed shots and the two *Al-Qassam* fighters would never lift a weapon again.

"What the fuck! Blow the fucking tunnel!" screamed Biedermann, scrambling for her rifle as Keller reached for his side-arm. At the same time Stegemann and the two *Al-Qassam* Brigade fighters dived to the floor half a metre short of the point where the tunnel sloped downward.

"We can't blow the tunnel, it'll wipe us out as well!" Stegemann shouted. "Arm the device, Jens! There's no way whoever is down there can hit us, the angles are all wrong. We'll spray bullets down the slope! Anyone moving up the slope will be hit! They're stuck down there! Arm it, Jens!! And then we get the hell away from here! Anne, open the tunnel-lid! Now!"

Neither Keller or Biedermann needed a second invitation. As Keller plugged the USB cable coming from the laptop into the device, Anne Biedermann pressed a switch that started a hydraulic motor. Slowly the lid of the tunnel exit began to push open. And then it stopped.

"*Verfluchte Scheisse!*" Biedermann stopped the hydraulic motor and tried again. The result was identical. The lid, which had lifted by 50 centimetres, did not budge any further. It had opened; Keller could feel the cold air draft coming through the crack, but nowhere near enough for a person to get out. What Keller did not know was that the cause for the jam. Above them, smack, bang, centre, right over the concealed lid, stood the stationary Merkava main battle tank of Lieutenant Ben Sachs. Moving a metre of earth was something the hydraulic system and pistons had been designed for, but not lifting a tank. The pistons pushed upward until the lid hit the bottom of the steel monster - and then tried to move an unplanned for additional 65 tons of weight! Something had to give and it wasn't going to be the tank, unless someone moved it.

The Ancient Synagogue of Ma'on, Israel

Lieutenant Ben Sachs was nowhere near his tank. He and three of his tank troops were at that precise moment having a chat to the driver of an older model Ford Transit panel van, who had, suddenly, and without warning, driven straight into the middle of the space occupied by the four concealed steel behemoths. And he had driven with the lights off! If that wasn't suspicious behaviour, then Lieutenant Ben Sachs didn't know what was.

Sachs immediately doubled the perimeter guard, ordering his troops to get their rifles on safety with one round in the chamber – the state of readiness prior to full-scale engagement. The man, professing to be a Palestinian living in Israel - and there were thousands of them - became more and more agitated as the minutes went by. Sachs was about to walk across to his tank and radio his Commander when, what had up until the appearance of the Ford Transit been an extremely uneventful night in the life of Lieutenant Ben Sachs, turned into one he would never forget.

As he approached his tank, he heard what sounded like ripping earth and then a dull thud. The noise came from underneath his tank. He stooped, flashlight in hand, to check what was going on. He couldn't believe what he was seeing. Three seconds later he was in the interior of the tank, shouting down the radio. His unit Commander came on the air immediately.

"What's up Lieutenant? And slowly, will you? Over."

"I think there's someone trying to come up from underground, except they can't, 'cause my tank's parked over what looks like an opening. Over."

"What?" All vestiges of proper military radio protocol went out of the window.

"An opening in the ground below my tank."

"Christ! Stay there, Lieutenant! Don't move! If anything else does move, shoot on sight! No, try to capture them. We'll be there in 10 minutes! And don't, whatever you do, screw this up – I'll have you peeling potatoes on the Golan Heights for the next ten years if you do!"

The IDF went into overdrive. Within minutes of Sachs having ended the conversation, there was a complete flight of F15s circling above them, and, from a distance, they could hear the sounds of approaching helicopters. Half the tank troops under his command had by then taken up position around Sachs's tank, their weapons trained on whatever could emerge from beneath the parked vehicle. The other half covered the area around them. The driver of the Ford Transit, who had tried - very unsuccessfully – to run away, was tied up in the back of the van with his mouth taped shut, a large, egg-sized bruise on his forehead.

When the first chopper landed and a platoon of Shayetet 13 Special Force soldiers emerged, Ben Sachs realised that whatever he had stumbled across was big, very big. Then Abel Sharon arrived, accompanied by a plethora of high ranking officers – including a General - and a man who clearly wasn't Israeli. Whatever was happening was way above his pay grade and Sachs ordered his troops to stand back as the others took over. Whoever was there below the ground didn't quite realise what was facing them above ground. *If I were them I'd run like hell,* thought Sachs, watching the proceedings as they unfolded. Next thing the General shouted at him to move his tank.

Below the ground, one of the hydraulic pipes connecting the hydraulic motor to the lifting pistons - unable to take the strain any longer - had eventually burst, spraying hydraulic fluid all over the place. Keller tried to keep control of the fast-deteriorating situation, Stegemann firing blindly down the slope of the tunnel. The two remaining *Al-Qassam* fighters had resorted to shouting at each other in Arabic. And Biedermann? She was at that point turning into a dysfunctional wreck. It was utter bedlam! Then above them Ben Sachs started up his tank, the roar of the engine audible to the three trapped Meinhof Kollaboration terrorists. Not able to get back down the tunnel, which was blocked by Grey, van Rensburgh and van Tonder, nor to the surface because of the jammed opening, they had nowhere to go. To Keller it boiled down to one thing. They were caught. But, if they were history, then so would the Israelis be. He scrambled across to the laptop and hit ENTER. As the clock started counting down, two canisters dropped from above though the small open space, hit the ground and, with a barely audible bang, exploded. Keller, Biedermann, Stegemann and the two fighters watched in abject horror as a nebulous cloud filled the space they occupied. The last thing Keller noticed as he slipped into unconsciousness was sand falling away from the one side of the jammed tunnel lid. The Israelis were digging their way in.

Grey, van Rensburgh and van Tonder, who had made one futile attempt to move up the incline, but had been stopped by the spray of bullets from the AK-47s at the top of the slope, were trying to figure out their next move when they heard a distant, muffled shout.

"Grey??!!"

"Sharon?!" he shouted back.

"Yes, it's me!" came the echoing response. "It's safe! You can come up!"

Five minutes later they were standing next to Sharon in the fresh air. By then the lid concealing the tunnel had been prised open fully. A metre away from them, three metres down, bathed in the glare of a number of hastily erected spotlights, they could see the nuclear device on the trolley. Stooped over a second laptop that communicated via Bluetooth with the unit that displayed the timer was Billy Mclaughlin, dressed in his usual attire of jeans, sneakers and a T-shirt. Someone had given him a jacket to wear but he had tossed it to one side. Even if it had been well below freezing, McLaughlin would not have noticed. Muttering and mumbling, his fingers virtually flying over the keyboard, he plugged away. At one point Grey thought he heard him saying something like "clever fuckers, aren't they?" No one said a word as McLaughlin worked, not daring to disturb the man. Suddenly McLaughlin stopped.

"Right! Got it."

Grey and Sharon looked down into the open pit. "Got what?"

"How this thing works." McLaughlin stepped back, scratching his head. "And it's not good."

"Why's that?" demanded Sharon. By then the timer was at 41:54:27 – 42 minutes to go.

McLaughlin looked up. "You can't stop it, that's why."

Sharon felt his blood freeze. "You've got to be kidding me!"

"Wish I was." McLaughlin pointed at his own laptop he had connected to the one displaying the countdown clock. "I had a look into the sub-routines that make up this software. I don't want to bore you with the detail so here it is in a nutshell. You can't disconnect the timer laptop from the device. You can't shut down the power. You can't alter the software. Try any of that and this thing will explode."

"And we've only got what? 41 minutes left?" Behind Grey and Sharon, guarded by six Shayetet 13 Special Force soldiers, Keller, Biedermann, Stegemann, hands and feet taped together and unable to move, by then conscious once more, watched the scene unfold. Keller was grinning manically, Biedermann spewing forth an ongoing string of profanities, while Stegemann merely glared. The two fighters of Shabaan's *Al-Qassam* Brigade, plus the driver of the Ford Transit, who had by then soiled himself, had been spirited away for some rather intense and unpleasant interrogations.

Sharon spun around, pushed his way past the soldiers and pointed at Anne Biedermann. "Will someone shut that fucking bitch up?!" One of the soldiers grabbed Biedermann by the head, holding it in a vice-grip, as a second soldier unceremoniously plastered a wide strip of duct tape across her mouth shut. Sharon bent down in front of Keller. "And you, you motherfucker! You stop this thing now, got it? 'Cause if you don't, I'm going rip your balls off!"

"Screw you, Jewish pig!" Keller leant forward as far as he could and spat in Sharon's face, the glob of sputum landing on Sharon's cheek. Sharon slowly wiped his face with the back of his hand. Suddenly he hauled out, about to punch Keller in the mouth, when Grey grabbed his arm.

"Don't, Abel," he said quietly. "You're lowering yourself to his level. Leave him, we'll deal with him later." He felt Sharon's arm relax and helped him back to his feet.

The two men stepped back, away from Keller, who was laughing like a demented maniac. "You will all die, you Jews! You cannot stop it! Pigs!"

"Not yet, Keller." Grey and Sharon turned, perplexed. McLaughlin, less than a metre away from them, was grinning. "Sorry gents. I hadn't finished yet. We still have time; I'd say around nine hours if the battery life indicator on that laptop is correct."

"But the clock! It's on less than 39 minutes!"

"Relax, people! What I didn't tell you is that the timer can be re-set to 60 minutes. It was probably the one fail-safe Amir Azadi built into the device, just in case something went wrong and more time was needed." He glanced across at Keller who had suddenly gone very quiet. "Didn't think I'd find out, did you? ... Asshole!"

Sharon felt the weight of a mountain drop off his shoulders. "You mean if the timer's down to - say one minute - we can re-set it to 60 minutes, let it run down again and keep on re-setting it?"

"Yeah, that's about the size of it."

"So we can hook this thing up to an external power source and keep on re-setting for the next 100 years if we wanted to?"

"No, not really. Nine hours is the max. Asadi removed the socket for the power supply so you can't plug in an external source. Cute little fucker, this Asadi! Knowing someone might try to stop it, he actually went and left a message on the machine stating precisely what he'd done to booby-trap it. And what he's gone and done is pretty much foolproof."

"Why'd he do that? Was he mad or something?"

"No, not mad, not at all. I reckon he was simply damned sure of himself. Thing is, any normal person was never going to find the message. No, this Asadi probably thought that someone like me might get into the system. So he leaves this message. Like it's a challenge along the lines of, *I'll tell you what I've done, now see if you can beat me.* Thing is, we can't even open the laptop; the casing's been fitted with hundreds of small pressure sensors. The minute we do so and one of the pressure sensors is activated, it will also set off the device. Can't drill into it either."

"So this thing will blow, no matter what?"

"That's pretty much the size of it. You see, the laptop software and the device software have been connected. Once the timer was started, the software inside the device started talking continually to the software outside the device, on the laptop. Any disruption in the communication loop has the same result as the timer hitting zero. It will detonate. In nine hours from now the battery will die, which is pretty much the same as disconnecting the power and therefore stopping the communication loop. Same effect once more... boom."

"Nine hours. That's it?"

"Yes. I suggest that by then you find a spot where this thing can go bang without killing anyone."

Sharon said nothing for a minute or so. Nor did anyone else, watching him pace backwards and forwards. The scene was almost surreal. Suddenly he stopped in his tracks.

"Nine hours. So be it. Excuse me for a few minutes, gentlemen. I have a call to make." He took his cell phone from his pocket and stepped away into the darkness. Five minutes later he was back and beckoning Grey, McLaughlin, the General and the Shayetet 13 Special Force Commander to join him. When they were well out of earshot of all the others, he stopped. "I've just spoken to Roni Ezra. Here's what we do. General. Your instructions first..."

Ten minutes later an IDF transport truck equipped with a mobile crane rolled up the short stretch of dirt road and came to a halt. Without much fuss and bother, the device, together with the trolley it was resting on, was lifted slowly out of the pit and into the back of the truck. The driver, who'd been wondering why a couple of mattresses had been thrown into the back of the truck prior to his hasty departure, realised, when he saw what was being lifted out of the pit, what they were for. Cushioning. Whatever it was, and it looked sinister enough, clearly had to be handled with care. And he had to drive the bloody thing?

"Okay gents, all loaded and ready to go," called McLaughlin, who'd been supervising the loading and the strapping down of the trolley with the device. "Mike, Abel. Can I have quick word with you?"

"Sure," replied Sharon, puzzled. "What's up?"

"Well," said McLaughlin, "I'm not sure how to say this, but someone will need to re-set the timer in...," he looked at the laptop connected to the device, "16 minutes from now."

"Yes? And?"

"We don't know if it'll work, do we?"

"But you said..."

"I know what I said. But, until someone does it, it's all theory. It's never been tested before, not on a live device, has it?"

"Fuck!"

"Yup. My thoughts exactly." McLaughlin had gone very quiet. "Tell me, what's the best straight line direction to the most unpopulated area around here?"

"Straight from here to the 241, then right down the 23," replied Sharon. "That'll take you somewhere past Hatzerim and then into open wasteland. But you'll never get there, not in the next 15 minutes."

"I know," said McLaughlin. "Still, the further we get, the lower the death toll if this thing does explode. Listen," there was urgency in his voice, "your driver doesn't have to do this, but we need to go. I'll be in the back of the truck with the bomb and re-set the timer when the clock reaches the last 60 seconds. What I need is a volunteer to drive the truck."

Grey stepped forward. "That's me and no questions. If this doesn't work, for whatever reason, then you and I go out together. Might be with a bigger bang than most..."

"Then let's get the hell out of here."

"One condition though," Grey pointed at the three Meinhof Kollaboration terrorists. "They're coming with us."

Two minutes later the truck moved slowly away from Ma'on, leaving the ancient monastery behind them. As the lights faded, Abel Sharon ordered the remaining men into the pit and down the sloping tunnel, knowing full well that the next ten minutes would determine the fate of Israel and the Middle East. As the tail-lights of the slowly-moving truck vanished into the darkness, dawn still some two hours away, Abel Sharon whispered to no one in particular.

"God help us!"

Grey drove as fast as he possibly dared, considering the contents in the back of the truck, hearing McLaughlin shouting at him to take it easy every few seconds. How long they'd driven for he couldn't calculate; to one part of him it felt like an eternity, to the other like seconds. Sweating profusely, even though it was cold in the cab of the truck, he carried on, each jolt, however slight, enough to make him cringe.

"Stop!! Now!!" McLaughlin, in the back of the truck together with the device and the three Meinhof Kollaboration terrorists, noted the timer go below the two minute mark. The truck ground to a halt. Grey climbed out of the cab, the engine on idle, sprinted around to the back and climbed into the load bay. They had just crossed the Hbshor River, the small village of Urim ahead of them in the distance. If Grey was sweating, McLaughlin was positively dripping.

"This is it, Mike," whispered McLaughlin as Grey crouched down next to him. "I'm going to re-set the timer now. If I don't get it right on the first attempt, there'll hopefully be enough time for a second try." By then the counter had dropped below 01:30:00. Grey watched in morbid fascination as McLaughlin began to key in a series of numbers.

"Christ almighty!!!"

"What?!"

"The timer! I can't re-set it! It needs a verification code!"

"WHAT??!!"

"A goddamned verification code! Mother of God! Where the hell are we supposed to get that from?" He pointed at the message on the screen - ENTER VERIFICATION CODE.

Below the message the clock had just dropped below the one minute mark, 00:59:36.

Orlando, Florida, USA

Gerald Hopkins climbed out of the taxi and made his way to Room 301 of the small motel close to Sand Lake, not far from the Interstate 4 heading out to the Disney World pleasure resorts. The place was mediocre, catering largely for the budget tourists who made their way to Disney World by the thousands. He took one final look at the SMS he had received less than 12 hours earlier. *Meet me in Orlando in next 24 hours. Adverse developments. We must protect ourselves. Blake...* followed by the address of the motel. Hopkins, not usually an alarmist, attempted to call Blake Wellington four times, each of the calls going straight to voicemail. This caused all sorts of alarm bells to go off in Hopkins's head. What he did not know was that the SMS, although it had come from Wellington's phone, had not been sent by Wellington. It had been sent by the Mossad operators, who had quietly removed Wellington from his residence in Tampa a day earlier. By then Hopkins knew that Gary Simms had been killed in a car accident, Brent Delgardo had disappeared off the face of the planet and Marty Trump wasn't answering his phone either.

Had Hopkins known he was the last member of The Patriots, still a "free" man, he would not have knocked on the door of Room 301, he would have been running like hell. As it happened, he knocked on the door. It was yanked wide open from the inside; a hand appeared and Hopkins was propelled into the dim interior of the room. As the door slammed shut behind him someone clamped his mouth shut, twisted his arm behind his back and forced him up against the wall.

"Mr Hopkins! What a pleasant surprise!" came a voice from

the one corner of the motel room. Hopkins couldn't see who was speaking; it definitely wasn't Blake Wellington. Next thing his hands were being tied behind his back and he was rammed onto one of the four cheap chairs that stood around a rickety table next to the large double bed.

"Who are you?" spluttered Hopkins. Across the table sat a dark-skinned, young man holding a rather large and evil-looking pistol with a silencer attached to the long barrel. Next to Hopkins appeared a second man, a muscular, 6ft2" bald individual.

"Aahh... now that would be telling, wouldn't it?" The young man leaned forward, studying Hopkins intently, and then sat back. "Yossi," he spoke to the bald man, "gag him. And fetch Wellington."

Moments later, his mouth stuffed with cloth rag, Hopkins watched as the young man's side-kick frogmarched a dishevelled Blake Wellington from the bathroom and unceremoniously deposited him on the vacant chair next to him.

The young man with the gun smiled. "Well, well, gentlemen. I see I have your attention. You've been rather naughty boys, haven't you?" He watched as his colleague started emptying the contents of a sports bag onto the bed. It was an assortment of erotic men's gear, most of it leather, including two leather hoods, some leather straps and a whip. "You see," he waved the gun at the two men tied up opposite him, "my name's Ben Stiller. I'm an Israeli. And it really isn't very nice of you to try and blow up my country, is it? Oh, before I forget. Brent Delgardo and Marty Trump. Those names mean something to you?"

Hopkins gagged as Wellington slumped forward on his chair. "Aha. So they do." The young man got up, gun in hand, and sat nonchalantly on the edge of the table, facing the two men. "They're dead, you know. So is Simms, but you already knew that. Which, as it stands, leaves you two as the last remaining members of The Patriots. With me so far?"

Hopkins vomited. With the gag in his mouth there was nowhere for the vomit to go. He swallowed, but it went down the wrong pipe. He tried to cough, yet that didn't work either. He began to choke. Unable to suck enough air in through his nose, and began to suffocate. Next to him, Wellington had fainted.

"Let me tell you what will happen now." He young man watched dispassionately as Hopkins struggled to breathe. "You two are actually a kinky bunch of gay bastards. You met here and played a sex game, a snuff session. You know what that is? No? Let me tell you. It's when someone strangles a consenting partner for sexual gratification. Normally the one doing the strangling lets go before the one getting strangled dies. But in your case something went wrong and you both expired. Sad, isn't it? In a few days from now – maybe earlier – your bodies will be found. And the reports will all state the obvious, death by asphyxiation. " He paused, watching as Hopkins's eyes bulged in their sockets. "You don't have much time left, but remember this. You fuck with us the way you did and you pay the price, assholes." He turned and faced his bald colleague, who had completed laying out the erotic gear on the bed. "Yossi. It's time." Hopkins, busy suffocating, felt two large hands encircle his neck and begin to squeeze gently.

CHAPTER 11
A SECOND SUN

Urim, Israel

00:59:36.

A missing six-digit verification code. Closer to death than he had ever been before, even the events in Ismailia paling into insignificance, Grey went into a mode that had kept him alive so often before. He didn't know why or how it happened, yet it was the one thing that set him apart from other equally able-bodied men, the ability to deal with extreme pressure when it really mattered. A second became like a minute, a minute an hour, the clarity of thought absolute.

"Billy! Try Keller!!"

McLaughlin, wet with perspiration despite the chill, typed.

"No-go! Next!"

Grey, his mind racing, glanced across at Keller. What had the bastard thought of? It wasn't Asadi who determined the verification code, was it? No, it had to be Keller. And there was no way Keller would tell him, would he?

00:37:46

"Baader!!"

Again McLaughlin typed, his fingers hitting the keyboard faster than even he thought he was capable of.

"Fuck! Wrong spelling!" He re-typed. "No-go! Error! Next!"

00:21: 15

"Meinhof!" shouted Grey.

"Too many letters! We're fucking dead!!"

00:15:47

"Fuck!!! ...BAADER!! Capital letters!!!" screamed Grey.

McLaughlin punched in the letters...60:00:00

McLaughlin slumped backwards, hands clasped behind his head. "Holy crap!! It's re-set..."

Grey leant out of the back of the truck and threw up. *No*, he thought, *there has to be a better way of making a living...*

"Christ! Was that close or what?" ventured McLaughlin from the depths of the load bay of the truck. "Another two seconds and we'd have been toast." He took a look at Keller. "Thought you had us there, didn't you?" McLaughlin stopped short and burst into tears, not of sorrow or pain, rather of rage. "You MOTHERFUCKER!!"

Not much later Grey was back in the cab of the truck. He was finished, emotionally drained. But it wasn't over yet. He took his cell phone and called Abel Sharon. Sharon, who had moved all the men with him into the tunnel, answered immediately.

"Mike! You did it!"

"How the heck do you know?" replied Grey, phone jammed between ear and shoulder, shifting the truck into first gear.

"The time's up! No flash of light, no explosion, no nothing! Or..."

"No, Abel, you're right. We re-set the thing. But it was closer than you'll ever imagine. The bastards had a verification code built into the re-set mode. I'll tell you over a beer one day..."

"Christ almighty...!!"

"Yeah, we made it by some two seconds... damn nearly shat myself!"

"What next?" asked Sharon.

"Meet us at Hatzerim. And get Khalid and Labuschagne there as well. We've got under nine hours left."

Hatzerim Airbase, Israel

The Lockheed C130, the same aircraft that had air-dropped Max Preston into the Gaza Strip, sat on the far side of the airbase, bathed in the shrill glare of the pylon mounted floodlights surrounding the open expanse of concrete apron. Dawn was fast approaching, the faint glow of red backlighting the horizon in the distance, as a number of people made their way to the aircraft and walked up the open ramp lowered from the back of the fuselage. It was akin to a funeral procession. The first to head up the ramp were Grey, Mclaughlin, van Rensburgh, van Tonder and the pilot. Following them were the three members of the Meinhof Kollaboration – Jens Keller, Anne Biedermann and KarlStegemann – as well as Francois Labuschagne, in a wheelchair and still alive – barely - and Ben Khalid. The last two had been flown in from Tel Aviv. Each was accompanied by a heavily-armed IDF soldier. Behind the procession a further six Israeli soldiers pushed a trolley with the nuclear device. From a distance it resembled the shape of a coffin.

Sinai Desert, Egypt

At precisely 05h45 the four turboprop engines spluttered into life. The ungainly aircraft taxied towards the end of the runway, the pilot revved up the engines and released the brakes. Less than a minute later the nose lifted and the C130 took off, banked towards the south and made a bee-line for the Egyptian border. Up front Michael Grey sat next to the pilot. In the back, McLaughlin sat in a canvas bucket seat next to the securely strapped-down device, watching the countdown clock. The counter had been re-set a second time, easy now he knew the verification code. Next to him van Rensburgh and van Tonder watched the device in silence as the seconds and minutes went by. Facing them from the other side of the cabin, trussed up like chickens and handcuffed to a steel rail mounted to the inside wall of the fuselage, were the five individuals who had caused all the misery. None of them were able to say anything, their mouths still taped firmly shut.

Fifteen minutes after takeoff the plane reached an altitude of six thousand metres, crossed into Egyptian air space, changed course to a south-south-west bearing, and headed out towards the desert wastelands of South Sinai.

As Grey looked out of the window, the sun beginning to rise over the distant horizon, two Egyptian Air Force Mirage 2000 fighter jets popped up next to them, less than 200 metres away to the left of the C130. Grey listened as the voice of the lead pilot came over the radio.

"Israeli C130, this Major Mubarak, Egyptian Air Force. We have orders to accompany you. Acknowledge. Over."

"Major Mubarak, this is Colonel Levy of the IAF. Acknowledged. You've been advised of proceedings? Over."

"We have, Colonel. Don't worry about us, just don't go and crash your C130, will you? And verify your course. Over."

Colonel Levy laughed wryly. "No, I won't crash this bus. Course set for bearing 195, altitude remains as is. Will that do? Over."

"It will, Colonel. And good luck! Out." The two Egyptian Mirage fighters peeled away and tucked in approximately one kilometre behind the Hercules.

As Colonel Levy switched off McLaughlin popped his head into the cockpit. "Gentlemen. We have 45 minutes left. I suggest we get ready?"

Grey nodded at the pilot. Levy made one final minor course correction, set the autopilot and got up. "Time to leave." He strapped on the parachute he had dumped behind the pilot seat and followed McLaughlin out of the cockpit, Grey close behind.

Inside the cargo-hold van Tonder too was getting ready, except that he had a second, extra harness. He tossed McLaughlin the second harness and Grey helped him put it on. At the back of the aircraft Colonel Levy was busy lowering the cargo ramp. Grey made sure the harness on McLaughlin was tight and secure and mated up the attachment parts with the main harness worn by van Tonder. The two men, McLaughlin's back firmly joined to van Tonder's chest, shuffled towards the open cargo ramp. Grey watched as McLaughlin tightened the strap of the helmet he'd been given and put on a pair of goggles.

"Mike!" McLaughlin shouted, barely audible above the noise of roar of the wind. "Whatever you do, don't touch the thing! Sure you don't want me to stay? And do I really have to jump? I hate bloody heights!"

"No! I won't touch the bloody thing!" Grey shouted back. "And yes! You have to jump! We'll be fine! Now go!"

Colonel Levy gave Grey the thumbs-up, walked calmly to the end of the ramp and dived out into the void, followed by van Tonder and McLaughlin, who were jumping in tandem. McLaughlin, who had never before in his life jumped out of anything apart from his bed, screeched as they left the plane. Grey held on to the airframe and watched as the two figures plummeted towards the ground far below. *Any time now, any time...* and suddenly the two parachutes deployed, one after the other in quick succession. McLaughlin, van Tonder and Levy were on their way to safety.

As the C130 continued on its way into the Sinai Desert, Grey walked back down the cavernous cargo hold to where van Rensburgh, who'd already strapped on his own parachute, was keeping an eye on Keller, Biedermann, Stegemann, Khalid and Labuschagne. Grey grabbed the last remaining parachute and put it on.

"Looks like it's the two of us once again, eh?" he grinned at van Rensburgh.

"As always," replied van Rensburgh, "never a dull moment when you're around, is there?" He pulled a cigar from his top pocket, bit off the end and lit it with a Zippo lighter.

"Where the hell did you get that thing?"

"Bought it on the way from the States. It's a Cuban Hoyo de … and I forgot the bloody rest... cigar. Fucking expensive, it was! Always wondered what they tasted like so I decided to get one. Might not get a second chance if this thing decides to go bang all by itself." He patted the steel casing of the nuclear device. "Listen, don't you think we should get the hell out of here as well?"

"We'll jump with ten minutes to go. That'll put more than enough distance between us and the plane when this thing blows." He looked at the clock on the device. 25:43:19. "Gives us 15 minutes to kill." He looked across at Keller. "Time enough for me to have a little talk to my all-time favourite asshole."

He moved across to where Keller was tied up and sat down in the empty canvas bucket seat next to him.

"Keller. Hmm... So tell me, what's it feel like when you're staring death in the face? Let's see, 24 minutes to go. Nice feeling, isn't it?" For the next two minutes Grey said nothing. Suddenly he turned, looking straight into Keller's eyes. "You know, Keller, I always wondered what makes someone like you tick. What causes someone to turn into the kind of low life, bottom-feeder you are? Did you get bullied in school? Was your mother some sort of control freak? Did she jerk you off? I suppose it doesn't really matter, does it? No matter what happens, nothing's going to change who you are, will it?" He could see the naked hatred spewing from Keller's eyes. "I see I've sparked something. Good. Well, let me tell you what I've got in mind for you. You're not going to die on this plane. That's far too nice." He took a small key from his pocket and held it up in front of Keller. "See these? I'm now going to open your handcuffs." He reached behind Keller and unlocked him. "Now get up."

Keller, hands still tied behind his back, unable to talk because of the tape across his mouth, staggered to his feet.

"Move!" Grey pushed Keller in the small of the back. "Stop!" Keller stopped. "And now," Grey pulled his combat knife from its sheath and cut the plastic tape the Israelis had used to tie Keller up with, "it's you against me."

Grey took a step back and watched as Keller, his hands free, spun to face him, ripping the tape off his mouth at the same time. Grey held his hands up. "See? No weapons. But that wouldn't be fair, so I've decided to make things a bit more even. Here," he slid the combat knife across the floor towards Keller. "Don't want anyone to say it wasn't a fair fight, do we?"

A few metres away, van Rensburg, cigar in his mouth, watched proceedings, saying nothing, as did Biedermann, Stegemann and Khalid. Labuschagne, more dead than alive, did not react at all.

Keller snarled and reached for the knife. "I'll kill you, you bloody Jew-lover!"

Slashing wildly he hurled himself at Grey. Grey ducked, the knife whizzing through the air above his head. Using Keller's forward motion, he spun him around and punched him in the mouth, breaking three of the front teeth. Keller stumbled backwards, spitting out blood and broken bits of teeth.

"Bastard!" he snarled.

Again he came for Grey, this time slower, more controlled. Or so he thought. He slashed at Grey and missed. Grey, however, didn't miss; ramming his fist into Keller's nose, breaking it in two places, followed up with two quick jabs, each jab opening a cut above Keller's eyes. Keller dropped the knife, his hands reaching up for his damaged nose, blood pouring down the front of his shirt. As Keller staggered backwards, Grey moved in. He grabbed Keller by one arm, twisted it around his back and started to run him down the length of the aircraft. By the time Keller realised what was happening it was too late. A metre away from the end of the open ramp Grey let go. Keller, not able to stop, shrieked one last time as he fell, dropping away to the desert floor and his death.

"Way to go, Mike!" Van Rensburgh came across, picked up

the knife and handed it back to Grey. "Not much of a fight, was it? Why'd you do it anyway?"

Grey bent down to put the knife back in its sheath and looked up his friend. "Keller didn't give a shit about dying. What he did give a shit about was success. Had he lived to see the bomb explode, even if he'd died in the process, in his mind he'd have won. Now he'll never know, will he?"

"Why not simply throw him out of the back of the plane and be done with it?"

"Because it would have put me at his level. I don't murder people. I will however protect myself. And Keller came at me with a knife, didn't he?" Grey stood upright, adjusted the straps of the parachute and took a look at the countdown clock. 00:12:28. "Time to go."

Van Rensburgh nodded, pulled on his goggles and made his way to the ramp, followed by Grey. He waited for Grey to pass him, watched as he jumped, turned to face Biedermann, Stegemann, Khalid and Labuschagne, and gave them a mock salute.

"*Ciao,* mother-fuckers! Have a blast!" Then he jumped himself.

As the C130 flew on, the autopilot doing precisely what it had been designed to do, Grey and van Rensburgh landed safely on the ground. They gathered up the parachutes and stood there, watching the tiny spec of the Hercules getting smaller and smaller. By then it was light, the sun a yellow orb rising slowly in the east. Grey checked his watch. Three minutes.

Twenty kilometres ahead of them, the C130 Hercules continued on its way. The two Egyptian Mirage 2000 fighters had dropped back, circling some fifty kilometres behind the Israeli transport aircraft.

In the cargo hold of the aircraft, Biedermann, Stegemann and Khalid were frantically trying to get out of their handcuffs, Labuschagne no longer capable of attempting to free himself. At some point Stegemann gave up. For the first time in his life he began to pray, to a God he'd never before bothered with, hoping he'd be forgiven for all he had done. So did Khalid, except his prayers went out to Allah. Only Biedermann continued trying to free herself, the flesh covering her wrists torn off, bone scraping against steel as she tried to force her hands out of the handcuffs. 00:01:76 ... 00:00:54 ... 00:00:00 ...

As Grey and van Rensburgh watched a second, far brighter, sun appeared in the sky. Of the C130, Biedermann, Stegemann, Khalid and Labuschagne nothing remained, vaporised in a microsecond. Grey and van Rensburgh, blinded by the intense flash of light created by the exploding 18 kiloton nuclear device, heard the boom of the explosion before they felt the warmth of the fast dissipating blast wave wash over them.

It was over.

Geneva, Switzerland

The old man walked quietly down the carpeted corridor of the plush hotel overlooking Lake Geneva. At the end of the corridor was the Presidential Suite. Someone inside the suite must have seen him coming, the entrance door opening when he was still three metres away. He gave the man who opened the door a curt nod and entered the luxurious suite, making his way straight to the expansive living area. There, looking out of the window, waited a grey-haired, olive-skinned man, immaculately dressed in a three-piece Armani suit. He turned to face his visitor.

"Mr Berkovich. You would be Roni Ezra's envoy, yes?" He moved forward and held out his hand.

Thomas Berkovich took the offered hand and shook it, slowly. "Yes, I am. And thank you for seeing me. I trust you are fully aware of what caused the incident in the first place?"

"Oh yes, I was informed all along as events unfolded."The grey-haired man in the Armani suit gestured at three sofas placed around an ornate coffee table. "But, please, have a seat." The two men sat down and he continued to speak, "It is not often that one embarks on a discussion such as the one we are about to have, Mr Berkovich. Certainly not in our day and age." He stopped for a brief moment, then continued, "Yet, there are times when such discussions must take place if some form of sanity is to prevail. May I offer you some coffee? Or tea?"

"Coffee would be excellent, Ayatollah..."

EPILOGUE
NUCLEAR TERRORISM – A SIMPLE TRUTH?

This book has dealt extensively with what could happen if a terrorist organisation obtained a nuclear device. The real question however is this: Can an amateur or terrorist organisation actually build a device? And, if so, why has it not been done? The following is an attempt at an answer.

One could always start off by talking to John Aristotle Phillips. Also known as the "A Bomb Kid", Phillips, a junior undergraduate at Princeton University in 1976, designed a nuclear device using only books, documents and other papers freely available in the public domain at the time, and handed in his work as a term paper. The upshot of the entire exercise was that Phillips, an underachieving student hoping his work would get him a good enough grade to be able to continue at the University, got a bit more than even he had bargained for. His design was actually deemed to be functional, which was verified by one Dr Frank Chilton, a California-based nuclear scientist specialising in nuclear explosion engineering. At the time Dr Chilton went on public record stating that Phillips's design was "pretty much guaranteed to work." There were, of course, those in the scientific community who argued it would not, but this did not prevent the FBI from confiscating the term paper, as well as the mock-up of the device Phillips had built in his room at Princeton.

If Phillips was able to design a rudimentary atomic device based on information freely available in the public domain in 1976, imagine how much more information is available to the aspiring amateur atomic device constructor in the early part of the 21st century. Hence, if step one in the process of building an atomic bomb is the design of such a weapon, then the brutal reality is that there are many engineering and physics graduates who would be more than capable of coming up with a workable blueprint for an atomic device.

As to the kinds of devices, there are two generic types - fission and fusion. Fusion devices are by far the more complex of the two as they require a fission device to get the fusion process going, in other words a nuclear device requiring another nuclear device to make it work. Thus the simpler devices are, by consequence, the fission types. Both atomic bombs dropped on Hiroshima and Nagasaki were fission devices, one of them a so called "gun-triggered" device called Little Boy and the other an "implosion-triggered" device called Fat Man. From a sheer engineering perspective the easier of the two to design and build is the gun-triggered version.

The principle behind the gun-triggered device is the firing of a sub-critical mass of fissile material into another sub-critical mass of fissile material, thereby causing the resulting mass to go critical and then immediately super-critical, initiating the required explosive chain reaction. Another way to describe it would be the firing of a "doughnut" made of fissile material from one side of a tube onto a "spike" made of fissile material on the other side of the tube, as was the case with the Little Boy bomb. Clearly it is not quite that simple, there are numerous additional elements that need to be included in the design, such as tampers, initiators, conventional explosives to accelerate the fissile material, as well as a handful of other bits and pieces. Yet it is the fissile material that forms the heart of the device.

At this point the prospective nuclear device constructor, workable design in hand, is faced with the one challenge which has, to date, prevented the wholesale manufacture of atomic bombs by all and sundry, and has probably saved the human race from annihilation. The challenge is to obtain fissile material.

Of all the materials known to man, there is only one fissile material found naturally in any meaningful quantity, the isotope Uranium 235, a component of uranium ore. The problem is that uranium ore contains over 99 percent of the isotope Uranium 238, and less than one percent of Uranium 235 - never mind a wide variety of other minerals which happen to make up the bulk of uranium ore when it is mined. Contrary to popular belief, Uranium 238 is worthless to the builder of the device, as it happens to be fissionable, but not fissile. What is needed is the fissile Uranium 235, and lots of it (depending on the concentration or the degree to which it has been enriched). The first obstacle therefore is that the host of other minerals in the uranium ore need to be removed. Once this has been achieved - a process involving the crushing of the ore and copious amounts of acids, alkalis or peroxide (there are various ways of doing this), where the uranium is leached out – one is left with what is termed "yellow cake", a powdery, pungent substance today commonly brown or black in colour. The term "yellow cake" comes from early mining operations, where the colour of the product was indeed yellow.

Having yellow cake is one thing, selling it a different issue entirely. Although available in large quantities, one cannot simply go and purchase yellow cake on the open market. Subject to some of the most stringent controls ever devised, the manufacture and sale of yellow cake is a highly regulated affair - both the purchaser and seller would certainly have to answer a number of very probing questions as to the purpose of the transaction. It should be noted that, in 2003, some 64 000 tons of yellow cake were produced, and, as more mines come on stream, this volume is expected to increase.

Let's assume the aspiring bomb designer has somehow or other managed to obtain a substantial amount of yellow cake. Now what? First the Uranium 238 has to be removed from the yellow cake, leaving the Uranium 235. This involves converting the yellow cake into Uranium Hexafluoride, which allows it to be enriched. Because Uranium Hexafluoride can be turned into gas it is perfect for the enrichment process, which, in the main, takes place in a gaseous state. The general idea is to remove the Uranium 238 from the yellow cake to the point that what is left consists of 85 percent Uranium 235. This is done commonly by using a series of centrifuges. After subjecting the Uranium Hexafluoride to what is called a cascade of centrifuges, the Uranium 238 is gradually removed, leaving Uranium 235. The resultant product is called highly-enriched uranium, or HEU. Another term used to describe uranium enriched to such a degree is weapons' grade uranium.

There is of course a further fissile material, Plutonium 239, but this is not found naturally, it is produced in a nuclear reactor – or what is termed a "fast breeder". For the purposes of building an atomic device, one requires far less Plutonium 239 than Uranium 235, which means a physically smaller bomb can be manufactured, but it also means one has to use the implosion method and not the gun-triggered method, as the Plutonium 239 – and here it gets highly technical - is far more unstable than the Uranium 235, largely due to the inevitable presence of Plutonium 240. Without going into further detail, this fact alone makes Plutonium 239 unsuitable for a gun-triggered device.

Hence, for the purposes of this exercise, we will stick to the gun-triggered device and the need for highly enriched Uranium 235. Of interest perhaps is that the energy released by one Uranium 235 isotope splitting is roughly one million times greater than the energy released by a petroleum molecule burning up in a motor vehicle engine, a truly good indicator of the violent force the explosion of a nuclear device unleashes.

The process of enriching uranium is, however, very complex and only a few nations on earth have the technology available to do so. In addition, any nation commencing dabbling in uranium enrichment - never mind a nation or individual wanting to purchase yellow cake - is immediately subject to intense scrutiny by the world's atomic watchdog, the International Atomic Energy Agency, the IAEA. It is an organisation whose sole function it is to ensure the purchase of items such as yellow cake, the development of enrichment technology, as well as the manufacture and purchase of any other materials needed for generating nuclear energy, are closely monitored to prevent anyone with nefarious intentions from acquiring these items.

The conundrum is that the nuclear power plants scattered across the world need enriched Uranium as fuel for the nuclear reactors, albeit enriched to a far lower degree of between three to five percent. Although many countries do operate nuclear power plants, only a few have actual enrichment capability. As it stands, there are 11 countries which, between them, enrich virtually all of the world's uranium, albeit that ownership of these plants is often split amongst several nations. For example, France, Belgium, Italy, Spain and Iran – yes, Iran – hold an investment interest in the French Eurodif enrichment plant. But, once a country has developed enrichment technology, irrespective of who ownership of the enrichment plant may rest with, who can say whether the enrichment technology is used only for peaceful purposes, or also to enrich the uranium until it is deemed weapons' grade or HEU, hence suitable for the manufacture of nuclear devices? Or, for that matter, what prevents countries owning the right type of nuclear reactors – fast breeder units - from harvesting Plutonium 239?

It is precisely this predicament which the world has with the Iranian nuclear program. Iran, never mind the interest in the Eurodif plant, purportedly has the ability to enrich Uranium, yet states categorically that this is being done for peaceful purposes, to provide fuel for the country's nuclear power station as well as for medical purposes. Israel, together with a number of other nations, say Iran is not being truthful, that the intention has always been to build nuclear weapons. Even worse is the situation of North Korea, that pariah of nations, a country that does have enrichment capability and does build atomic weapons.

Back to Uranium 235. The amount of material needed to start a chain reaction is called the critical mass. In the case of 85 percent HEU, critical mass is achieved when one has a sphere of HEU of just over 17 centimetres in diameter, weighing around 56 kilograms, at which point the chain reaction will start by itself. The implication is never to have 56 kilograms or more of highly-enriched Uranium 235 lying about as a single unit; while you may not have an atomic bomb, you may, unless you immediately remove some of the Uranium 235, end up with an extremely hot, highly radioactive and deadly puddle of molten uranium to contend with. Or, in nuclear terms, you could have a meltdown. But the device needs to explode, and not simply to melt down, hence the atomic bomb requires what is called an initiator, a material such as polonium, which, during the explosive cycle, releases a blizzard of neutrons that collide with the Uranium 235 isotopes, causing them to split and resulting in the cataclysmic, unstoppable chain reaction.

This state of affairs is called the super-critical stage, where the chain reaction is totally uncontrolled and extremely quick. Can critical mass and subsequent super-criticality be achieved by using less fissionable material? It can, but it is difficult, as one has to compress at least a part of the available mass of fissile material into a volume far smaller than it would have in its natural state – which, as previously mentioned, usually involves the use of Plutonium 239 rather than Uranium 235. Gun-triggered devices, however, as they do not use plutonium, typically need a minimum of 56 kilograms of Uranium 235, plus the initiator, to go from critical to super-critical.

In short, the builder of the gun-triggered device, workable plans available, needs at least 60 kilograms of HEU, if not more – one has to include an allowance for machining waste, HEU is after all a metal - to put theory into practice. Unless he or she has access to the yellow cake and the enrichment production facilities, in which case the device constructer would, in all likelihood, have to be state-sponsored, the fissile material would either have to be stolen or bought on the black market. There are, of course, a handful of individuals on the planet who could possibly finance the entire process which could throw the proverbial spanner into the works. So far, this has not happened; it is an unlikely, yet not entirely unrealistic, scenario.

Taking into account the above, where then could one steal or illegally buy 60 kilograms of HEU? It is, to put it rather plainly, not really possible.

In summary, is it possible for an adequately trained amateur or a terrorist organisation to design a nuclear device? Yes, it is. Could they then actually build one? No, it is highly unlikely, largely due to the immense difficult of obtaining the fissile material required.

And for that, humanity as a whole, has cause to be thankful.

ABOUT THE AUTHOR

Born in Germany in 1962, Klaus Schirmer has lived in Europe and
South Africa, as well as, briefly, in the United States.
He has travelled extensively throughout Africa, Europe
and the Asian sub continent.
With a passion for current affairs and modern day history,
he combines fact and fiction in this novels.
Married with two daughters, he currently lives in South Africa

The Ninth Device is Klaus Schirmer's second novel.

www.ingramcontent.com/pod-product-compliance
Lightning Source LLC
Chambersburg PA
CBHW030413180626
46812CB00005B/1988